Bryce's laugh vibrated through her body. "Has anyone ever told you that you are the most stubborn person in the whole world?"

"Apart from you?"

"Apart from me."

She nodded. "Yes

"I'd like to meet the...

You never will. The thought jerked her back into reality. "I'll be fine now, Bryce. You can go. Thanks for your help."

"Yeah, like that's going to happen." The sarcasm in his voice was withering. "I'm just going to walk out of here and leave you when you can't even crawl to your own bed."

"You don't have any choice. I don't want you here." With a determined effort, Steffi pushed herself away from him and tried to sit up straight. It was a mistake. Behind the tinted lenses, the edges of her vision went black. Everything swam out of focus. She heard Bryce call her name in alarm and the last thing she felt was his strong arms catching her...

* * *

Sons of Stillwater: Danger lurks in a small Wyoming town

* * *

If you're on Twitter, tell us what you think of Harlequin Romantic Suspense! #harlequinromsuspense

Dear Reader,

The Soldier's Seduction is the second book in the Sons of Stillwater series, and it tells the story of Bryce, the youngest Delaney brother.

Stillwater is a small Wyoming city, set in the cradle of some beautiful mountain scenery. In Stillwater, everyone knows everyone else's business...or they think they do. On the surface the town is all laid-back Western charm. But scratch beneath the surface and nothing is what is seems.

Bryce attempts to disguise the trauma of what happened to him in Afghanistan by continuing with his daily routine. Stillwater allows him to hide in plain sight, until a new employee turns his routine upside down.

Steffi Grantham is a thorn in Bryce's side from day one. Belligerent and uncooperative, she still manages to be the only person who makes him feel alive again.

When Bryce discovers Steffi's true identity, he comes to her aid, and their adventure takes them across the country on a search that brings them face-to-face with danger and passion and forces them both to confront their fears.

I loved writing these characters. They were both badly hurt by their pasts, and they really needed to find each other! Giving them their happy ending was one of the most satisfying things I've done as a writer.

I'd love to hear from you and find out what you think of Bryce and Steffi's story. You can contact me at www.janegodmanauthor.com, on Twitter, @JaneGodman, and on Facebook at Jane Godman Author.

Happy reading,

Jane

THE SOLDIER'S SEDUCTION

Jane Godman

HARLEQUIN® ROMANTIC SUSPENSE

Recycling programs
for this product may
not exist in your area.

ISBN-13: 978-0-373-40220-5

The Soldier's Seduction

Copyright © 2017 by Amanda Anders

Printed in U.S.A.

www.Harlequin.com

Jane Godman writes in a variety of romance genres, including paranormal, gothic and romantic suspense. Jane lives in England and loves to travel to European cities that are steeped in history and romance—Venice, Dubrovnik and Vienna are among her favorites. Jane is married to a lovely man and is mom to two grown-up children.

Books by Jane Godman

Harlequin Romantic Suspense

Sons of Stillwater

Covert Kisses
The Soldier's Seduction

Harlequin Nocturne

Otherworld Protector
Otherworld Renegade
Otherworld Challenger
Immortal Billionaire
The Unforgettable Wolf

Harlequin E Shivers

Legacy of Darkness
Echoes in the Darkness
Valley of Nightmares
Darkness Unchained

Visit the Author Profile page at Harlequin.com for more titles.

This book is dedicated to my editor, Carly Silver. She makes every book we work on together the best it can be, and she has been a wonderful cheerleader for the Sons of Stillwater miniseries!

Thank you, Carly.

Chapter 1

Bryce Delaney was at a point where anger was threatening to tip over into fire-storming rage, and he wasn't sure
why. This sort of thing happened all the time. Delaney
Transportation was a large organization. Dealing with employees who stepped out of line was part of his job. He was
used to the inevitable frustrations that came with being in
charge. Even so, as he made his way toward his brother's
office, he needed to find an outlet for this unexpected fury.

When Bryce kicked the door closed behind him,
Vincente looked up from one of his complicated color-
coded financial spreadsheets. As he took in the expression on Bryce's face, he immediately closed the lid of
his laptop, indicating the chair on the other side of his
desk. "What has she done now?"

Bryce didn't know whether to be annoyed that his
half brother had interpreted the source of his mood cor-

rectly, or relieved that there was no need for lengthy explanations.

"She didn't turn up for the weekly drivers' meeting. Again." Bryce flopped into the chair, running a hand through his hair in frustration. "This is the third time since she started with us. Last time I gave her a warning. I told her if it happened again, I would fire her stupid, stubborn, skinny ass without any further discussion."

Vincente leaned back in his own chair, tenting his fingers beneath his chin. "If you gave her a warning and you don't act on it, the other drivers will think you've gone soft."

"I know they will. It's just—" Bryce leaned back, gazing at the ceiling as some of the fight went out of him. "What the hell is she playing at? This is a good job. We pay well. Delaney Transportation is a great company to work for. But it's like she has to go out of her way to thwart me any way she can. It's not just the meetings. She's forever telling me how I can do my job better, finding fault with the schedules, wanting me to change routes I've planned weeks in advance. Steffi Grantham has been a goddamn thorn in my side from the day you hired her."

"Whoa, don't turn this around and make it my fault. If I remember rightly, you told me I did a good job when I hired her. You said she was a good driver." Vincente rose and moved to the coffee machine. He held up a mug and Bryce shook his head.

"She is a damn good driver. When she quits belly-aching long enough to get behind the wheel."

Bryce couldn't explain his feelings to Vincente. Couldn't explain them to anyone, least of all himself.

How could he possibly disclose the real reason he didn't want to fire Steffi, no matter how hard she pushed him? Where did he start? *How about with the truth?* That, if he let Steffi go, he would lose the one thing that had made his miserable existence worthwhile these last three months?

After two years of bleak nothingness, the truth was there had been a bright spark in his life just lately…and Steffi was responsible for its ignition. *But what sort of sorry specimen does that make me?* Bryce wasn't about to confess to anyone, least of all the brother with whom he had only recently begun to repair a prickly relationship, that the only thing getting him out of bed in the mornings these days was the prospect of an argument with a woman whose only interest in him seemed to be to tell him what he was doing wrong.

Vincente returned with his own coffee, setting the steaming mug on the desk. His expression was thoughtful. "I'm not happy to part ways with a good driver. And you know how hard I've been working to make sure we recruit and keep more women onto the team. Part of that drive has been to make sure we find ways around any issues they may have with things like attendance at meetings outside of their usual shift patterns. We've done a lot of listening to the other jobs some of our female employees do. Childcare, looking after elderly relatives, keeping the home going…we have to find ways to ensure we don't put anyone who is dealing with all those things at a disadvantage."

Bryce clenched a fist on his thigh. "You know I support that, but Steffi can't keep defying me like this. I can only help her with her issues if she talks to me about them. She won't."

"It's your call. Managing the drivers is your responsibility." Bryce got the feeling Vincente would have liked to say something more, but, after a brief pause during which he sipped his coffee, he remained quiet.

"She made me so mad today. This is one time I'm actually going to enjoy telling someone they're fired. In fact—" Bryce glanced at the clock on the wall "—I'm going to stop by her place on my way home."

Vincente frowned. "Is that a good idea? You're angry, and Steffi is headstrong. My advice is to call her, or wait until she shows up tomorrow. And don't rush into firing her until you've heard what she has to say."

Bryce wavered. Vincente was right, of course. Damn him. He shouldn't do this while he was angry, and he probably shouldn't do it face-to-face. But no one had ever gotten under his skin the way Steffi Grantham could. Since she had started working for Delaney Transportation three months ago, he had given her chance after chance and she'd thrown every one back in his face. He wanted to look her in the eye when he told her that today was the day she had used up those chances. Wanted to see if there was even a flicker of remorse there. Of course, it was just about impossible to see her eyes behind those huge, tinted glasses she wore all the time.

"Don't worry. I'll keep it brief and professional."

"That's not what I meant." Vincente's dark eyes were fixed on his face. "By going to her home and being alone with her, you'll make yourself vulnerable. She could accuse you of anything and it would be her word against yours."

Bryce frowned. "I hadn't thought of it that way. But although she's a hornet, I can't imagine Steffi would be vindictive. It's not her style. And she's the one who has pushed this by not turning up today. After our last confrontation over the drivers' meetings, she must know what's coming."

Vincente had been born and raised in Wyoming, but some of his gestures unconsciously betrayed his half Italian heritage. The shrug he gave now was as Italian as the taste of Chianti or the roar of a vintage Vespa's engine. "Your call."

Half an hour later Bryce was pulling into the parking lot at the Wilderness Lake Trailer Park and wondering if his brother might have been right. Maybe he should have waited. The edge was gone now from his anger. He viewed his surroundings and felt a flat, uncomfortable dejection. This was not the sort of place he had expected to find Steffi calling home. What the hell was it with her? How did she manage to make him feel so many conflicting emotions every time he thought of her?

Stillwater was a beautiful place. The city itself was cradled low in the embrace of a towering Wyoming mountain range. It was becoming increasingly popular with the tourists who recognized it had as much to offer as neighboring Yellowstone, and several new trailer parks had sprung up recently. Bryce's other brother, Cameron, was the mayor of Stillwater and he, together with the council, fought an ongoing battle to ensure these places stayed within municipal regulations. Bryce was fairly sure this one didn't. It was a run-down eyesore.

Roughly divided into sections, there was an area for fixed trailers, a larger one for visiting recreational vehicles and a cluster of tired-looking log cabins. Next to these, a tumbledown sign invited visitors to Inquire About Our Rates! Several cabins had broken windows, and the wooden structures looked like they hadn't been varnished for years. Weeds grew wild between the paving stones of the path, and garbage was piled in the pathways between the cabins. Bryce didn't imagine the owners got many inquiries about rates. As he drove along the narrow road in front of the cabins, he made a mental note to tell Cameron about this place.

Steffi's cabin was set slightly apart from the others. *Typical Steffi*, Bryce thought grimly as he parked in front before treading up the shallow step and rapping on the scarred wood of the door. She always chose to set herself apart. There was no answer, but her beaten-up car, the one that looked like it was held together with rust and prayers, was parked out front. He took a step back and looked at the broken-down building.

He couldn't reconcile the feisty woman he knew with this place. His drivers didn't make a fortune, but they earned a decent wage. Enough on which to live well. It occurred to him that he knew nothing about Steffi, except that she wasn't from Stillwater. Why had she chosen to live here? *None of my business.* As soon as the thought came to him he dismissed it as unworthy. He might be about to fire the woman, but no one deserved to live in this hellhole. Whatever had brought her here, if she needed a helping hand, he would offer it. He almost laughed. *Just be prepared to get that hand bitten off, Delaney.*

When his second knock still got no response, he walked around the cabin. His impression of the place didn't improve upon closer contact. It was falling down. When he got around the back, Bryce pushed his way through the weeds and got up close to the window. Steffi would flay him alive with that acid tongue of hers if she knew what he was doing, but he pressed his face to the grimy glass of the window...and recoiled in shock at what he saw.

Steffi was lying curled up on the bedroom floor, clutching her hands to her stomach as her features twisted in an expression of pain.

Steffi could see the clock on her bedside table from where she lay and its digital display told her the only thing she needed to know. The drivers' meeting had finished hours ago. Bryce Delaney would be burning up with rage. Even though she had lain awake all night with stomach cramps after throwing up most of the previous day, she had done her best to get ready for work that morning. Struggling to the shower, she had shivered under the pathetic stream of water that never quite seemed to heat up enough. Getting into her clothes had taken forever and by the time she'd managed it, she was shaking all over and as weak as a kitten. As she'd snatched up her car keys and cell phone, her legs had given way and she'd hit the floor. That was the last thing she remembered for some time.

Now, having faded in and out of consciousness for most of the day, she supposed she could have called Bryce and offered him an explanation for why she'd missed his precious meeting. Her lips tightened. *He wouldn't believe me. And I won't grovel. Let him fire me. It was bound to happen sooner or later.*

She closed her eyes again, only to have them jerk open abruptly at the sound of splintering wood. *They've found me!* The thought hammered panic through to every nerve ending and she tried to scurry into the only available hiding place. Her weary limbs refused to fully obey the promptings of her brain and she was only halfway under the bed when a man burst into the room. She cowered, wrapping her arms around her head, wanting to fight him as he reached out a hand to her, but not having the strength.

"Steffi, it's okay. It's me. It's Bryce."

He knelt beside her. She risked uncovering her head to look at him. The expression in his dark eyes was a mixture of shock and concern. She could never see those eyes without noticing how beautiful they were. And then giving herself a mental kick for noticing. She couldn't allow herself the sort of weakness that came with attraction. No matter how handsome Bryce might be—and he was oh-so handsome—she had to fight the magnetic pull that drew her to him. She had more important things to focus on. Like staying alive.

A thought penetrated her weariness. *Focus. Eyes. Something about eyes...*

"Don't let them get me." She clutched his arm, momentarily too afraid to reinstate the barriers she was always so careful to maintain between them. "I need to see him first."

"Who, Steffi?" Bryce's voice throbbed with anxiety. "What are you afraid of?"

By the time he'd finished speaking, every reason why she needed to shut him, and everyone else, out of her life had returned. The fear of being discovered receded, replaced by the more immediate fear of allowing Bryce to get too close. Antagonism usually did the trick. She quickly slipped into the familiar role.

"How did you get in here?" She wished her voice

didn't sound so pathetic. Where was her cloak of prickliness when she needed it?

"I kicked the door down."

"You did what?" That was better. That tone had something approaching her usual fire.

His grin peeped out. The boyish one that had an annoying habit of disarming her just as she was in full tirade. "Oh, come on, Steffi. I could have blown on it like the wolf in the kid's story and gotten in here. It will take me two minutes to patch it back up again. Five minutes and I'll have it in better shape than it was before. Now tell me what's wrong."

She tried to inject every bit of energy she had into her next words. "Get out of my house."

Evidently every bit of energy she had wasn't enough, because he scooped her up in his arms and deposited her on the bed. She should try to fight him, but it was taking every ounce of stamina she had just to keep her eyes open. She slumped back onto the pillows, scowling at him from beneath lowered brows.

"Tell me what I can do to help you."

She didn't want his help. Accepting it was the very last thing she wanted to do, but she was weak as a kitten. Maybe if she conceded and allowed him to feel useful he would go away. She had a feeling it was a vain hope. "Some water would be good. And you could hand me my glasses."

"You don't need those tinted lenses in here. It's gloomy as hell."

"I can't see without them." It was a lie, but she'd remembered what it was about eyes that bothered her. Part of it.

He found her glasses on the bedside table and handed

them to her before making his way toward the tiny kitchen. She heard him moving around in there and lay back, too wrung out to do anything else. When he returned with a glass of water, Steffi found to her shame that she couldn't struggle into a sitting position. Without hesitation, Bryce placed the glass on the bedside table and, sitting on the bed next to her, slid an arm around her waist. Lifting her so she could lean against him, he held the glass to her lips. She submitted, grateful for both the cool liquid and his strong arms.

"We have to get you to a doctor."

She shook her head, the action causing her cheek to rub against the hard muscle of his chest. It was both comforting and disturbing at the same time. Disturbing because she didn't do physical contact. Closeness meant opening up to another person. That meant trust. The last time Steffi had trusted someone, she had been five years old. The person she trusted had brought her a new doll, then murdered her parents. She had never made that mistake again.

"No doctor." *Not a chance.*

"Steffi, you are clearly unwell. If this is about money…"

With an effort, she lifted her head to glare at him. Even behind the dark glasses, she had perfected the expression so it had maximum impact. "I said no."

His laugh vibrated through her body. "Has anyone ever told you that you are the most stubborn person in the whole world?"

"Apart from you?"

"Apart from me."

She nodded. "Yes."

"Your family? I'd like to meet them."

You never will. The thought jerked her back to reality. "I'll be fine now, Bryce. You can go. Thanks for your help."

"Yeah, like that's going to happen." The sarcasm in his voice was withering. "I'm just going to walk out of here and leave you when you can't even crawl to your own bed."

"You don't have any choice. I don't want you here." With a determined effort, Steffi pushed herself away from him and tried to sit up straight. It was a mistake. Behind the tinted lenses, the edges of her vision went black. Everything swam out of focus. She heard Bryce call her name in alarm, and the last thing she felt was his strong arms catching her as she fell back onto the pillows.

Steffi would kill him for ignoring her wishes, Bryce decided as he ended his call. If she couldn't find something to do to him that would cause more pain than death. He checked on her again in between waiting for Leon Sinclair to answer his summons and fixing the pathetic front door. Her breathing seemed way too shallow.

Stop panicking. Leon will know what to do.

Bryce was pleased to have found this decisiveness within himself. It was a trait that often went missing at the most important times. Day to day, he could function. No one would know there was a problem. At Delaney Transportation, he knew the drivers viewed him as a good boss: tough, uncompromising, a little picky about the details. It was when the unexpected happened, if he was faced with an emergency, that it all came back to him. The explosion, the blood, the *guilt*. That was when his mind and body froze and he ceased to function. But he had made this decision about Steffi without hesitation. The thought brought with it a new and unexpected tingle of pride.

He prowled restlessly around the little cabin. In contrast to its ramshackle exterior, the inside was scrupulously clean and neat. In the midst of this squalor, Steffi had tried to make the place comfortable. Somehow, the sight of the bright cushions and throw on the sofa brought with it a feeling of sadness. He frowned. If she suspected him of pitying her, Steffi would be outraged. In the bedroom, the quilt on the bed was a colorful, cozy patchwork and there were vases of wildflowers throughout. The whole cabin smelled fresh and clean. There was a TV in the tiny den and a smaller one in the bedroom.

Even so, there was nothing about this place that made it Steffi's. The few prints on the walls were landscapes. There was nothing personal, no photographs, no knickknacks, nothing that claimed it as hers. It was as bland as a vacation rental or hotel room. If she walked out of here right now, no one would know who had lived here. The only unusual thing was the stack of newspapers—she must read several each day—and celebrity gossip magazines. He wouldn't have figured Steffi was the type to enjoy those. He shrugged. It just confirmed how little he knew about her.

When Leon arrived, Bryce studied him cautiously. Both men were veterans of the war in Afghanistan, but their career paths could not have been more different. While Bryce had been an explosive ordnance disposal—EOD—specialist, or bomb disposal expert, Leon had been an army doctor. Bryce's promising career had been brought to an end two years ago by a roadside bomb. His physical injuries had healed quickly, leaving him with only a slight limp. He knew his brothers would say he had been left with other, deeper scars. Bryce didn't encourage such comments, even if he knew them to be true.

Although Leon retained his medical license to practice, he had been given a medical discharge for mental health reasons. He had come home to Stillwater just over a year ago and had proceeded to make a name for himself by getting drunk and raising every kind of hell he could come up with. He had achieved the distinction of getting himself thrown out of every bar in the city and beyond.

Leon's arrival in town had coincided with a period in Bryce's life during which he had wondered whether alcohol might be the answer to his own problems. Since he didn't even know what the question was, he soon found out it wasn't. He and Leon had been on some spectacular benders while he tried to find out. Bryce had quickly sobered up, but it took Leon a lot longer. A spell in rehab had followed and he was still fighting his demons day by day. His reputation lingered and Bryce was the only person in Stillwater who didn't believe it was still Leon's ambition to drink the town dry.

Although Bryce knew how hard Leon was working to fight his addiction, he was secretly relieved to see that Leon was perfectly sober.

"Where's the patient?" The slight stammer that disappeared when he had been drinking was evident now as Leon held up his medical bag.

"Through here." Bryce led him through to the bedroom. "She was on the floor when I found her. Although she was conscious then, she passed out again after I lifted her onto the bed."

"Who is she?" Leon had removed Steffi's glasses and was checking her pulse.

"One of my drivers. She didn't show up for a meeting today—" He broke off as Steffi blinked.

"Oh, for God's sake, Bryce." Although her voice was weak, she still managed to sound belligerent. "I told you I didn't need a doctor."

"As the only doctor in this room, I'm going to overrule you." Bryce had never heard that sort of authoritative tone from Leon before. "I expect you would prefer it if Bryce left us while I examine you?"

Steffi subsided back on the pillows, nodding submissively. So that was all it took? Somehow Bryce doubted the high-handed manner Leon had used would work for him. Before he left the room, he overheard a brief doctor-patient exchange.

"When did you last eat?" Leon asked as he opened his medical bag.

"What day is it?"

"Wednesday."

Steffi seemed to be struggling to work something out. "That means I was sick all day Tuesday, my day off. So I may have had a snack on Monday evening."

Bryce closed the door quietly behind him. *Damn it, Steffi.* How the hell could she not know when she last ate? What was he going to do about her? There must be a story behind why she was here, but the chances of Steffi letting anyone get close enough to know what it was were remote to nonexistent. The chances of Bryce being the person she chose to confide in… He shook his head. Worse than nonexistent. Stillwater was a small city and Delaney Transportation had its own grapevine. Bryce had overheard the inevitable speculation about Steffi when she first arrived in town. He knew she had been a disappointment to the gossips, who had been unable to discover anything about her. He was fairly sure she had no friends in Stillwater. Who did Steffi talk to? Who knew anything about this intensely private and prickly woman?

Bryce gazed out the kitchen window at the hayfield of lawn surrounding the cabin. He knew what his brothers would say. Bryce was good at collecting waifs and strays. It was what he did instead of dealing with his own problems. He had a sixth sense for people who were in trouble. And when that sense kicked in, he had no mechanism for walking away. Was that what he was doing here? Maybe there was no problem with Steffi other than her current illness. Okay, this cabin she lived in was a dump. There could be a good reason for that. Eccentricity. Debt. Maybe she was getting out of a bad relationship and didn't want to be found. It was her business. She didn't want him here. He should just walk away, leave her to it.

Oh, hell. I'm already involved. Walking away wasn't an option.

The sound of a door opening drew him away from his thoughts. He went back to the hall where Leon was closing the bedroom door behind him. "I've told her to get some rest."

"What's wrong with her?" Bryce scanned his friend's face.

"A nasty case of stomach flu," Leon said. "It's been going around." His expression was grave. "In Steffi's case it's been much worse because she doesn't look after herself. What's her story?"

"I don't know. She's only been working for me for a few months." Bryce ran a hand through his hair. "What does she need?"

"Medication doesn't help with this particular strain. She needs rest and plenty of fluids. Then light meals for a few days. After that she needs to build up her strength. From what she was saying, she rarely eats more than one meal a day and even then it's not well balanced." Leon gave Bryce a sidelong glance. "Is money a problem?"

"It shouldn't be. We pay our drivers well." Bryce heard the defensive note in his voice and was annoyed. He had no need to uphold the company's reputation.

Leon nodded. "Even so, if she had money trouble before she got here, her debts might eat up all her income."

It was exactly what Bryce had been thinking. He withdrew a roll of cash from the pocket of his jeans. "Can you go to the store, get some provisions and bring them back here?"

Leon raised a brow. "People don't generally trust me with their money."

"I know it won't end up behind the bar of..." Bryce paused. "Is there anywhere in town still serving you?"

Leon pretended to give it some thought before shaking his head. "Bartenders don't have much faith in the word of a recovering alcoholic. And I find the bigger the distance I put between myself and any bar, the better it is for everyone concerned."

The words might have been frivolous, but the look in his friend's eyes was anguished. "I trust you to come back." Bryce handed him the cash.

Leon grinned. "Damn. Now you've guilt-tripped me

into it." He made his way to the door, turning back with a slight frown. "I asked Steffi about her eyes. She said her vision is fine and her only problem is light sensitivity."

"Her eyes?" Bryce tried to remember if he'd ever really seen Steffi's eyes. He didn't think he had. They were always hidden behind those tinted glasses she wore.

"Yes, it's a condition called coloboma. It causes an irregularly shaped iris. In Steffi's case, it means she has very striking-looking eyes, but I don't think there is anything for you to worry about as her employer. She told me she doesn't have any of the other complications that can be associated with the condition. She's certainly safe to drive, and she has insurance that covers her condition."

Bryce had no idea what Leon was talking about. He was worried about Steffi, but his concerns had nothing to do with her eyesight.

"I'll be here when you bring the groceries back. I'm staying with her tonight."

Chapter 2

As Steffi came slowly awake, she was conscious of two unexpected things. One was a sense of well-being, something she hadn't felt for the last three long, fraught months. The second was the low murmur of the TV in the corner of the room. When she turned her head, she realized that Bryce was seated in a chair at the side of her bed. His head was turned away from her as he watched the screen. She took a moment to study his strong profile in the flickering light.

When she had arrived in Stillwater, her whole focus had been on survival. Finding somewhere to live had been her first priority. An undemanding job had been next. When she had been hired by Vincente, he had introduced her to his brother, her new boss. With everything that was going on in her life, the last thing Steffi had expected was to be blown away by a man. But that was what had happened the first time she had set eyes on Bryce Delaney. And the impact hadn't gone away. It hit her every time she looked at him.

With his dark, wavy hair and deep-set brown eyes he was a striking man. High cheekbones, an aristocratic nose and a perfectly proportioned mouth, with slightly full lips, would have made him stand out in any crowd. Add in a muscular, athletic body, and Bryce Delaney came as close to the ideal image of masculine perfection as it was possible to get.

But it wasn't like she hadn't seen a good-looking man before. She had been around plenty of them day to day and never once experienced the sort of fizz of electricity Bryce Delaney induced in her. And to feel this now? Shouldn't she be immune to anything but the way her life had recently been turned upside down in the most destructive way imaginable?

Bryce's presence explained the noise from the TV. The feeling of well-being? She had no idea where that was coming from. All she knew was she felt safe. Which was ridiculous. She wasn't safe and it would be madness to try to fool herself. If she allowed herself to slip into a mind-set where she stopped being watchful, she would make a mistake. She had been scrupulously careful; she wasn't about to throw it away now just because, for some reason, she'd managed to snatch a few hours' sleep. And that was another thing. After three months of insomnia, how come she was suddenly able to slumber peacefully?

Her thoughts caused her to stir restlessly. The movement brought Bryce out of his chair and to her side in an instant.

"Hey." He switched on the lamp. "Let me get you a drink of water."

Steffi managed to shuffle into a sitting position so she could accept the glass from him. It wasn't dignified, but from the moment he had found her sprawled on the floor her self-respect had taken a nosedive. "Why are you still here?"

"Because you need someone to take care of you."

Instead of firing up with anger at his high-handedness, Steffi felt sharp, unaccustomed tears sting her eyelids. Bryce couldn't know what he did to her with those words. He had no idea what the last few months had been like. For the first time in forever, she had no razor-edged comeback. Everything slipped away. The role she played, the barriers she put up, they were all gone as she gazed up at him.

"Say something quick, Steffi, or I'll think you're dying." There was a trace of amusement in Bryce's voice.

"Go to hell." The words had no bite and she sank back onto the pillows.

"That's more like it." He took the glass of water from her, scanning her face. She saw his eyes widen.

Damn. She was used to that look. It was the reaction she got whenever people first saw her eyes. Her unusual, beautiful eyes. In the early days, they had been her passport to success. Now they might just be her downfall.

"Is there something wrong?" She might as well call him on it.

Bryce collected himself with obvious difficulty. "No. Not unless you count the fact that Leon thinks you need to take better care of yourself."

Steffi hunched a shoulder. "He had no right to tell you that."

"He was concerned about you. *I'm* concerned about you."

She watched his face. She preferred him snapping and snarling. In this mood, he was too breathtaking. And Steffi lived in a world where breathtaking men were commonplace. *Used to live*, she reminded herself. *Those days are gone.* Forever? *I guess so...unless I can bring this nightmare to end.* She had come to Stillwater with that aim in mind, but her quarry had remained stubbornly elusive. The man she had come here to confront seemed determined to stay away, although she didn't flatter herself that her presence in Stillwater had anything to do with his absence. But, until she could meet him face-to-face, she had to avoid being found by his thugs. If they got to her, she was unsure whether their instructions would be to kill her or take her to their boss. Steffi wasn't taking any chances. She had come here for answers, even if getting them meant putting herself in danger.

"I thought you stopped by here to fire me."

His expression told her she'd hit a nerve. "That was the plan, but then I found out why you didn't show up yesterday."

"Yesterday? What time is it?" Steffi turned her head to look at the clock. "Seriously, Bryce, haven't you got better places to be at two a.m.?"

She blushed slightly at the implication of her own words. Even in the short time she'd been in Stillwater, she'd picked up on Bryce Delaney's reputation. He slept around. A different date, if not every night, at least every few days. The man was a walking shot of testosterone and it seemed the ladies of West County were only too happy to indulge his need to be the local stud.

His lips quirked into a smile that told her he understood the reason for her blush. "As it happens, I don't." He frowned slightly, changing the subject abruptly. "When I broke in here, you were afraid of something. You said, *'Don't let them get me.'* What was that about?"

She shrugged, hoping the gloom disguised her blush. "Did I? Maybe I was delirious or something."

It was a lame explanation, but, although he gave her a searching look, he didn't push it. "Go back to sleep, Steffi. I'll be here if you need me."

She should probably challenge that. Get mad. Throw him out. But she was still so tired and, even if she only admitted it to herself, having him here was comforting. Snuggling back down into the bedclothes, she closed her eyes and listened to the voice of the newsreader. A train had derailed, causing major problems. There was an ongoing debate about the minimum wage. Steffi was just feeling sleep tug at the edge of her consciousness again when the focus switched from local issues to celebrity news.

"Police still have no further information on the whereabouts of actress Anya Moretti. Moretti, who has been missing since the murder of her boyfriend Greg Spence and an unknown woman three months ago, is best known for her roles in films such as..."

"Turn it off, please." Steffi spoke more sharply than she had intended.

Bryce looked up in surprise. "Sorry, I didn't know it was bothering you." He flicked a switch on the remote control and the room was plunged into darkness and silence.

* * *

Sleep didn't come easily to Bryce. When it did arrive it was brief and filled with nightmares from which he woke sweating, having relived every minute of the living hell of that roadside explosion. Perhaps that was one of the reasons why he never chased slumber, why he tended to find other—more interesting—things to do during the hours of darkness. Sleeping in the uncomfortable upright chair in Steffi's bedroom was damn near impossible. After shifting his long limbs into various positions, Bryce gave up. He didn't want to switch on the lamp and disturb Steffi, but he did want to check on her before he left the room.

Stepping into the narrow hall, he flicked on the light. Returning to the bedroom, he gazed down at her in the gloomy half-light flowing through the open door. She was sleeping peacefully, her short, chestnut curls clustered like a halo around her head. In sleep her features seemed less sharp than in wakefulness. Steffi was one of those women who would never be able to lay claim to classical beauty. Taking each feature in turn, there was a flaw. Her nose definitely turned up at the end in a defiant, go-to-hell gesture. Her mouth was way too wide for prettiness and the gap between her front teeth caught the eye almost as much as her full lips. Then there was that stubborn, determined chin. The one she tilted upward at him during their frequent arguments. Yet when you put those features together, they made an unforgettable face. It wasn't beautiful. It was mesmerizing.

Because she kept them hidden behind her dark glasses, Bryce hadn't seen Steffi's eyes until just now. They had taken his breath away. The golden-brown irises had elongated downward notches that made them look like cat's eyes. He had never seen eyes like them. What had Leon called the condition that caused it? Coloboma, that was it.

She was an enigma. Bryce didn't care what she said; Steffi had been scared out of her wits when he broke in here, trying to hide under the bed and covering her head with her hands. His first guess had been that she was running from a bad relationship. *Don't let them get me?* Them. Plural. That made it sound less like she was running from a vengeful ex. One thing was for sure; she clearly wasn't ready to confide in him. Another thing was certain; Bryce wasn't leaving her until he knew she was both well *and* safe. To hell with what his brothers might say about his knack for collecting waifs and strays. This was Steffi. She was different. He didn't know why; it was just a conviction, solid and unshakable, sitting in the center of his chest.

Treading softly back out of the room, Bryce made his way into the den. There was a TV in here as well, but the walls were so thin he was afraid of waking Steffi. With a sigh of resignation, he picked up one of her celebrity magazines and began to flick through it. After twenty minutes of thumbing through the magazines and newspapers, he came to the conclusion that Steffi had a bit of an obsession with the very story she had interrupted when she asked him to turn the TV off so she could go to sleep. Either that, or it was a coincidence that all these journals she had stockpiled contained articles about the disappearance of Anya Moretti.

Bryce hadn't paid much attention to the case. Celebrities didn't interest him, and the sort of happily-ever-after romances in which Anya Moretti starred weren't his style. He knew it was a sordid story, typical gossip column fodder. Greg Spence, Moretti's boyfriend, had been found shot through the head. The story was that another woman had been with him at the time. She had been shot as well, also through the head. Although the woman had still not been identified, rumors were rife on social media about the compromising position in which the couple had been found. Anya Moretti had not been seen since the day of the murders. The inevitable conclusions had been drawn. Moretti, once Hollywood's darling, had already been tried and convicted in the press as the woman who had killed her boyfriend and his lover in a jealous rage.

Bryce thought again how he just hadn't seen Steffi as the type to enjoy this sort of trashy reporting. He started to cast aside the magazine he had been thumbing without reading the story, when one of the pictures caught his eye. Most of the articles had gone with the same photographs. Moretti in the role that had brought her into the public eye as an accident-prone speedway rider, shaking loose her waist-length curls as she sat astride a bike and removed her helmet. Or on the podium when she received her Oscar, her arm held high as she raised the statuette above her head in a celebratory gesture. One had gone with a red carpet picture of her smiling into Spence's eyes as they held hands. He was a tall, handsome man with dark brown hair drawn back into a ponytail. The caption beneath the picture stated that they hadn't been together long, but there was already talk of an engagement. Most articles included pictures of the crime scene outside Spence's luxury apartment on the morning the bodies were found.

Emergency vehicles converged on the building, and shocked onlookers waited behind a makeshift barrier.

This picture Bryce studied now was different. This article included a photograph of a younger Anya Moretti. Her chestnut curls were drawn back in a ponytail and there was a wistful smile on her face as she turned to look at the photographer. She wasn't exactly pretty, but you could tell she had that special something that would always draw the camera to her. It was her eyes that held Bryce's attention. Her golden-brown eyes with their unusual downward notches. They were cat's eyes. They were Steffi's eyes.

It was fully light when Steffi woke again and she lay still, blinking slightly as she recalled the events of the previous day. Turning her head, she confirmed that Bryce was in the chair where he had been when she fell asleep. But something in his demeanor had changed. The concerned look had gone. He was watching her, but there was a frown in his eyes. She didn't need to ask why. It was obvious. He knew. Somehow, between her falling asleep and waking, Bryce had discovered the secret of her identity.

"How did you find out?" It didn't occur to her to try to deny it. Subterfuge wasn't Steffi's style. It almost felt like a relief that, at last, someone knew who she was.

"There was a picture in one of your magazines. It showed a close-up of your eyes."

Steffi sighed, pushing herself into an upright position. Although she still felt weak, the stomach cramps were a thing of the past. "I knew my eyes would give me away. I usually wear contact lenses so I don't draw attention to them. In the early days, when I made my first films, it didn't bother me too much. Then the comments started to get intrusive and I decided I'd rather have normal eyes. But I'd been out jogging that day and I didn't have time to pick my contact lenses up…" Her voice trailed off as the memory of that awful morning came back to her. Swallowing hard, she focused on Bryce. "What will you do now?"

"I guess that depends on you." His eyes never left her face. "Did you kill them?"

"No, but I don't know how I can prove that to you."

Although she had known Bryce Delaney for only three months, Steffi had gotten to know enough about him in that time. He was fiercely moral and totally honest. If he thought she was the person who killed Greg and the woman he was with, Bryce would hand her over to the police without hesitation. He wouldn't accept anything less than the truth from her. But how could she convince him about her version of events, particularly when everything she had told him since her arrival in Stillwater had been a lie?

He seemed to be following her thought process. "How about you tell me all of it and let me judge for myself?"

"Can I get a shower first?" She tried out a smile, but it went wrong somewhere in the middle and ended up with her lower lip wobbling pitifully.

She saw Bryce's dark brown eyes soften slightly. "I'll make coffee and toast while you get ready. Then we'll talk."

Standing under the lukewarm water, Steffi tried not to let the flashbacks get to her. It was useless. Ever since that day, she had lived with a constant series of images playing inside her head. Bright sunlight pat-

terning the sidewalk as she jogged up to the entrance of
Greg's apartment building on that lazy Sunday morning. The man who exited the elevator as she stepped in.
The strange feeling that had hit her in that instant. She
tried to conjure up his image. His shades and the cap
tilted low had disguised his looks. All she could recall
was the tattoo on the back of his right hand where he
gripped the gym bag he carried. The tattoo was an eye.
A perfect, blue, bloodshot eye, gazing up at her from
the back of his hand. An eye she had last seen when
she was five years old.

It was the same sign the men who had killed her parents had on the back of their right hands. It wasn't similar, or an imitation. It was the *same* tattoo. There was
no way Steffi could be mistaken. Not when that symbol
had featured in her nightmares for all these years. Not
when, as a child, she had obsessively drawn that bloodshot orb over and over. Not when she could count the
number of hours she had spent hunched over her laptop,
searching the internet for gangs who used that mark.

The men who killed her parents had never been
found, and the only information she had discovered
about the tattoo was in connection with a Russian crime
organization called the Sglaz, or Evil Eye, which had
operated around the time of her parents' death. Since
the gang had disappeared from public record around
the same time, Steffi had been unable to find out any
more about them.

Exiting the elevator in a rush, she had fumbled her
way into Greg's apartment, calling out his name. Even
then, she had known something was very wrong. When
she walked into the den Greg had been seated in his favorite chair. He was naked and his legs were splayed. A

girl knelt between them. A girl whose hair was a mass of brilliant gold corkscrew curls.

As soon as she saw the blood Steffi had run. So much blood. She had narrowly avoided stumbling over the two suitcases in the hall as she had tugged open the apartment door. The memories had come flooding back and she had just kept on running. She was six blocks away when she tugged her cell phone out of her purse and called 911. Stammering out the details, but withholding her name, she had fought a losing battle with her nausea. Doubling over, she had let nature have its way. When her stomach was finally empty, she had kept running, her only instinct to get away and stay away. Her rational self told her she should go to the police and tell them what she knew. Her flight instinct was stronger, overruling reason. What she knew was nothing. What she *thought* she knew sounded crazy.

Blood and that tattooed eye. They were the images that played on a loop in her mind. Keeping her awake at night and haunting her during the day. Twin memories. Her parents and now Greg. The thought made her close her eyes as feelings of love and loss welled up inside her. To have Greg taken from her like that in the same way her parents had been. *Just as we had found each other.*

The coffee and toast smelled good. The thought surprised her as she returned to the bedroom wrapped in a towel. For the first time in forever, she actually felt hungry. She dressed quickly in jeans, boots and a lightweight sweater, rubbing a towel over her hair. It had cost her a pang when she took a pair of scissors to her long locks that first night in a cheap motel room, but she was used to her short curls now.

As she pulled back the drapes, she felt a loosening of

some of the tightness around her heart. Could she tell Bryce all of it? Could she trust someone for the first time in her life? She wouldn't know until she tried. In recognizing her, Bryce had forced her into a situation where she would have to make the attempt. Maybe it would be comforting to finally talk to someone.

She was about to turn away from the window when she caught a glimpse of movement in the trees beyond the lawn. Her heartbeat stuttered and she narrowed her attention on that area. Was it a breeze stirring the trees? An animal? There it was again. Her heart gave a downward lurch. Someone was standing just within the cover of the trees, watching the cabin.

"Bryce?" Steffi was running for the door when the window shattered.

Chapter 3

Bryce took a sip of his coffee and examined the surreal situation. He had been going over and over it in his mind since he first saw that picture in the magazine. Steffi was wanted for a double murder. It was hardly a minor thing. He should just get her into the car and take her downtown. Hand her over to his sister-in-law, Laurie, Cameron's wife and the Stillwater Police Department Detective Division's newest recruit, and let her deal with it. By not doing that, he was making himself into an accomplice.

So why was he standing here, waiting to hear her story, remembering the way her lip had trembled when she tried to be brave as she asked if she could have a shower before they talked? *Damned if I know.* But he was going to let her tell her side of it before he decided what to do. Although, at this moment in time, even though he was determined to uphold his promise to keep her safe, he couldn't see any alternative to handing her over to the police.

He ran a frustrated hand through his hair. It was still early, but, picking up his cell phone, he sent Vincente a message, letting him know he wouldn't be at work. Since Bryce never took a day off, it would no doubt cause his brother to raise those expressive dark brows of his. Bryce shrugged. Let Vincente speculate. The truth was a lot more far-fetched than anything that imaginative mind of his could come up with.

He heard Steffi moving around in the bedroom and poured another cup of coffee for her. His hand was poised in the act of refilling his own cup, when he heard Steffi call his name. Bryce had barely a moment to register the panic in her voice before there was an almighty crash.

"What the…?"

Bryce erupted from the kitchen in time to get a back view of a man forcing Steffi out of the bedroom and down the short hall toward the front door. One hand was clamped over her mouth and although she was making a wild attempt to fight him, he had his other arm around her waist. Bryce took a moment to register what was happening. The intruder was huge, shaped like a barrel, with thighs like tree trunks and fists like hams. Towering over Steffi, he was able to ignore her struggles and propel her along with him.

Bryce launched himself at the man. Even in the urgency of the moment, a thought flashed through his mind. *Not even a second's hesitation. Nice work.* Starting in a crouch, Bryce barreled into the intruder's midsection, knocking him off his feet. Steffi went down as well, but, lithe as a cat, she broke free of her captor's hold, rolling to one side. As the two men hit the floor, they came together in a tangled mass of limbs.

A blur of fists flashed back and forth. The intruder might have been bigger than Bryce, but Bryce was faster. Years of mixed martial arts training in addition to the strict exercise regime of the army meant he had endurance and discipline on his side. They switched places repeatedly. Eventually, Bryce pinned the other man down, straddling him and holding on to his shirt as he pounded his right fist into his face. Then, with a sudden surge of enormous strength, the intruder let out a bellow of rage and threw Bryce off. Reversing their positions, he forced Bryce into the floor and drove his fists into his rib cage, one after the other. It felt like twin sledgehammers were slamming into him over and over. The breath was being systematically driven out of his lungs, until Bryce struggled to draw in even a gasp of air.

Just as he thought he was about to pass out, Bryce heard Steffi call out his name in a warning. Looking up, he saw her standing over them. As he ducked his head out of the way, she brought a vase of flowers crashing down onto the top of the intruder's skull. Although the other man remained conscious, the blow slowed him down long enough for Bryce to land a powerful, uppercut punch to his jaw. He followed this up immediately with two more slugs and the man toppled over. He hit the floor, his head bouncing off the wooden boards with a dull thud that signaled he wouldn't be getting up again for some time.

Grimacing and clutching his ribs as he rose to his feet, Bryce leaned against the wall as he caught his breath.

"How did he get in?" He managed to gasp out the words.

"He came in through the bedroom window. The whole frame gave way under his weight."

"What are you doing?" He glanced down at Steffi as she dropped to her knees beside the intruder.

"Just checking."

Her body was partially blocking Bryce's view, but she seemed to be turning the man's right hand so she could get a better look at it. Whatever she saw prompted an unexpected reaction. Without warning, Steffi bolted. In one fluid movement, she was on her feet and running. Out of the cabin, out into the sunlit morning, out in the direction of God knew where.

"Steffi, wait…"

Before he followed her, Bryce spared a glance down at the intruder. What had she seen to cause her to run like the hounds of hell were at her heels? The back of the man's right hand was covered in a tattoo. A pale blue, bloodshot eye gazed unblinkingly up at Bryce.

It's my turn. First my parents. Then Greg. Now me.
They were the only thoughts in Steffi's mind as she ran out of the cabin. Straight into the arms of another man.

"*Zdravstvuyte*, Stefanya." Hearing the Russian word for "hello" along with her full first name made her blood run cold. "The Big Guy has been looking for you. Keeping him waiting is never a good idea."

She was aware of Bryce skidding out of the cabin behind her at the same time as she was scooped up and thrown onto the back seat of a waiting car. Bryce shouted for her abductor to stop and got a stream of Russian curses in response. As she bounced into a sitting position, Steffi saw the Russian pull a gun out from the waistband of his pants and take aim at Bryce. To her relief, Bryce ducked behind his Range Rover just in time to avoid the bullet. Her captor jumped into the driver's seat of his own car and gunned the engine. Screeching away, he drove way too fast for the narrow tracks that crisscrossed the trailer park. Steffi risked peeping out the rear window and saw Bryce's vehicle following close behind.

"Get down," the man in the front seat growled at her as he exited the trailer park gates and swung wildly onto the highway, narrowly avoiding a collision with an oncoming truck. "Lie on the seat and don't move."

He waved the gun back between the seats with his right hand in a threatening gesture. Although she obeyed his instruction and curled into a ball, Steffi remembered his words. If "the Big Guy" wanted to see her, he would want her alive. It was no consolation, but it meant this man wasn't going to shoot her. Not yet.

Three months ago, she had come to Stillwater in search of the Big Guy. She wanted answers. And now, it seemed, he did, too. She wasn't sure why it had taken him twenty-two years to decide to speak to her. Until recently, she hadn't known his identity. Could he have been in prison or living overseas all this time? Whatever the reason, it seemed he had lost track of her after he'd executed her parents. He had resurfaced with grisly results, resulting in the deaths of Greg and the unknown woman. Since she was on her way to see him, Steffi supposed she would find out the truth soon enough.

They were traveling fast and erratically. Steffi was thrown around by the movement of the vehicle as her abductor wove wildly back and forth across the road. He was swearing under his breath and, unable to figure out the reason for his strange behavior, Steffi risked shifting into a half-sitting position so she could glance out the rear window again. The cause of his annoyance soon became obvious and her heart gave an optimistic bound.

Bryce was still tailing them…and he was gaining on them. Even though it was impossible to see his face across the distance between the two vehicles, Steffi could imagine his expression. The determined set to his jaw. The stubborn glint in his dark eyes. The way he held his whole body rigid. It was a look she had provoked often enough. She never would have believed the time would come when Bryce Delaney's obstinacy would be such a welcome sight.

There was little early-morning traffic, which was just as well, since her abductor was veering across to the other side of the road in an attempt to throw Bryce off his tail. With a feeling of mingled horror and elation, she figured out what Bryce was attempting to do. He was going to try a PIT, or precision immobilization technique, maneuver. It was a pursuit tactic from one of her movies. Although a stunt double had been used in the driving scene, Steffi had been fascinated by the maneuver itself and the skill it took to pull it off.

Had Bryce been trained to do this? She knew he had been in the army, but she had no idea of his role. From what she could see, it looked like he knew what he was doing as he pulled alongside the Russian's vehicle. Carefully aligning his front wheels with the fleeing car's back wheels at such high speed was no easy task.

"I told you to stay down," the Russian growled at Steffi. The words lacked any heat as he struggled to avoid Bryce's next move.

Steffi ignored the warning, watching with her heart in her mouth as Bryce swung his wheel and made contact with their vehicle before steering a sharp quarter turn into its side. The Russian let out another furious stream of curses as his car spun out and came to a stop.

"Stay here."

Like that's going to happen.

As he grabbed up his gun and leaped out of the car, Steffi slid the door on the opposite side open. The vehicle had come to rest at the edge of the highway, right at the point where the tarmac ended and the road sloped down to a steep wooded bank. Crouching low, she used the vehicle to shield herself from view as she slithered down the incline on her bottom. Her boots squelched into a narrow creek, and she bent almost double, following the muddy water away from the car as fast as she could. As she reached the shelter of a line of trees, she heard a single gunshot and bit back the cry that rose to her lips. If Bryce had been killed because of her...

For several heart-stopping minutes nothing happened. Not daring to risk leaving her hiding place, Steffi waited in silence for some clue to what had gone on.

Eventually, she heard footsteps and a voice called out, "Steffi? Where the hell are you?"

It was Bryce and this time she allowed the cry to escape her lips. She had intended to shout his name, but instead it came out as a strangled sob. Emerging from the trees and looking up the slope, she saw him at the top. Leaning down, he offered her his hand. Reaching for him, she twined her fingers into his and let him haul her up the bank. Glancing over at the Russian's car several yards away, she saw her abductor writhing on the ground, clutching his left knee and groaning. Blood was seeping through his fingers and dripping onto the road. Even though he was clearly in agony, he raised his head and glared at her. Through clenched teeth, he muttered a warning. "You think you can outrun the Big Guy? Think again, Stefanya."

Steffi felt her own knees begin to wobble and was glad when Bryce slid his arm around her waist as he led her toward the Range Rover. "Let's get out of here before someone calls the cops."

"Damn." Bryce felt the unmistakable drag on the wheel as he pulled out onto the highway.

"What is it?" Steffi slewed around in her seat. "Are we being followed?"

"No, we have a flat tire. It must have been damaged when I immobilized his vehicle."

She made a sound that might have been the start of a hysterical laugh. It tailed away as she looked his way again. "Do we have to stop?"

In normal circumstances, Bryce would not have driven with a flat tire. He had no desire to run up a hefty repair bill, and he knew the damage he would do to the rim if he didn't pull over and change the tire. But these circumstances were far from normal. Whatever was going on with Steffi, he had to get her away from a situation where these guys, whoever they were, could catch up with her again.

"Not yet. But I don't understand why you won't call the police." Bryce looked across at Steffi as she returned to her huddled position low in the passenger seat. She looked like someone who was trying to disappear into herself. He had tossed her his phone as they got into the car, but all she had done was stare at it as if it was a coiled snake. "Don't tell me you don't know who those guys are."

"If we call the police, I will have to tell them who I am." Her voice was a quiet monotone. He got the feeling she had said those words many times, maybe just not out loud.

"You said you didn't commit those murders." Bryce kept his voice low, sensing she was close to a breaking point.

She pushed her curls back from her face with a hand that shook. "I didn't, but you have no idea what I'm up against."

"Tell me." He risked glancing away from the road again and was shocked at the raw fear he saw on her face.

"Can we get off the highway first?"

"Steffi, that guy isn't going to be moving anytime soon. There's no way he's following us."

"He won't be alone." Those haunting eyes were wide with fear. "Please?"

Bryce gave it some thought. His house was on the opposite side of town, and he was seriously concerned about Steffi's well-being if she stayed in the car much longer. She was walking a knife-edge between stability and hysteria, swaying precariously back and forth from one to the other. He had no idea what was going on, but it was clear she was scared half to death. He also had the issue of a shredded tire and an increasingly damaged rim to take into account.

They were driving along Lakeside Drive. On their left was Stillwater Lake, the huge body of water that bordered the city. His brother Cameron had a house here, a beautiful designer property that was tucked away in the trees above its own private lakefront view. Since his recent marriage, Cameron had moved into a sprawling ranch on the road out toward Park County. He and

Laurie were restoring the old property and were planning to sell the lake house. It was so private, it should reassure Steffi that no one could find them. Once they were there, maybe she would be able to calm down and tell him what the hell was going on. His ribs gave a twinge. And maybe he could take a look at his injuries at the same time. That guy back at Steffi's cabin had used his fists the way other people took a mallet to a fence post.

He turned the car off the highway and down a narrow, winding track that led between tall pine trees. Steffi eyed him suspiciously. "Where are we going?"

"My brother's house." Correctly interpreting her look of horror, he quickly attempted to reassure her. "Don't worry, no one else will be there."

Although she didn't seem convinced, Steffi remained silent as he pulled up to the wrought iron gates, waiting while the sensor on his windshield opened them automatically. She glanced around her nervously, but seemed relieved when the gates closed behind them. The same sensor opened the double garage. As Bryce pulled into the gloomy interior, the fluorescent lighting kicked in. From there, they could mount an internal staircase into the house itself. Bryce had a key, and he also knew the code to the alarm system. He was convinced they hadn't been followed, but he was keen to calm Steffi's nerves by showing her he was taking her apprehension seriously. Pocketing the gun he had returned to the Range Rover's glove box after shooting Steffi's abductor, he led the way into the house.

The lake house was stunning, but its story was tragic and Bryce no longer felt comfortable in the beautiful glass-and-wood dwelling. It had been designed by Cameron's former girlfriend, Carla, who had died on the lake. At the time it was believed it had been a boating accident. It was only recently it had emerged that she was one of the victims of the serial murderer known as the Red Rose Killer. The city, and the Delaney family in particular, were still reeling from the impact of that investigation. It was the reason Bryce drove around with a loaded gun in his glove box.

Steffi appeared not to notice her surroundings. As Bryce made coffee—adding several heaped spoons of sugar to her cup—she hugged her arms around her waist and gazed out of the full-length window. He took the drinks through to the large family room and set them on the glass-topped driftwood table. Although the weather was cool, he opened the glass doors that led out onto the deck, allowing the breeze to filter through from the lake. Sitting on one of the large, squishy sofas, he gestured for Steffi to join him. She perched stiffly on the edge, apparently poised for flight.

"I think it's time you told me." This situation was totally out of the scope of his experience, but he did his best to keep his voice gentle. He could only help her if he knew the truth.

Steffi was gnawing her lip so hard he thought she might bite right through it. "I don't know where to start."

"Just talk and let's see where it takes us."

She nodded decisively. "Greg Spence wasn't my boyfriend. Everyone thought he was because we were so close. The press even speculated that we were about to get engaged. It made us laugh." She took a deep breath, lifting her eyes to his face. "His real name was Gregori Anton, and he was my brother."

Chapter 4

"When I was born, my name was Stefanya Anton."
Bryce was right. Once she started talking, it became
easier to keep going. Until now, Steffi hadn't figured
Bryce for someone who might be easy to confide in,
but he surprised her. Her story wasn't an easy one to
tell, but it felt like he was really listening, rather than
judging her.

"Our parents died when I was five and Greg was
eight. We were placed with separate adoptive families
and we lost touch. Although I became famous, he hadn't
recognized me from my movies. It was sheer coincidence that we met again. He had a minor part in one
of my films. There was something about him—" she
smiled reminiscently "—I couldn't place what it was.
Then, one day, I got something in my eye while we were
shooting a scene together. He came to my assistance,

saw my eyes and knew right away I was his sister. He remembered my cat's eyes from when we were children."

"But you let people believe you were an item?"

She bit her lip. This was the hard part. "There were reasons why we couldn't tell anyone our true identity."

Although he wasn't judging her, it was clear Bryce wasn't going to let that go. "You're going to have to tell me all of it, Steffi. Two people are dead and I shot a man today to help you escape. If I'm going to help you, I need to know why."

He was right, of course. It was just so hard to talk about something she'd kept locked up inside herself for so long. "Although we lived in America when our parents died, Greg and I were born in Russia." She drew in a long breath. "Our father was involved in organized crime. More than involved. He was the leader of one of the largest gangs in Russia, and he brought his criminal activities with him to this country."

There. She had said those words aloud. Words that had, until now, only been spoken between her and Greg. It was only recently, since their reunion, that they had pieced their story together, realizing with dawning horror who they were and what they had witnessed all those years ago.

Steffi watched Bryce's face, waiting for his reaction. She was unsure what to expect. Disgust? Rage? Contempt? Any combination of those would be natural, she supposed. She was the daughter of one of the most notorious Russian mob bosses of all time. She herself was a wanted alleged killer who had tricked her way into Bryce's employment. He was hardly likely to pat her arm and say it was all going to be okay. She bit back the sob that tried to rise in her throat. It was never going to be okay.

His expression remained carefully neutral. "Go on."

"I was too young to remember much of my life before his death. Greg told me we moved to America when I was about three. My father was very wealthy, as you can imagine, and he had connections in high places."

She thought back to that night. To the shouts and running footsteps. To her mother dragging Steffi and Greg from their beds and pushing them up the stairs to the attic, her whispered voice urging them to stay there.

"No matter what you see or hear." Steffi could still hear the terror in her mother's tone as she said those words.

They had huddled together, lifting the trapdoor that led from their parents' bedroom to the attic space an inch or two while they watched the scene below…even though they didn't want to see. Men had crowded into the room, all of them dressed in black. All of them with the tattooed eye on their right hands. Steffi hadn't seen what happened to her mother, but she had pressed a hand to her mouth as they beat her father. Then another man had come into the room. A big man with dark hair. The atmosphere changed with his arrival. He didn't have the tattoo, but he was in charge.

Steffi had known this man. He was her father's friend. He visited their house often, bringing presents for her, and spending hours playing with her by the pool. Greg used to be jealous of the time this man spent with Steffi. He teased her and said she was the favorite. This man wouldn't hurt them. Why, only a few days earlier, he had brought Steffi the doll she wanted. She had turned to smile at Greg in relief and saw his eyes widen in horror. A shot rang out and Steffi had looked back in time to see the big man lower his gun as her father's body crumpled to the floor.

"Find the children." His pleasant voice with an American accent had sounded different as he strode out of the room.

The men had started to search the house, and Steffi could still recall the choking sense of panic when two of them pointed up to the trapdoor. As one of them pulled up a chair and prepared to stand on it, police sirens could be heard approaching the house, and the other man cursed, pulling his friend by the arm; they both ran off.

"The police found us eventually. Mama had told us not to come down, so we didn't," Steffi said as she finished recounting this memory to Bryce. Tears sparkled on the ends of her lashes, but she blinked them away. "We told the police what we saw, but no one was ever convicted of the crime."

"Didn't you know his name? The man who pulled the trigger?"

"We knew him as our Uncle Waltz, although we had heard our father call him 'Big Guy.' The police couldn't trace him from either of those names. Looking back, I'm not sure how hard they tried. My father wasn't exactly a law-abiding citizen. Perhaps they were glad his murderer had put an end to the activities of his criminal organization." She gave a rueful smile. "I went to my new home, became Steffi Grantham, had counseling, of course, and started a new life. Greg's adoptive parents and mine tried to keep in touch for a while, but it was hard and eventually we lost contact with each other."

"Until recently," Bryce said.

"Yes." Steffi felt a tiny, reminiscent smile touch her lips. "Our mother was an actress, and I suppose we both inherited the gene. It was all I ever wanted to do and it seems Greg was the same. The chances of us ending up on the same movie together were crazily remote, but we liked to think it was fate's way of bringing us back together. Once we found each other again, we spent so much time together, the press invented this big romance and we decided it was easier to go along with it than tell the truth."

A shadow passed over her features and Bryce observed it with a frown. "Tell me the rest, Steffi."

"We talked about the way our parents died, of course. We were curious to find out why it happened. So we set about discovering exactly who our father really was. It wasn't easy. Getting information about him from Russia was hard, and he had covered his tracks well, but we managed to piece enough together from a number of sources. It was a shock to learn just what he had been involved in." Steffi turned to look directly at Bryce. "To learn that the father you loved did some horrible things…that's not an easy discovery to make. But it got worse." She covered her face with her hands as the memories came flooding back. "It got so much worse when we realized who the Big Guy was."

Bryce fixed more coffee and finally delivered the toast he'd promised hours earlier. When Steffi shook her head, he tried for the authoritative tone Leon had used the previous day. "You have to start taking care of yourself. You've been ill and you haven't eaten properly for days."

He was worried about her. Those pictures in the celebrity magazines had shown a woman with a stunning figure. The Steffi he knew was thinner than the Hollywood actress they depicted. Now she had lost even more weight and her illness of the last few days had given her an air of fragility. Her cheek and collarbones jutted and her pale skin appeared almost translucent. Whatever ordeal Steffi had to face next, whether it involved the police and the media or more running, Bryce wondered if she would have the strength to deal with it.

Her story so far was a wild one, but he believed it. Although he hadn't known Steffi very long, his gut told him she wasn't a liar. That might sound like a bizarre claim to make since she had gotten a job in his company under false pretenses, but he was prepared to stake his honor on it. And his honor meant more to Bryce than anything.

His ribs were aching as he left Steffi begrudgingly nibbling on a slice of toast and made his way to the bathroom. Pulling his T-shirt over his shoulders was a painful process and, when he checked his reflection in the mirror, his sides were a patchwork of marks in varying shades of red, pink and purple. He winced as he felt his way around, but decided there were no bones broken. His body might be hurting, but his mind felt clearer than it had in a long time. When it had mattered most, the nightmares of flames and blood hadn't intruded. The doubts and fears hadn't held him back. He had done what he needed to do. He had gone to Steffi's aid and fought the bad guys. It felt like he had defeated a monster. A monster that had lived inside him for a long time.

Opening the medicine cabinet, he rummaged around for the salve he knew Laurie kept in there. He remembered her talking about the natural remedy she had purchased at the monthly farmers' market in Stillwater and about how well it worked on bruising and swelling. Taking the salve and a roll of bandage back into the family room, he presented them to Steffi. She regarded him with raised brows.

"I can't reach all the way around to get this stuff on my back. And, if I try to put my own dressing on, I'll look like I've been engaging in a bondage ritual."

Although she attempted a smile, Steffi's lip trembled slightly as she viewed his injuries. "I wouldn't have dragged you into this for anything."

"Just tell me you really do have a commercial driver's license, and you haven't been driving my trucks around illegally these last few months," he said, shivering slightly as her fingertips connected with his flesh and she began to smooth the salve over his bruises.

"Of course I have one." She glanced up from her task, her expression indignant. "Vincente checked out my qualifications when he employed me."

His curiosity was aroused by her words and he thought again how little he knew of her. "Why would a Hollywood actress need a CDL?"

"I had to play a truck driver in one of my movies and, although the actual driving was done by a stunt driver, I wanted to make the close-ups look realistic. So I got a license."

That statement summed Steffi up, Bryce decided. It told him more about her than anything else. It epitomized the determined, unyielding, downright bullheaded way she approached the world. Knowing something of her story, he now knew where that came from. There were still so many things he needed to ask her. There was the whole story about the murders. His instinct from the start had been to believe Steffi when she said she hadn't murdered Greg Spence and the woman who was with him. It was hard to say why. He barely knew her, but he knew he trusted her. She might drive him crazy on a daily basis, but he had never once doubted her integrity. She hadn't told the truth about who she was when she came to work for him, but she hadn't lied, either. She had simply hidden her identity. Once she told him Greg was her brother—with genuine love and grief in those amazing eyes—he had known for sure she wasn't responsible for the deaths. Even so, she still had a lot of explaining to do.

"If you didn't kill them, why did you run?"

"I found their bodies." There was a haunted look in her eyes. "And, just before I did, I saw a man with a tattoo on the back of his hand leaving the elevator in Greg's apartment building. It was the same tattoo I'd seen on the hands of the men who killed my parents. The same one that was on the man who broke into my cabin today." Her voice trembled on something close to a sob. "I panicked and ran."

There were other questions battling for supremacy, and, as Steffi's soothing fingers continued to apply the salve, Bryce struggled to make sense of and prioritize them. Why had she fled? Why had she come to Stillwater? Who were the men who had pursued her—Bryce had heard an accent and a smattering of a language he didn't know. He had guessed Eastern European and knew now it was Russian—and how had they found her?

In the end, as Steffi wound the bandage around his waist, he went for the question that seemed the least important, but the one that, for some reason, really mattered. "Should I still call you Steffi?"

She paused, her hand resting on his abdomen. Her touch sent a shimmer of heat through to his nerve endings. It felt a lot like arousal, but that couldn't be right. How totally out of place would that be in this situation? And anyway, this was *Steffi*. He might like sparring with her; she might be the only person who could hold his attention for longer than five minutes these days, but did that mean he felt something for her? And if he did, he should shake that aside fast. His head and his heart were in such an almighty mess that neither of them was in any state to consider sharing their contents with another person.

In spite of everything, there was a hint of mischief in Steffi's eyes as she smiled. "My full name is Stefanya. I use Anya as my stage name, but my family—and my friends, the few I have—have always called me Steffi."

"Do I qualify as a friend?" He didn't know why, but it was important to know the answer to that question.

The smile changed and he got a glimpse of full-on Hollywood charm. It nearly knocked him off his feet. "Engaging in a car chase and shooting the bad guy for me? I think you qualify."

Steffi finished winding the bandage around his torso and neatly tied the ends. Bryce shifted from side to side. It wasn't comfortable, but hopefully it would help him heal. "I'll get one of Cameron's T-shirts and then you can tell me the rest of the story."

Steffi nodded, her smile vanishing and nervousness taking its place. He turned away, intending to make his way to the bedroom…just as the front door came crashing in.

* * *

The three men who burst through the door clearly meant business. Bryce sprang into action, reaching for the gun he had placed on the table. Before his fingers could close over the butt, one of the intruders aimed a kick at his head. Steffi heard the sickening crunch of a boot connecting with Bryce's skull and watched in horror as her only hope crumpled to the floor.

"Shall I finish him off?" The man who had kicked him spoke with a pronounced Russian accent as he trained his gun hopefully on Bryce's unconscious form. Steffi recognized him as the giant, tattooed intruder who had burst into her cabin and been in the process of dragging her down the hall when Bryce had knocked him out. The darkening bruise on his chin confirmed it. Her heart thudded uncomfortably as she waited for a response to his question.

"No." The man who answered him had a shaved head and an air of authority. There was barely a trace of an accent when he continued. "The Big Guy doesn't like it when people he knows nothing about get involved in his business. He'll want to ask this guy some questions before you get to put a bullet in his brain and throw him in the lake."

Even though the future didn't sound hopeful for Bryce, it was a reprieve. Of sorts. Steffi began to slowly back up toward a side table on which a large piece of rose-colored quartz was the centerpiece. If she could just get her hand around that chunk of mineral…

The man who was in charge turned his attention to her. Like his companions, he had the tattooed eye on the back of his right hand.

"You have led us on quite a chase, Stefanya. Yuri has

a bullet in his knee courtesy of your friend here. Luckily, he was able to notice you had a flat tire as you drove off. We followed the shredded rubber and the marks your rims made on the asphalt. They led us right here." He shook his head with mock sadness. "The Big Guy is not happy at the delay." He signaled to his companions. "Erik, pick up the guy, get him in the car. Sergei, bring Stefanya. Let's get moving. No more screwups."

Erik was the huge man who had kicked Bryce. He tucked his gun into the waistband of his pants. Placing his hands under Bryce's armpits, he began to drag him across the floor toward the door. Sergei, who until now had remained in the background, made a move toward Steffi. Even as her instincts for self-preservation went into overdrive, her fear for Bryce's well-being kicked up a notch. She wanted to run to him and check he was okay, to shove the thug who was hauling him aside and cradle his head against her breast. The tender feelings welling up inside her were new, unexpected and highly inconvenient.

As Sergei reached out a hand to grab her, Steffi ducked under his arm. He called her an unflattering name and moved in closer. Steffi came up to one side of him, grabbed the piece of quartz and swung the heavy object into the side of his head. It made a satisfying crunch as it connected with his temple. He staggered backward from the impact, clutching a hand to his head as blood blossomed between his fingers. It bought Steffi a few precious seconds, but as she darted toward the open glass doors that led to the deck, she heard him coming after her.

When she reached the deck rail, she turned, taking Sergei by surprise as she gripped the wood with her hands and used it to support her weight. The years of dance training she had engaged in during her time at performing arts school came to her aid and, springing up with the full power of her body behind her, she kicked Sergei in the groin with both feet. He dropped onto the deck like a stone.

She didn't have time to waste on feelings of gratification. The leader of the group burst through the door seconds later, gun in hand. There was only one way for Steffi to go. It was a long way down, but the alternative didn't bear thinking about. Taking a deep breath, she placed both hands on the deck rail and vaulted over, propelling her body outward to avoid the jagged rocks.

As she landed on the pebbly lakeside beach, her left foot turned at an awkward angle and she gave a sharp cry of mingled pain and dismay. Struggling to her feet, she attempted to break into a run. It was impossible. Sharp, screaming agony shot from her ankle right up through her calf. She closed her eyes and swallowed hard. She couldn't even walk. With a sob of frustration, she sank back down onto the pebbles.

"Go down there and get her." There was a note of smug pleasure in the leader's voice as it drifted down from the deck above her. "And Sergei?"

"Yes, boss?"

"Try not to screw up this time."

Chapter 5

Bryce felt like he was crawling through a long, dark tunnel. Getting to the other side was taking too much time and effort. His head hurt like hell and the closer he got to the end of the tunnel, the more it hurt. Maybe he should just give up. Staying inside the tunnel wouldn't be so bad, would it? He couldn't remember why he wanted to get out, but something nagged at him. There *was* a reason why he had to get out. An important one.

He could hear voices, but they were fading in and out of his consciousness in a peculiar manner, like a radio with an intermittent signal. One of them was familiar and he focused his attention on that one. It was a woman and she was doing what she did best. She was arguing. There was only one woman he knew who was that skilled at disagreeing.

Steffi. His memory came back to him in a rush and

with it came the impulse to let loose with his fists. He guessed, from the pain in his head, that any attempt to put up a fight right now would get him another trip straight back into that dark tunnel of unconsciousness. He stayed where he was, lying on his side in the back seat of a fast-moving vehicle. The driver was cutting corners, swinging wildly, with an occasional squeal of tires adding to the cinematic car-chase effect.

He had no idea where they were going, but at least he and Steffi were both alive. For now.

Through his half-open eyes, Bryce could see the driver. His shaved head was the giveaway. Bryce had a vague memory of him being the first one through the busted-down door of the lake house. Next to him was another of the thugs who had been with him. In the seconds before he lost consciousness, there had been enough time for Bryce to take in the details of his appearance. Bryce couldn't turn his head, but he knew Steffi was next to him from the amount of squirming and complaining that was going on. From the occasional exasperated grunt he could hear, he figured the third guy was on Steffi's other side. That must be the muscular guy who had kicked Bryce in the head, the same one who had been in Steffi's cabin.

"Can't you shut her up?" The man in the passenger seat turned his head and Bryce caught a glimpse of congealed blood on the side of his head. He was seized by a fierce sense of pride. It was obvious Steffi hadn't succumbed to this abduction without a fight.

"Like you did, you mean? You got whacked around the head with a rock and kicked in the balls." The man on Steffi's other side snarled the words. "I sure as hell wish I *could* find a way to shut her up."

Bryce could have told them they were wasting their time. He'd known Steffi for three months and he'd never found a way to silence her once she got started. If they ever got out of this, he made a promise. He would never again make the attempt.

"And another thing." Steffi bumped against Bryce's leg as she struggled against the man who held her. "My DNA will be all over the coffee cup in that house at the lake. You do know I'm the most-wanted woman in the country, right? Now Sergei's blood is in that house, as well. It won't take the police long to link you to me."

The driver said something in Russian. Although Bryce had no idea what it was, it sounded a lot like a curse. "She's right." He half turned to look at Steffi. "Who owns that house?"

Bryce lifted his foot and pressed it down on Steffi's in a warning gesture. It was the lightest of touches, but she squealed so loud he almost started upright in shock.

"What in God's name is wrong with you now?" It was clear Steffi was seriously testing the driver's patience.

"My foot hurts."

"Maybe you should have thought of that before you jumped off that deck." He suspected the man's response involved gritted teeth.

Bryce's admiration for Steffi kicked up a notch higher. She'd jumped from the lake house deck? If he wasn't pretending to be unconscious he'd have given an admiring whistle. That must have taken some guts. He was finding out that one thing Steffi had in abundance was courage.

"Where are you taking me?" She was back to haranguing her abductors.

"We told you, Stefanya. The Big Guy wants to talk to you."

"There was no need for all this fuss." She really was amazing. Her tone of voice was that of a schoolteacher scolding a group of naughty pupils. "Why do you think I came to Stillwater? It isn't some random place I chose by sticking a pin in a map. I've been trying to get to see him. You should tell him to try coming home more often."

Bryce tried to process what she had just said. There was a lot of information in those few sentences. Steffi's words implied that this "big guy" they kept talking about lived in Stillwater. How was that possible? Bryce's hometown might be the county seat, but it was still a small city in West County, Wyoming. Stillwater was a place where everyone knew everyone else. He had complained more than once, when he had been subjected to the scrutiny of the local gossips, that everybody knew a little *too* much about each other's business. Bryce did a mental review of his acquaintances. Not one of them struck him as the sort of person likely to be involved with Russian organized crime.

"No one tells the Big Guy what to do."

A slowing in the car's pace and a change in the road surface signaled that they had left the highway. Bryce's years of driving army vehicles came in handy and he judged they were on a gravel drive of some sort. When they halted, he did some quick thinking. His cell phone was in the front pocket of his jeans. If his captors found it—and, let's face it, if he kept it on him, they *were* going to find it—he would give them everything. His identity, his contacts…his family. He had to find a way to get rid of that phone. Fast.

When they came for him and began to drag him out of the car, he opened his eyes and took a look at his surroundings. The unusual, intricately styled mansion built at the base of a mountain told him what he needed to know. With its quirky architecture and rolling gardens, Woodland Lodge was instantly recognizable. The Big Guy's identity was no longer a mystery. It was a shock, but it wasn't a mystery.

"Sleeping Beauty is awake, is he?" Sergei's voice grated on Bryce's nerves. "Good. That means I don't have to carry you."

There was an ornate pond and an elaborate arrangement of fountains in the marble courtyard in front of the house. There. Bryce needed to get to that pond. As Sergei, his hand clamped around Bryce's upper arm, marched him past it, Bryce made a performance of staggering and falling, using the action to fumble his cell phone from his pocket into the palm of his hand. With a snarl, Sergei dragged him to his knees. Bryce put out his hand as if to use the marble surrounding the pond to help pull himself up from kneeling to standing. There was only the tiniest *plop* as he slid his cell phone into the water.

He breathed a sigh of relief and allowed Sergei to manhandle him the rest of the way inside the house that belonged to Walter Sullivan, billionaire businessman and aspiring senator.

Walter owned several factories in Wyoming and retail outlets throughout the country. He was one of the biggest employers in Stillwater. Born and bred in the city, he was fond of boasting about how he liked to give some of his wealth back to his hometown. Bryce hadn't heard anything about his involvement with Russian gangs, but he had heard it wasn't a good idea to get on the wrong side of Walter.

Which didn't make his and Steffi's future seem a whole lot brighter.

* * *

When Steffi had run from Greg's apartment after she found the bodies, her only thought had been to keep running and find a place where she could hide forever. She had returned from filming in Italy the day before and the purse she carried still contained her passport and driver's license with the name of Steffi Grantham— which was, of course, her real name—some cash, and the card for her checking account.

For the next few days, she had used the card to withdraw the maximum amount of cash. Once she knew she was the main suspect in the murders, she disposed of it in case it could be used to trace her.

Sitting in a cheap motel, hacking at her hair with shaking hands, she had finally drawn a breath and stopped to think. Fear was still her overriding emotion, but anger had started to creep in. Was she going to live with this feeling for the rest of her life? Look over her shoulder every minute of every day? Or was she going to take this fight to the man who had started it and bring it to an end...one way or another?

Her decision made this meeting the ultimate irony. She had come to Stillwater intending to see Walter Sullivan on her terms. When she and Greg had realized the identity of the man they used to call Uncle Waltz, they had been stunned.

Although Steffi's adoptive parents lived in Sheridan, Wyoming, she had moved to Los Angeles six years ago. And she really didn't pay much attention to politics. It had been Greg who had found the article about Walter Sullivan, the Wyoming businessman who was predicted to sweep his way to a seat in the national Senate.

They had both stared at the accompanying photograph in horror. He was a little grayer at the temples, had a few more lines around his eyes. But there was no question about it. Walter Sullivan and Uncle Waltz were the same person. Then Greg had been killed by a man with an eye tattooed onto the back of his right hand and Steffi's world had been turned upside down.

Am I next? That was the first of the many questions Steffi wanted to ask Walter. Maybe coming to Stillwater and planning to meet with him in private wasn't the smartest move, but it was the only one she could live with. She could run, but she couldn't outdistance the nightmares.

When she'd fled, she hadn't run *from* Walter. She'd run *to* him. Her biggest fear had been that his men would find her and kill her before she could look him in the eye and demand to know why.

For the last three months she had driven out this way every few days, studying his unconventional mansion for signs that its owner was in residence. There had been nothing. The place had been closed up, the gates locked, the windows shuttered on the outside. Impatiently, she had followed his whereabouts on social media, hoping to discover his intentions. Walter relentlessly documented his progress on various sites and he had not stepped foot in Stillwater throughout the time Steffi had been in the city. Since he had announced his intention to run for a Wyoming seat, he had traveled all over the state. One of the few places he hadn't been was his hometown. Possibly he believed his popularity there was so great he would win without too much campaigning. The media and polls seemed to agree with him.

Now, instead of putting into practice her plan to sneak into the house and confront Walter on her own terms, Steffi was being carried through the front door by a thunder-faced Erik. Behind them, Sergei was dragging Bryce along with him. The bald man, who clearly had some sort of seniority within the group, strode on ahead of them. Steffi risked a brief glance in Bryce's direction. A vivid bruise was already standing out on one side of his face and he looked pale, but, as she gazed at him, one eyelid drooped ever so slightly into a wink. It was just enough to give her waning spirits a boost. She didn't know why it should. They were hopelessly outnumbered, in the hands of a group of murderous thugs, and about to be brought before the ruthless killer responsible for the murders of her parents and brother. Even if she was able to escape, she couldn't run anywhere on her injured ankle. She very much doubted she could walk. But somehow that tiny gesture from Bryce mattered. It told her she wasn't alone. It gave her a glimmer of hope.

That glimmer lasted about as long as it took for Erik to march into a luxurious dining room and deposit her on her feet beside a vast mahogany table. In acknowledgment of the cooler weather, a fire blazed in the huge grate. Heavy, full-length crimson drapes had been pulled across the windows, giving the disconcerting effect that night had fallen, even though it was afternoon.

Steffi winced as her injured ankle protested at the sensation of bearing any weight. Sergei shoved Bryce through the door so that he stood next to her. While Erik remained in the room, Sergei, walking with the delicate gait of a man in some discomfort, left.

The man sitting at the head of the table pushed aside an empty plate, wiped his lips with a snow-white napkin and regarded them from beneath hooded lids. Walter Sullivan was one of the most famous men in the state. His business interests, the factories and retail outlets he owned all over the country, raised him to the status of a celebrity, and his charitable giving had made him hugely popular. His darkly handsome features had graced television news programs and newspaper spreads almost daily in the past twelve months. His rise to prominence and his recent campaign had been stylish and intelligent. This was a man who was destined for greatness. Even though he was just beginning his campaign for the Senate, his name was regularly mentioned in connection with a possible future presidency. Now that Greg was gone, Steffi seemed to be the only person who knew what lurked behind that charming exterior.

It scared her that she was the only thing standing between Walter and the political power he wanted, but she wasn't going to let that fear show through. Tilting her chin, she met his gaze bravely. He had unusually dark eyes. It made reading his expression difficult. The last time Steffi had looked into those eyes, she had called this man Uncle Waltz. What frightened her more than anything was that he was regarding her with the same amused, affectionate smile she had seen from him all those years ago.

"You have caused me a great deal of inconvenience, Stefanya." Walter's voice expressed the same mild irritation with which he would rebuke a troublesome child. She had heard his voice on TV recently, but being in the same room as him, hearing those cultured tones up close…that was what took her right back to the night he'd murdered her parents. It took every ounce of her strength to keep from screaming.

"You killed my brother." She was pleased with the way the words came out clearly, betraying no trace of the nervousness she felt. "I wasn't in the mood to make things easy for you."

Something shifted in the depths of Walter's eyes. Something dangerous. Something she guessed he wouldn't want the voters to see. It was gone in an instant, to be replaced immediately by the public smile he showed the world.

"I haven't got time to waste sparring with you. Where is the cell phone?"

Steffi took a moment to consider the question. Her heart was pounding uncomfortably, causing the pulse in her throat to hammer wildly. It was an unpleasant choking feeling. She had no idea what he was talking about. She knew nothing about any cell phone, but she sensed giving Walter that piece of information might not be the smartest move she could make right then.

"Why should I tell you that?"

"Because you have no idea how much I can hurt you if you don't." Next to her, Bryce made an impulsive movement in Walter's direction, only to be stopped short as Erik caught hold of him by his upper arms. Walter turned his attention to Bryce, his eyes narrowing. "Ah, yes. We'll discuss your involvement later. But first we need to return to the subject of Gregori's cell phone. What have you done with it?"

Although Steffi might not know why he was so focused on Greg's cell, she sensed she may be able to use its existence to her advantage. "It's safe."

"Where?" Walter's voice was silky. That silkiness made her shiver.

It was a long shot, but she decided to go for it. "If I

told you that, you wouldn't have any reason to keep me alive, would you?" While she was being brave, she decided it was time to ask the question that had haunted her since she was five. "Why did you kill my parents?"

He seemed to debate whether to answer her, then he shrugged. "I first met your father when I visited Russia about a year before your birth. Our friendship and business partnership continued after your parents moved to America. Aleksander Anton was the leader of the Sglaz, one of the most feared criminal organizations in the world. But he made a big mistake when he tried to cheat me."

Steffi frowned. "If the men with the eye tattoo were in the Sglaz, why were they working for you on the night you killed my parents? Why do they still work for you now?"

"Money, Stefanya. Your father thought he could double-cross me, but I was one step ahead of him."

"And my mother?" It hurt to ask, to remember her mother urging her and Greg up the attic stairs that night, but she had come this far. She had to know.

For the first time, Walter appeared shaken out of his calm. Steffi thought she saw a glimmer of emotion in his eyes. "Ekaterina was…" He shook his head. "No. No more. This is ancient history."

"Did you kill her because she could identify you?"

Walter gave a harsh laugh. "You know nothing about my motives, Stefanya, but you and your brother are two of a kind. He made his first mistake when he recognized me in Los Angeles. He should have had more sense, walked away, let the past lie. He had no idea what he was dealing with. Instead, he insisted on a meeting."

It took every ounce of Steffi's acting ability to listen to what he was saying and not allow the surprise she was feeling to show. At the start of her career, she had spent a season traveling the country, working in masked theater, an old tradition that was rarely performed by modern actors. The experience had taught her how to hide her emotions behind a blank expression. Even so, her thoughts were raging out of control. A meeting? What had Greg been thinking of?

"You agreed to meet him." She managed to keep her voice level, midway between a question and a statement. It seemed safe to assume Walter *had* met with Greg.

His face contorted as if a twinge of pain had caught him unawares. "He told me he had proof I was guilty of murder. Even though I was sure he was bluffing, I wasn't going to take a chance. When we met, it turned out I was right. The *proof* he was talking about was his own memory. I couldn't believe his nerve. He started rambling about Aleksander and Ekaterina, talking about my men and the tattooed eye on their right hands, talking about what happened that night when your parents died. As if I was an idiot who couldn't remember every detail of my own life. And he assumed I was still involved with Russian organized crime. My involvement with your father was my first and only foray into that world. Even though our partnership made me billions, I was never tempted to repeat it. Your father's men may work for me now, but they are my security guards, not my gang members." Walter shook his head, clearly still struggling to believe Greg's audacity. "That was your brother's second mistake. It was only later he sent me a message to let me know he had been recording that conversation on his cell phone."

Slowly, Steffi exhaled the breath she had been holding. So that was what this was all about. That recording was the key to all of this. It was the reason Greg and the mystery girl he was with had died. "That recording confirmed everything."

Walter's lips twisted into an unpleasant smile that told her all she needed to know. Walter's ego was so huge he had responded to Greg's questions truthfully. Maybe he had even boasted about what had happened all those years ago when he killed their parents. A horrible sick feeling squirmed low in Steffi's stomach.

"Gregori was an idiot." Walter gestured dismissively. "If he'd asked for money, taken that recording to the press, or walked out of that meeting and gone straight to the police it would have been all over for me. But no. By hesitating, he gave me time to make a move against him. Three days after he made that recording, he was dead."

Steffi bent her head, hiding the rush of tears that threatened to spill over. Why hadn't Greg told her what he was planning to do? As Walter had begun his campaign and risen to prominence over the past twelve months, they had watched with mounting horror, recognizing that unforgettable face. Once they had known who the Big Guy was, they had discussed ways of bringing him to justice, but they had never come up with a satisfactory solution. They had been so young when their parents were killed...

And the man they were accusing was *Walter Sullivan*. He was one of the most powerful men in the country, and, with his political ambitions, his might was growing. Without any evidence, their story was too far-fetched. Going public would mean they would have been labeled attention-seekers. They would have given up their anonymity, drawing Walter's attention to them. And they would announce to the world that they were the children of Aleksander Anton. Putting their murdering, crime boss father's activities in the spotlight would not have been the smartest move two Hollywood actors ever made.

Now it seemed Greg had not only confronted Walter, but he had actually managed to get a confession from him. Even better than that, he had recorded it. But instead of going straight to the police, her brother had done nothing. Why? Greg might have been honorable, but he wasn't stupid. He wanted Walter brought to justice as much as she did. She had no idea where the cell phone was now, but by hiding it, Greg might just have given her a chance of survival. *If I can find the phone.* That was one huge *if.*

"A word of warning." As Walter's voice intruded on her thoughts, she felt Bryce move infinitesimally closer as though attempting to offer her comfort. "You may be tempted to pick up where your brother left off and take that recording to the police." His gaze hardened. "Let me advise you against it, Stefanya. Even if I was temporarily detained by the forces of law and order, Alexei would find you and ensure you met the same fate as Gregori. And I can assure you that my many friends in police forces all over the country would ensure the recording was destroyed before it ever reached a courtroom."

Steffi raised her head, looking Walter squarely in the eye. She had no doubt he meant every word of his threats. "I need time to get it."

He frowned. "Surely you have it with you? I figured you came to Stillwater because you had listened to it and you wanted to ask me for money. Even a movie star would be drawn by the prospect of billions."

Her instinct was to react with anger instead of fear.

How dare this man—this *murderer*—suggest she would attempt to make money out of her brother's death? "I don't want or need money from you."

As his eyes narrowed, she realized too late she had placed herself on dangerous ground. "So why did you come to Stillwater?"

Think fast. "I thought this was the last place you would look for me."

He gave a snort of laughter. "You were right. My men have been scouring the country for you since you staged your little disappearing act. Luckily, my guys are just a little smarter than the police. I already had your adoptive parents' address, so I knew you were not with them."

She took a hasty step toward him. "If you have hurt them—"

Walter's face hardened and, for a moment, Steffi was swept back to the night she looked down on him as he turned away after killing her father. Even through her fear, she refused to back down. Maintaining eye contact, she injected as much menace as she could muster into her gaze. She doubted Walter would feel intimidated, but it made her feel better as he stared back at her.

"Don't push me, Stefanya." His voice was low.

"Then don't threaten my parents. They are good people."

"I know that." *I know that?* The words sent a chill down her spine. How could Walter know anything about her parents? How much pressure had he put on them during this search? "It was clear June and Todd knew nothing of your whereabouts. I'm not sure the police have made that connection, even now, that they should be searching for Steffi Grantham instead of Anya Moretti."

"Tracking me down must have been difficult." Steffi couldn't imagine how he had done it.

"You made it so much easier by choosing to come to Stillwater. Even so, finding you was a lucky coincidence." Walter dabbed his lips again and rose from the table. "My men came here ahead of me when I was preparing to return. I have a rally in Cheyenne next week, but my campaign bus broke down. They called ahead to see if Yuri could organize a replacement. He went into Stillwater and stopped by at the offices of Delaney Transportation to see what they could do. Guess whose name he saw on the wall with the list of other drivers?"

Steffi sensed, rather than saw, the slight movement from Bryce at the mention of his firm. She was surprised that he had so far remained completely quiet, but she guessed there was a reason for his silence. During the time she had known him, she had come to trust his judgment. Her instincts told her now that she could count on him in this situation, and that he was waiting for the right moment to make a move.

"Now, it could have been coincidence, of course. I have no way of knowing how many Steffi Granthams there are in America, or even in Wyoming. But Stillwater is a small city. It also happens to be my hometown. It seemed like something that was worth checking out. It didn't take Yuri long to discover that the Steffi Grantham who worked at Delaney Transportation showed up in town around the same time Anya Moretti went missing. So he and Erik went to your place this morning to talk to you."

Walter's expression darkened again as he turned to Bryce. "Which is where your friend here entered the equation."

Chapter 6

"Who are you, and why the hell are you sticking your nose into my business?"

Keeping quiet during Steffi's exchange with Walter had been one of the hardest things he had ever done, but Bryce had been biding his time, doing what he did best, processing every bit of information available to him while sizing up the opposition. He knew the moment would arrive eventually when Walter Sullivan would turn his scrutiny from Steffi to him. He was just grateful the change in focus hadn't come in the form of a bullet to the head. At least he'd had enough time to think up a story. Would it hold up? He was about to find out.

"My name is John Andover." He felt Steffi's eyes probing his profile, but to his relief, she showed no surprise at his use of the fake name. Johnny Andover had been killed by the same roadside bomb that had injured

Bryce. He had also been one of Bryce's best friends. Johnny wouldn't have objected to Bryce using his name this way. Hell, no. He'd have wished Bryce luck and just been sorry he couldn't be here to help when he wiped that smug smile off Walter Sullivan's face. "I work with Steffi. I stayed the night at her place."

Bryce heard Steffi's sharp inhalation. Thankfully, Walter was farther away and seemed not to notice. "So this is the new boyfriend?"

"Not exactly. It was just a one-night stand." Even in a situation where she was in extreme danger, Steffi achieved a note of indifference. Bryce reminded himself that she was an actress and this was an imaginary situation. It wasn't a comment on his bedroom skills. They had never been called into question... *Focus, Delaney.*

"For a casual lay, you did a pretty good job of taking out two of my guys." Walter sounded suspicious.

Bryce knew this was going to be the tricky part. By bringing him here, Walter had made a loud, clear announcement. Bryce was disposable. Once he had seen the face of the man behind the operation responsible for killing Greg Spence and the girl he was with, Bryce was never going to be allowed to live. It wasn't a question of *if* Walter decided to give the order to kill him; it was a question of *when*. That decision about timing would influence Bryce's own actions.

Right now he only had Erik and Walter to deal with. He figured Erik was his biggest problem. Walter Sullivan might be known as the "Big Guy," but that was a reference to his status rather than his muscle. Although Walter was tall and heavyset, he clearly lived an easy life. He didn't have the same toned physique as his bodyguards. Bryce had taken Erik out once today and, although his ribs cringed at the prospect of a re-match, he knew he could do it again. It was probably a good idea to provoke Walter into making a move now, before Sergei or Alexei came back into the room and his chances grew slimmer.

"I'm ex-military. Some instincts never die. Like squashing a cockroach." Bryce maintained eye contact. "Although I prefer cockroaches to some people."

This time Steffi's indrawn breath was loud enough to be heard. Walter gave a short, disbelieving laugh before nodding to Erik. "I've heard enough. You can get rid of him…any way you choose. Just make sure the body can't be found."

Before Erik could move, Bryce took a step closer to Walter and hit him just below his left ear with the full force of his right hand. The blow had exactly the effect he had hoped for. Walter's head snapped sharply to one side and he instantly dropped to the floor.

Swinging around, Bryce saw Erik reaching into the inside pocket of his jacket. Deciding he didn't have enough time to grab the other man's arm before Erik drew his gun, Bryce moved so he was at a forty-five-degree angle to him and delivered a kick to the meaty part of Erik's thigh. Erik gave a grunt of pain and went down on one knee. Offering up thanks for the years he had spent in illicit mixed martial arts fights while he was in the army, Bryce tackled him from behind. Grabbing him by the hair, he smashed Erik's face into the polished rosewood floor several times. It wasn't a pretty or sporting move, and he could tell from the look of shock on Steffi's face it wasn't doing much to enhance Erik's looks, but it had the desired effect. When

Bryce let Erik go, the Russian wasn't getting up again anytime soon.

Rummaging in Erik's pockets, Bryce found his gun and car keys. He turned to Steffi, who was regarding him with an expression of astonishment. "Can you walk?"

"I might be able to hobble." She sounded doubtful.

"No time to find out." Pocketing the car keys and tucking the gun into the waistband of his jeans, he scooped her up into his arms. "Hold on tight."

In the three months since he had met her, Steffi had never followed an instruction from him without question. Bryce was glad she chose this as the time to change. Placing her arms around his neck, she clung on to him as though her life depended on it. Technically, he supposed it did. She was also uncharacteristically silent. So that was all it took. Sideswipe one bad guy and pound another into the floor. With those actions he had not only reduced Steffi to sweet docility, he had also gotten rid of any trace of his own demons.

While he was pleased to wave his monsters goodbye—even if it was a temporary arrangement—it sure as hell was a strange time to discover he wasn't happy about submissive Steffi. *Don't get me wrong. I don't want her fired up and fighting right now. But this quiet, passive version isn't the Steffi I...* He paused. What had he been about to say? *It's not the Steffi I know. I prefer the firebrand.*

Bryce had a basic mental map of the first floor of the house in his head, which he had gleaned upon their arrival. What he had seen wasn't helpful to a getaway. Too many rooms opened off that central hall. All it needed was for someone to exit one of those doors as they were leaving the house and they would be right back to where they started. The room they were in was at the side of the house, so he figured the best exit route would be through one of its full-length windows.

He kept hold of Steffi with one hand under her thighs, relying on her to keep herself anchored with her arms around his neck. With his other hand, Bryce pulled aside the heavy velvet drapes.

The window had an old-fashioned sash mechanism that initially resisted his efforts to push it up with one hand. Bryce used brute force to push harder and the wood gave a weary creak. Slowly, the lower part of the window rose.

He ducked down, checking what was outside. On this side of the house there was a quiet garden area. There was no one around. Underneath the window was a pretty flower bed, useful for a silent exit. Bryce lowered Steffi through the window, carefully setting her on her feet before following her.

Okay. He allowed himself a momentary feeling of relief. They were free of the house, but there was no time for whooping and hollering. Although this part of the garden was secluded, they were out in the open and vulnerable. Some fast thinking was necessary.

His ideal escape would have been on foot, using the mountainous terrain he had hiked for years, and knew so well, as cover. Reluctantly, Bryce dismissed that option. Steffi was injured, meaning she just wasn't up to that sort of exertion. He pursed his lips, aware of Steffi's eyes on his face. With her vivid, golden gaze came the full force of his responsibility to her. He had seconds to get this right. If he screwed up, he risked her life as well as his own.

A shiver of anticipation ran down his spine as he expected the thought to be accompanied by the doubt and fear that had stalked him for the past two years. It wasn't. All he felt was the same steely determination that had gripped him before a mission in Afghanistan. Before the explosion that had changed his life.

"We have to get back around to the front." He drew the car keys from his pocket and handed them to Steffi. "I'll get you as close as I can to the car we were brought here in, then I'm going to create a diversion. When I give you a signal, I want you to get across and unlock the car. I know you can barely walk, but I need you to do this for me, even if you have to crawl on your belly."

Steffi's expression was determined as she nodded her understanding. "I'll do it." From the look in her eye, Bryce didn't doubt for a second that she would give it 100 percent.

"Once you get into the car, put the keys in the ignition. Then get down in the footwell of the passenger seat. Stay there, even when I get in and start driving."

"What will you do to create a diversion?" Those mesmerizing eyes were huge, dominating her face as she gazed up at him.

He grinned, a surge of energy and something suspiciously like the old pre-mission excitement powering through him. "I'll think of something."

Steffi barely had time to register what Bryce was doing when he indicated for her to duck behind a clump of finely cut gray-green ferns. Peeping out from behind the aromatic fronds, she watched in surprise as he doubled back the way they had come and climbed into the room they had just left.

What the hell was he thinking? Having just escaped the lion's den, he was now deliberately returning to place his head in the big cat's jaws one more time. The only consolation was that Walter and Erik were both unconscious. Since they wouldn't remain that way forever, Steffi was strongly of the opinion that she and Bryce should be making the most of that situation by moving rapidly in the opposite direction.

From her fragrant vantage point, Steffi kept her gaze fastened on the windows of the dining room. It didn't take long before Bryce's intentions became clear. Pulling back the drapes and hoisting up the other three windows, he disappeared briefly from view. From then on, she caught disjointed glimpses of him as he moved around inside the room. As he drew close to the windows again, he was carrying a lit taper. Fascinated, Steffi watched as he proceeded to set light to the drapes at each of the windows except one.

Having assured himself that the drapes were fully alight, Bryce climbed back out of the only window that wasn't surrounded by a ring of fire. Throwing the taper back into the room, he joined Steffi behind the fern bush.

"Walter has got himself a sophisticated sprinkler system, so the bad guys won't be barbecued while they are out cold. I give the smoke detectors another minute." He slid an arm around her waist, pulling her upright and against his side. "Time to get moving."

Although it was painful, Steffi found she could walk with his assistance. She had no idea where they were in relation to the front of the house. The contours of the quirky building seemed almost to have been designed to throw her into confusion, but Bryce had no such problem. As he followed the outer wall of the house, keeping Steffi pinned tight against his side, he navigated the twists and turns as if he had an internal GPS system.

She marveled at his ability to have assimilated so much detail while under pressure. He must have known that Walter had brought him here with the intention of killing him, yet he had taken the time to notice the fire safety features, storing the information up, finding a way to make it all work for him. It even looked like he'd factored the flammability content of the drapes into his plan.

And it was working. Alarms were already screeching out a warning inside the house, and, as they reached a corner from which they could view the front of the house, Steffi could hear shouts and running footsteps.

Looking up at the man at her side, she encountered an unaccustomed feeling. As she observed the total concentration on Bryce's face, she realized that, for the first time ever, she was placing all her reliance on another person. It had never happened before. Not once throughout her life with her adoptive parents. Not even when she had encountered Greg again after all those years. So this was what trust felt like. This warm, pleasant, scary as hell emotion must be what having confidence in another human being felt like. Steffi took a moment to examine it and decided she didn't like it. She might have to tolerate it for now, but she wouldn't be doing it again.

Hand control of my life over to someone else? No, thank you.

Even as that thought kicked in, she had to admit that Bryce had done a pretty good job so far of keeping her safe. She felt secure with him, like he knew what he was doing. The knowledge that he would get them out of this wrapped itself around her like someone draping a warm blanket around her shoulders on a cold day. For someone who had spent her whole life keeping the world at a distance—usually relegating it to the other side of a camera lens—it delivered a powerful jolt to her system.

Bryce was doing this for no other reason than that was who he was. Okay, now it was about saving his own life as well as hers, but prior to Walter's involvement, Bryce could have just walked away and left her to sort out this mess on her own. He didn't know her well enough to get involved, didn't owe her anything. It occurred to Steffi that she didn't know many people who were genuinely good. There was no one in her life on whom she could rely totally the way she was doing with Bryce right now. *I don't know many people.* Anyone examining her Hollywood life under a microscope would believe it was filled with friends. The truth? People had drifted in and out of her world without making any real impression. It suited Steffi because she didn't do closeness. The reality was that her perfect Hollywood life was lonely as hell.

Those thoughts flashed through her mind in the seconds before Bryce gave her a quick push toward the car Erik had left out front when he brought them to the house. "Go." His voice was low and urgent, but also encouraging.

As Steffi, biting her lip against the pain that flared through her injured ankle, crouched low and moved at a midspeed hobble to the car, part of her mind acknowledged the chaos unfolding around her. Although she didn't dare risk a glance back at the house, she was aware of people—*two, possibly three?*—spilling out from the front door onto the drive.

"They can't have gone far. Split up and find them." The order was barked out, and Steffi recognized the voice. It was Alexei, the leader of the group who had burst into the lake house. "When you find the guy, kill him."

Those words caused a little whimper to escape Steffi's lips as she reached the car. Her fingers felt numb as she fumbled with the key to press the button for the central locking system. After several attempts, she heard the click of the door. It was the sweetest sound she had ever heard. Keeping her head down, she opened the passenger door and, remembering Bryce's instructions, slid into the footwell.

Her heart was pounding in her ears as she felt her way around the steering column and slid the key into the ignition. The action seemed to be the trigger for a hail of gunfire. Like firecrackers going off in a constant, deadly stream, the shots were coming from the direction of the house. Steffi gnawed at her lip. Bryce had told her to keep down, but surely he didn't mean for her to ignore something like this? He should have given her options for different scenarios. What about if the shooting got too bad and he couldn't get to the car? If Bryce got shot, what was she meant to do? How was she supposed to help him?

Easing herself into a reclining position in the passenger seat, she peered over the edge of the dashboard. The scene that met her eyes was confusing. There was no sign of Bryce, and Walter's men appeared to be shooting randomly in the direction of the house. Angry orange flames had begun to blaze from the lower floor and clouds of acrid smoke poured out, filling the air with the bitter scent of destruction. As she watched, she saw Sergei, who was stalking across the lawn in front of the house, turn sharply as if in response to a prompt behind him. As he did, Bryce darted out from behind a row of bushes to Sergei's left and, keeping low, made his way toward the car. With a sigh of relief, Steffi dropped back down into the footwell.

Bryce barreled into the car, started the engine and screeched across Walter's immaculate lawn before he had even closed the driver's-side door. They bumped over an ornate water feature before settling onto the winding drive. Bryce took the twists and turns of this with the ease and skill of a rally driver. Steffi, expecting a volley of bullets to come through the rear windshield at any second, realized that he had used the advantage of surprise against his pursuers.

A sharp right turn and a dramatic increase in speed signaled they had left Walter's property and were on the main highway. Steffi heard sirens coming toward them and assumed the fire department had automatically been alerted when the alarm went off inside Walter's property. She uncurled slightly and looked up at Bryce. At his strong, capable hands on the wheel. His forearms were tanned and corded with muscle. From her angle beneath him, her distorted view of his face emphasized the determined lines of his jaw and the carved beauty of his mouth.

From nowhere, a sudden, overpowering desire to straighten farther, drape her arms around his neck and kiss those masterful, surprisingly full, lips hit her hard and low…at a point somewhere just south of her navel.

She drew in a sharp breath, surprised by the ferocity of the longing that gripped her.

Bryce's eyes flickered briefly from the road to her upturned face. "Are you okay?"

She decided now was probably not the best time to confess the unexpected turn her thoughts had taken. "How did you get them to shoot randomly in the direction opposite from where you were?"

"I threw stones. They were so jumpy, they started firing at the sound." Although Bryce's attention was back on the road, and she could no longer see the upper part of his face, she heard the frown in his next words. "How did you see what was going on? I asked you to stay down."

"I got scared that you might have been shot, so I took a peek at what was happening."

He was silent for a few moments. "If we're going to get out of this alive, Steffi, you are going to have to trust me and do as I say."

There was that word again. *Trust.* Could she do it? Steffi looked up at that uncompromising, stubble-shadowed jawline and that perfect mouth. Bryce was right. She was going to have to try.

Chapter 7

A few miles past Walter's place, Bryce left the main highway and followed a series of rough hunting tracks, some of them only half remembered hiking routes from his teenage years. The bumpy terrain was difficult to navigate, but the car he had taken was an SUV and it covered the ground easily. After about half an hour of crisscrossing the lower reaches of the Stillwater Trail with no sign of any pursuer, he decided it was safe to make his way onto the road into town.

Once he was sure they weren't being followed, he had allowed Steffi to leave her uncomfortable position. Seated next to him, she was now looking around her at Stillwater's center with wary suspicion. After the day they had just endured, it was hardly surprising.

The working day was coming to a close and Bryce took comfort from the familiar sights and sounds of his

hometown doing what it always did. Stores on Main
Street were closing up and he recognized people on the
sidewalks as they made their way home. On his return
from Afghanistan, this place, together with his brother
Cameron, had been his anchor. At that time, his relationship with Vincente had still been too antagonistic.
They had been half brothers in the remotest sense of
the word. Growing up, there had been nothing frater-
nal about their relationship. Vincente had been four
when Bryce was born, and their relationship had been
clouded by the jealousy Vincente felt for Cameron, the
brother Bryce worshipped. Childhood had set the tone
for an uneasy distance in adult life. Vincente had always known how to fire up his younger brother's temper. Despite his promises to Cameron that he wouldn't
let his older brother get to him, Bryce had continued to
fall for Vincente's jibes every time. It was only recent
events that had made them see they could be a formi-
dable team when they put their minds to it. It saddened
them both that it had taken a vicious murderer to force
them to realize that they were bound together by un-
breakable ties of love and loyalty.

"Have you ever heard of post-traumatic stress
disorder?" That was what the fresh-faced young doctor had asked Bryce on his return from Afghanistan.

Bryce had clenched his fist to keep from driving
it into that earnest, sympathetic face before walking
straight out the door. Had he heard of it? Giving the
monster that lived inside him a name didn't make it easier to live with. No amount of therapy would drive away
the images of good men and close friends being torn
apart before his eyes. Talking about it wouldn't banish
the guilt that they had died while he had survived…all

because he had made the wrong decision. Sitting in a discussion group with other sad-eyed people who had been diagnosed with the same disorder wouldn't take away the nightmares. None of those things would make him whole again.

Stillwater had done a good job of allowing Bryce to hide in plain sight. When he came home, everything was familiar. He had been able to slip right back into his old life with no outward sign of the scars the bomb had left on him. He had a slight limp, and now and then someone would notice and ask how his leg was healing. No one ever asked how his head was doing. Which was just as well. *Because the answer to that would be screwed.*

Cameron knew, of course. His older brother, the person he was closer to than anyone else in the world, had taken one look at him on his return and acknowledged the change in him. Bryce had seen sadness instantly cloud Cameron's eyes. From then on, Cameron had done practical things to help. The job at Delaney Transportation had been a lifeline. Helping Bryce purchase a run-down old house in town and undertake the renovations had been a project that had helped keep him occupied. Being there to talk, even though Bryce never mentioned feelings or memories, was another of Cameron's skills. Then Cameron's girlfriend, Carla, had died and the brothers had leaned on each other.

Now, as he drove through town and allowed Stillwater to work its hometown magic on him, Bryce realized he and Steffi needed help. He also realized he couldn't take this to the one person to whom he would usually turn with even the smallest problem.

Bryce loved his new sister-in-law. He thought Laurie

was perfect for Cameron. She had healed the hurt left by Carla's death in a way Bryce had believed might never be possible. But he wasn't about to ask her to compromise her duty to the police force by revealing the details of his plans to her. Because he had no intention of letting the forces of law and order take charge. Not yet. Walter Sullivan's face came into his mind's eye. This had become personal. Playing it by the rules wasn't an option. Walter would fight dirty. And Bryce was looking forward to fighting back in exactly the same way.

"Where are we going?" Steffi asked as he swung the car off Main Street and away from the downtown area.

He couldn't ask Cameron and Laurie for help, but lately there had been one other person in his life he could trust. Bryce felt his heart lift slightly in acknowledgment of that fact. "Vincente's place."

He registered the look of apprehension on Steffi's face as she swallowed hard. "I'm not sure…"

"Steffi, if we are going to clear your name, we have to get to California and get that cell phone. We can't do that without help. We have no money. We don't even have a change of clothes." He indicated his bare chest and the remnants of the bandages still clinging around his waist. "Walter will be on our tail as fast as you can blink. Vincente will help us."

Pulling over a few blocks from Vincente's elegant new apartment block, he took his hand off the wheel and reached over to place it on her knee. It was a simple gesture, intended to reassure her. As he turned his head to catch her eye, it became something more. In the space of a few seconds, the air in the car had become statically charged. Out of nowhere, everything changed. It hit him like a bolt out of the blue, driving out his breath and making him so hard his zipper was in danger of bursting. How had he reached this point? How had he gone from mild interest to wanting Steffi so much it hurt, all in the space of a nanosecond?

"Do you trust me?" His voice was husky with need.

"I want to." Some intuition told him those words cost her a lot. He heard his own hunger reflected in Steffi's voice, saw it in her eyes, and his heart leaped in response. "It's just that I didn't tell Walter the truth back there when we were in his house."

Bryce frowned, forcing himself to focus on what she was saying instead of on the plump cushion of her lower lip. "What do you mean?"

"I have no idea where Greg's cell phone is."

Vincente's apartment was on the second floor and the views from the full-length windows across the river to the mountains beyond were amazing. Although she had been in Stillwater for three months, Steffi hadn't grown accustomed to the raw power of the landscape. It could still take her by surprise, stealing her breath away like a skillful pickpocket, leaving her unaware that she had been robbed until it was too late.

As she sank into one of the leather chairs that had been placed to get the full effect of the view, she felt a pang of envy toward Vincente, who got to see this every day. She was aware of Bryce's half brother, the man who had hired her, casting curious glances in her direction as he went to fix coffee, but he had refrained from asking questions. He hadn't even mentioned his brother's lack of a shirt and the rainbow bruises that decorated his ribs and chest or the fact that one half of his face was swollen and discolored. As restraint went,

Vincente was displaying a level that went beyond remarkable and strayed into the superhuman.

When Vincente placed three steaming mugs of coffee on a central coffee table, Bryce gave an appreciative sigh. "Some food to go alongside it would be good. It's been a long day."

Vincente nodded. "Let me see what I can do."

Steffi gazed at his back as he retreated once more in the direction of the kitchen. "What will you tell him?"

"The truth." Bryce leaned across and took her hand, the action feeling comfortable and familiar. Steffi didn't want to pause and examine the way that made her feel happy and scared at the same time. "It's the only way I know how to do this."

She swallowed the sudden obstruction in her throat. *The only way I know how to do this.* It summed up Bryce and his approach to life. Unlike him, her whole life had been built around a lie. Playing a part. Pretending. They were polar opposites. He was open and honest. There was no subterfuge about him. With Bryce, what you saw was what you got. He was helping her because he had no choice. He would never walk away from a fellow human being in distress. The reality of her life would repulse him. She was the daughter of a notorious crime boss, a man who had murdered, dealt drugs and trafficked people for money. She hid her true nature so successfully behind a series of roles, she herself didn't know who the real Stefanya Anton, Steffi Grantham or Anya Moretti was. A woman who was so scared of relationships, she ran a mile whenever a man appeared in danger of getting close. Just like now. Gently, she withdrew her hand, forcing herself to ignore the flare of hurt the action provoked in Bryce's dark eyes.

He is being nice because that's who he is, she told herself, with a touch of exasperation. It was no good trying to fool herself that this was anything different. That this was about her personally, or that he returned that spark she'd felt back there when he parked the car—the one that was like a shot of molten heat straight to her core—or that this was anything unusual for him. That would be about as close to crazy as she could get. And Steffi wasn't about to let this situation drive her crazy. Not without a fight.

Vincente returned with half a cold, take-out pizza plus assorted chips and cookies, and Steffi hid a smile. Bryce, falling on the food like a starving man, didn't seem to notice that they had clearly caught Vincente unawares. It looked like he had been forced to raid his limited stash of bachelor fare for them. Somehow, the knowledge, together with the arrival of the food, stripped away the barriers between them, and Steffi chewed on a piece of cold pizza while Bryce summarized the story so far. Even though she was at the center of it, as she listened to the details, it sounded like the worst kind of paranoia.

Vincente Delaney's coloring was darker than his brother's and there was often a staccato restlessness about his manner that hinted at his half-Italian heritage. On this occasion he sat very still, his almost black eyes trained on Bryce's face as he listened intently to what he was being told. Steffi found it impossible to judge what he was thinking. Would he refuse to help? All Vincente had to do was call the police and her freedom was a thing of the past. She was surprised to find she could consider that option objectively. Now she knew about the cell phone, wouldn't it be better to turn herself in? To try to prove that she hadn't killed Greg and the girl he had been with? By running she had pretty much declared her guilt. If she came clean now, and told the truth, the police would have to check her story out. DNA tests would show she and Greg were related. She supposed it would at least lay to rest the theory that she had killed him in a jealous rage.

The problem with her story was that until the cell phone was found it was her word against Walter's. Steffi had a horrible feeling that, even if she was in police custody, the man who had killed her parents and her brother would be able to carry out his threat and find a way to get to her, as well. Even now, in the security of Vincente's apartment, she had to resist the temptation to keep looking over her shoulder. The compulsion to check each darkened corner for men with tattooed hands was overwhelming. All in all, she was relieved to see Vincente's own hands remained loosely clasped between his knees. He didn't reach for his cell phone while Bryce talked.

When Bryce finished his narrative, ending at the point where they had escaped from Walter's mansion, Vincente's expression was unreadable. Then he exhaled long and hard, taking a moment to study the ceiling.

"I hate to be the one to point this out, but Los Angeles is a big place—" Vincente gave a quick glance from his brother to Steffi, then back again "—containing a hell of a lot of cell phones."

Bryce paused with a handful of chips partway to his mouth. "It stands to reason that Greg must have kept this one somewhere safe."

Vincente turned to Steffi. "Do you have any idea where?"

She shook her head. "No, I only learned of its existence a few hours ago. But he would only have shared this information with someone he trusted. Greg and I are the only people, apart from Walter and the men who were with him that night, who know how our parents died. I think Greg would have tried to either get the cell phone to me, or get word about where it was to me. I was on location in Italy when he met with Walter and I only returned the night before Greg was killed. Because I didn't know about this recording, I wasn't looking for it before I left Los Angeles. Now I can go back there and search from a position of strength. While still hiding from the police, and now Walter, of course."

"What about your own cell phone?" Bryce asked. "Did Greg send you any messages just before he died that might have contained any clues?"

Steffi bit her lip. "He didn't send me a copy of the recording, that's for sure. But I threw my phone into a Dumpster when I took off after I found the bodies. I was scared the police might be able to use it to trace me." She frowned as she tried to recall her interactions with her brother over the few days prior to his death. "I didn't speak to Greg while I was in Italy. When I think back to before I left, I think maybe Greg did seem edgy, but I'm not sure whether I'm going back and ascribing a mood to him at that time that might not have existed in reality." She wrinkled her nose, not sure she was explaining herself clearly. "Because I now know what came next. You see?"

"Hindsight." Bryce nodded. "There might have been little things you didn't notice at the time that you're only remembering now."

Steffi nodded, grateful that he understood. "I got

back from Italy the night before he died and we were supposed to have dinner together before I went to an awards ceremony. Greg called me at the last minute and canceled. That *was* unusual. If ever we had an arrangement to meet, we always kept it. After all the years we'd spent apart, our time together was precious. When he called, he said something had come up, and it was unavoidable. He asked if I'd come over to his apartment for breakfast instead. He said he had something to tell me but he didn't want to do it over the phone." She frowned. "I'd almost forgotten. When we hung up, he almost immediately sent me the weirdest message. Just one word and four digits. It said 'Bliss 2713.'"

"Did that mean anything to you?" Bryce asked.

"Nothing at all. I messaged him back asking what he meant, but he didn't reply. I figured I'd be seeing him the next day, so I'd ask him then." She swallowed hard. "Only when I did see him…" That image swam into her mind. Greg with his head thrown back, that poor unknown girl kneeling between his legs. The blood. The guy with the tattoo stepping out of the elevator as she stepped in. She squeezed her eyelids tightly closed, trying to shut the pictures out.

"You are placing yourself at risk going back there." Vincente's voice was cool and businesslike. "Someone may recognize you."

Steffi exhaled the breath she'd been holding and opened her eyes. "You'll help us?"

He nodded slowly. "On one condition."

Bryce's frown wasn't encouraging. "Go ahead."

"You call me every night to let me know you're okay. Anytime you miss, I go to the cops."

"Damn it, Vincente. I'm not a kid checking in with my big brother while our folks are away."

Vincente shrugged. "Take it or leave it."

"It's not a bad idea." Even as she uttered them, Steffi could hardly believe the words were coming from her lips. "If we don't check in, Vincente will know there is a reason, probably a Walter Sullivan–related reason. That would be a good time to hand this over to him, let him take it to the police."

For a moment Bryce regarded his brother from under lowered brows. Steffi got the feeling this was nothing to do with her, or the current situation. It seemed to be a brotherly power struggle that transcended time or place. Bryce's stormy brown eyes met Vincente's darker ones. Gradually, the heat diffused and something else replaced it. It was hard to say that Vincente won. It was more that an understanding was reached, a balance achieved. Steffi got a strong sense that these men had battled their way to this point, but that they had built a relationship based on bonds of mutual trust.

Ah, that word. *Trust.* It was taunting her lately, dancing around just out of her reach. It was a thing other people had—fought hard for, in the case of these two men—but it continued to remain stubbornly elusive in Steffi's life.

Bryce nodded curtly. "You got it. And Steffi won't be at risk. Not while she has me with her."

He gripped her hand again, and this time she didn't pull away. She gave it a fleeting thought and then decided she liked it. Liked the feeling of his warm, slightly calloused fingers wrapped around hers. Liked the feeling of subdued strength she got from him, as if he could apply more pressure, but he was treating her gently because he was stronger than she was. Liked handing herself over, just this once, into his power.

Vincente looked down at their entwined fingers and smiled. Steffi thought what a charming man Vincente could be…when he wanted to. It was something she had thought when he first gave her the job at Delaney Transportation. Vincente could turn his charm on and off at will. It was a skill in itself. Just occasionally, when he thought no one was looking and the charm wasn't needed, there was a haunted look in those midnight-dark eyes that hinted at a hidden sadness.

"You'd better give me a list of what you need…starting with how we patch up your injuries."

Chapter 8

Catching a glimpse of their side-by-side reflections in a smoked glass window as they exited the bus station, Bryce was satisfied with what he saw. A woolen beanie completely covered Steffi's hair and a huge pair of shades hid the upper part of her face. Vincente had followed his instructions to perfection, and her dark, androgynous clothing, coupled with a pair of biker boots, meant she could easily be mistaken for a youth. Bryce bit back a smile as he observed her. She had even adopted a slightly moody swagger to go along with this new persona. It was partly to disguise the limp that lingered from her ankle injury and partly because, as an actress, she had automatically slipped into this new role. It was only on close inspection that her delicate features and slender curves gave her away.

He was dressed in a similar, grungy style, with two

days' worth of stubble adding to the effect. They both carried beaten-up backpacks, unearthed from Vincente's garage and containing a few changes of clothing.

Getting into Bryce's house to get his credit cards and clothes hadn't been a problem. When Vincente returned to his apartment with these items, they had discussed the problem of getting into Steffi's cabin.

"Walter will have someone watching it," Bryce had said with grim certainty. "There is no way you will be able to get in there to get Steffi's things."

"I don't keep my personal stuff at the cabin." There had been a spark of triumph in Steffi's eyes as she spoke. "My driver's license, passport and credit cards are in my locker at Delaney Transportation. I had nowhere in the cabin to lock them away, so I always felt they were safer there if I was recognized and needed to make a quick getaway."

From then on, Vincente had moved fast, buying Steffi the items of clothing she needed, getting Bryce a new cell phone and booking their bus tickets, hotel room and a rental car.

"It feels strange being here in San Diego when my house and Greg's apartment are both in Los Angeles," Steffi said now. She kept her voice low and made sure there was no one around as she made the comment.

"We need to stay one step ahead of Walter." That was one of the reasons why they had traveled by bus instead of flying. The other was the more obvious threat; the police would be on the lookout for Steffi's identification, and the scrutiny would be more intense, at an airport. "I have a feeling he will have a welcome party waiting for us in Los Angeles. Driving into town will make it easier to stay under his radar."

Steffi shivered and moved a little closer to him. It

wasn't much, but the gesture made Bryce's heart soar. There had been a few such moments over the past twenty-four hours, tiny movements on Steffi's part that made him feel like a man who had gained the precious trust of a wild bird. It was a fragile bond, and one he wanted to nurture. He wasn't sure why this woman was different. He just knew she was. Maybe it was this crazy mess they were in. He hoped it had nothing to do with who she was in her day job. He gave a wry smile at the image of himself as a starstruck fan. Maybe it was because he wanted her more than any woman he'd ever met. Whatever it was, he wanted to take it slow, savor it, see if it was still around when they came out the other side of this madness. *If* they came out the other side of this madness. Right now he should probably focus on that instead of thinking about grabbing her and kissing her into near oblivion every time she brushed up against him accidentally.

There had been a turning point when they had stayed in Vincente's apartment and his brother had made an assumption about their relationship. Having cleaned up Bryce's various cuts and bruises, Vincente had checked out Steffi's injured ankle. Although it was swollen and painful, there didn't seem to be any broken bones. Vincente had expressed his opinion that it was a sprain and had bandaged it. By that time, his visitors were tired and he had thrown open the door of the second bedroom in his apartment.

"I hope this is okay?"

Steffi, having viewed the king-size bed in silence for a second, had raised her eyes to Bryce's face. He had read the conflicting emotions that were darting across her expressive features. There was apprehension and anticipation, but there was also a definite spark of arousal.

He wanted to see that flame in Steffi's eyes. More than anything. He just didn't want it forced on her because the sleeping arrangements dictated it.

Before she could say anything, Bryce had spoken up quickly. "I'll take the sofa."

Her expression had changed to one of gratitude. Had he also caught a brief flicker of disappointment alongside it? *Your reputation as the Stillwater stud is going to your head, Delaney. What the hell do you have to offer Anya Moretti, darling of the paparazzi, queen of Hollywood awards ceremonies?* Somehow he didn't imagine a steak and a beer at Dino's, his favorite restaurant on Main Street, would compare to the fancy places she was used to. Hadn't he read somewhere that she was super-picky about the men she dated? Why was he even picturing this as if there was anything in their future? Hollywood actress and truck company boss? Like that would happen.

As Bryce organized the paperwork for the hired car and they made their way across the vast parking lot in the shimmering midday heat to collect the vehicle, he realized they would need to have the whole who-sleeps-where conversation again once they reached Los Angeles. They were booked into one hotel room. No way was he accepting a different arrangement. Until that cell phone with its incriminating recording was in the hands of the police and Walter Sullivan was behind bars, he wasn't letting Steffi out of his sight.

He sighed. It didn't need a clairvoyant to predict there was likely to be more sleeping on the sofa in his immediate future.

"Lighter or darker?"
Steffi barely registered Bryce's words as he stood

behind her, meeting her eyes in the mirror over the bathroom sink. His hands rested gently on her shoulders and although the gesture was casual, she had recently discovered that any physical contact with Bryce had the power to drive the breath from her lungs and rob her of the ability to think straight. The intimacy of this situation, with him standing so close she could feel the warmth of his body radiating through her own, was making her feel ever so slightly giddy. Every other thought was a new fantasy, each one just a little bit wilder, a little more daring and a whole lot of what she desperately needed. Right now she was picturing turning to face him, lifting herself onto that sink, and wrapping her arms around his neck and her legs around his waist…

Those chocolate-brown eyes seemed to be reading her thoughts. Heat and color flooded her face. "Uh… I don't…"

Bryce quirked an amused brow at her. "I'm not promising to deliver red carpet standard styling here, Steffi. The best we can hope for is to make you look radically different. So what's it to be?" He nodded at the two boxes of hair dye on the counter next to the sink. "Black or blond?"

Focus. This is about keeping you alive, not about how much you want to rip this man's clothes off. "Black."

Her eyes widened as he lifted his hand to reveal a pair of scissors. "Just remember, it will grow again."

Steffi gave a little moan as she ran a hand through her hair. "It's already short."

Bryce shook his head. "That might make a die-hard fan think twice if they pass you on the street. It might even stop the police from recognizing you. But Walter and his thugs saw you two days ago. I want to make you look as different as I can from the person they remember."

She sighed. "Do your worst."

He pretended to be hurt. "I'm going to do my best."

She closed her eyes, deciding the only way to get through this was to let Bryce get on with his task but to not look at the detail of what he was actually doing. His big hands felt capable and warm on her head and neck as he chopped at her hair, turning and tilting to get a better angle. When he had finished with the scissors, he stroked a hand over her head and Steffi shivered. She was fairly sure he was checking for loose hairs, but the gesture felt a lot like a caress.

Next came the sensation of the cold dye being massaged into her hair. Bryce moved closer, arching his body over hers, and Steffi bowed lower over the sink to make it easier for him. The intimacy of the position wasn't lost on her. His muscular chest was pressed against her back. The fronts of his thighs pushed into the backs of hers, forcing her up against the sink. She could tell Bryce was aware of it, too. Very aware. The hard ridge of his erection rammed into the soft roundness of her buttocks, making her long to remove the layers of cloth between them. Making her ache to push back against him. To grind her hips. To wriggle. Anything to relieve the building tension.

"We have to leave that for twenty minutes." Bryce's voice was husky when he finally finished applying the dye.

Steffi turned slowly. He held up hands that were encased in plastic gloves and covered in the same black gunk that coated her head. Those glorious brown eyes were alight with the same fire that invaded her limbs.

Without hesitation she rose on the tips of her toes and pressed her mouth to his. He responded instantly, his tongue parting the curve of her lips and tangling with hers. The heat that had been dancing on the surface between them for days pounded deeper, invading her blood and spreading like wildfire through her veins.

"You had to do this now?" Bryce raised his head, laughter and frustration in his eyes. "When I can't touch you?"

"Twenty minutes isn't so very long to wait," she murmured, brushing her lips back over his again. His mouth was warm and masterful as his tongue licked and tasted hers, building the desire between them to a peak. Kissing Bryce was like being in the center of a furnace; molten heat washed over her, drawing her in, filling her and searing her.

"Long enough to kill me." His voice was shaky as he looked down at her.

"Anyway—" she reached for his belt buckle, enjoying the flare of surprised pleasure in his eyes "—for the next twenty minutes, I *can* touch you."

Moving lower, she dropped to her knees on the tile floor as she slid his zipper down, pushing his jeans and briefs over his hips. Bryce gave a groan as her hand closed over him. She ran her fingers up and down his shaft, exulting in the feel of him. Silk-encased steel throbbed hot and hard beneath her touch.

Leaning closer, she flicked her tongue lightly over his tip, and his whole body jerked wildly in response. Electricity zinged through her own body at the same time. Parting her lips, she closed them over him, taking him fully into her mouth. As she began to suck his iron hardness, she moaned around him. The erotic anticipation that had been building within her broke free, out of control, flooding her body with its urgent demands. Excitement and hunger filled her in equal measures. Desire built and spiraled, leaving her quivering and aching for his touch.

Lost in the pleasure of what she was doing, she dimly heard Bryce's groans of approval, felt his hips moving in time with the rhythm of her movements as she rubbed her tongue along the underside of his erection.

"Hell, yes. Just like that."

She gazed up at him through half-closed eyes. He was watching her mouth, watching as he slid in and out between her lips. His expression was a mix of such perfect concentration and pleasure that a matching emotion pulsed through Steffi's own veins. The effect was like a shot of pure lust straight to her core.

As he began to throb and tighten, Steffi increased the pace of her movements. Bryce gave a single harsh cry as he climaxed, and she relaxed her mouth, swallowing the heated taste of him.

As she moved to sit back on her heels, easing his clothing back into place, his indrawn breath told her he was struggling to find the right words.

"Steffi, I…"

"Shh." She didn't want this to get awkward. They had enough problems without making this out-of-control attraction between them into one of them. "I think our twenty minutes are up and I don't want my hair to fall out."

He muttered a curse, indicating his hands. "Can you turn on the faucet?"

She got to her feet and busied herself with preparations for removing the dye while trying to ignore the lingering heat in her body. As Bryce leaned over to begin washing her hair, his lips brushed her ear, sending a frenzied shiver down her spine. "Just so you know, we are not done. I owe you an orgasm." His teeth nipped the lobe, making her gasp. "And I intend to deliver... with interest."

The words were so delicious that Steffi couldn't help the little moan that escaped her. It wasn't going to happen, of course. Bryce couldn't know that she had never been able to relinquish control sufficiently to climax. And she certainly wasn't going to tell him. She would just have to rely on her acting ability. It had never let her down before.

Just as he had planned, Steffi looked different. Different in a way that Bryce wasn't sure was an improvement, but one that continued to arouse the hell out of him. Or maybe it was the lingering memory of what had happened in the bathroom that was responsible for his permanent hard-on. All he knew was he would never look at a packet of hair dye in the same way again.

He had cut her hair so short it stood up on top of her head in spikes. Now a blue-black color, it accentuated the creamy pallor of her skin and the sharp delicacy of her features. When she wasn't wearing her glasses, her eyes appeared huge, dominating her face.

"I look like a pixie," she grumbled. "Or some other creature of the woodland variety."

They had agreed to wait until nightfall before they started their search for the cell phone at her house in Beverly Hills. Bryce had a feeling it was going to be a pointless undertaking, if they managed to get into the house at all...and, given that she was wanted for murder, there were no guarantees that they would. In the immediate aftermath of the murders, the police would have been all over Steffi's place. If Greg had hidden the cell phone in her house, or mailed it to Steffi in the days before he was killed, and it had turned up at her house after his death, Bryce would have expected the police to have it by now. Clearly, since Walter was still at large, that wasn't the case.

If Greg had hidden it somewhere in the house without telling Steffi where it was, their chances of finding it were slim to nonexistent. Always supposing it was still there. Walter's guys had probably gotten in there and searched the house from top to bottom. If they hadn't found the phone, it wasn't there. The same went for Greg's apartment, where they were planning to go next. Even though Bryce thought searching both places was probably a waste of their time, he also thought not doing it would feel like unfinished business. And it would make Steffi feel better that they were making an effort to find the phone.

Although, speaking of unfinished business...

He reached out a hand and caught Steffi by the wrist, pulling her to him. Her eyes widened and the breath left her lungs with a little huffing sound as he gripped her hips hard. "I owe you, remember?"

Those unusual eyes darkened to a deeper shade of gold as he bent his head and lightly kissed the curve of her neck. The scent of her perfume flared in his nostrils. It was light, summery and sexy, spiking his need for her up to superhuman proportions.

"You started this—" his voice was hoarse with longing "—and I'm going to finish it. But you'd better be sure you want to see this through, Steffi. If you don't, now would be a good time to tell me no."

She tilted her head back, staring at him with a faint look of defiance on her face. When she didn't speak, he swung her around, so she was facing the wall. Lifting her hands above her head and holding them at the wrists with one of his own hands, he used his taller, harder body to keep her in place.

The fingers of his other hand moved to the button of her jeans.

A soft whimper greeted him, but he knew from the tone, and the way she pushed back against him, that it was a plea to continue. He spread his hand over her abdomen, enjoying the way her muscles fluttered beneath his touch. He pulled the zipper down slowly, separating the material in its wake and sliding his hand into the opening. Tormenting himself as much as Steffi, he edged his hand below the elastic of her underwear, unable to hold back the groan that rose to his lips as his fingertips encountered soft curls.

Raw heat consumed him; at the same time some of the pain that tormented his soul was quenched. This was what he had been seeking on all those lonely nights when he searched for another warm body to lose himself in. Seeking and finding were two different things. He had never felt like this. Had never known this contrast between pure energy and total peace. Never experienced a feeling so right it scared him. Touching Steffi was addictive. He couldn't stop. He had promised her payback, but this was for him as much as for her.

His hand was shaking as he moved it lower. Using his knee, he moved her legs apart and she widened her stance, allowing him to slide his middle finger between her folds.

"Dear God, Steffi. You're so wet. So hot and wet and ready for me."

His middle finger found her clitoris as he spoke, feeling it throb and swell beneath his touch. Sliding his fingers lower, he parted her swollen flesh, probing her tight entrance. He pushed a finger inside with a single, hard stroke. Steffi gripped him, clenching tight around him. She cried out, tilting her head back against his shoulder and grinding her hips wildly.

He wanted to tug her jeans down around her ankles and bury himself inside her. Wanted to lose himself in her heat, and forget everything except the sensation of those tight muscles rippling around him. But he was determined to remain in control. To see this through and give her the climax he'd promised before he threw her down on that bed.

"Bryce." The pleading sound of his name on her lips as she circled her ass made his erection jerk wildly.

Responsive to her plea, he added another finger, thrusting harder while using his thumb to circle the sensitized bundle of nerve endings. Steffi was close. He could feel it in the low moans that spilled from her lips at each thrust of his fingers.

Just as he felt her tip over toward the point of climax, she threw back her head, calling out his name as she did a passable whole-body shudder. Her internal muscles clenched rhythmically around his fingers a few times. Then she was pulling away from him, reaching for the zipper on her jeans.

"What was that supposed to be?" Bryce spun her around to face him, stunned at what had just happened.

He saw a flicker of fear in the depths of her eyes. It

was gone almost as soon as it appeared. "I don't know what you mean."

His laugh was harsh. "Like hell you don't. I thought you were supposed to be an actress. That had to be the worst fake orgasm in history."

Her eyes dropped away from his as color flooded up from her neck to her cheeks. "Oh."

"Oh? That's all you can say?" He ran a hand through his hair in frustration.

She raised her eyes to his again. "I did my best, but it's hard to know what a real climax looks like when you've never had one."

"Never? Not even when you touch yourself?"

She shook her head. Her expression was both nervous and regretful. "I just can't let go. I freeze up on the inside."

"Damn it, Steffi, you are not frozen up on the inside." He had felt all that heat and quivering passion just waiting to spill over. "You were close as hell…until you put on that little show."

"It's always the same—I get close, but it never happens." She gave a little squeal of surprise as Bryce picked her up and carried her to the bed. "What are you doing?"

He stripped off his shirt, keeping his eyes on hers. "Trust me."

Chapter 9

Bryce's lips on her breasts were featherlight and teasing. He alternated sucking, licking and nipping until Steffi's hips began to lift and undulate in a rhythm all their own. *Trust me.* The memory of those words burned into her brain. She couldn't let him continue with this. He was used to women who lit up at his touch. He'd soon get bored when confronted with one who, no matter how much she enjoyed the preliminaries, couldn't get to the finish line.

"Is this how you got to be so skillful with your mouth?" His smile was teasing. "So you could use that as a distraction from what was going on with you?"

His perception was scarily accurate. The men she'd been with until now had seemed happy with her prowess at pleasing them and her noisy, back-arching fake climaxes. Add in the fact that she was Anya Moretti, and she'd have said they were ecstatic. A small, self-satisfied club of ex-lovers. With the emphasis on the *ex*. Steffi didn't do long-term.

"It's no good." As he trailed his fingers down over her abdomen, her voice was an embarrassed whisper. "It doesn't matter what you do."

"Steffi, stop thinking and relax. I like doing these things for you."

A slight frown tugged her brows together as she looked at him. Was that true? She had always believed that, for a man, sex was about chasing his climax. Could she have gotten this wrong? Bryce certainly looked like he was enjoying himself. His expression blazed passion, and the gold flecks in his eyes were alight with pleasure.

"Tell me what you want."

Steffi bit her lip. No one had ever asked her that before. Could she talk to him? Could she be honest? Because what she really wanted was him. Bryce. His dominance, strength and that hint of wickedness in his manner turned her on and swept her breath away.

As he moved lower and lips replaced his fingers, she gasped. Bryce had disposed of her clothing as well as his own and now, as he held her thighs open, she was exposed to his gaze. She felt her control slipping away. That was when fear hit her, hard and cold. She was going to disappoint him. That hungry look in Bryce's eyes would soon be replaced with contempt.

"Well, Steffi?" There was a harsh edge to his voice. He ran a finger down her center, pausing over her entrance. "I'm waiting."

"I...don't want safe." There. She'd said it. Something flared in the depths of his eyes in response.

"You want to let go of that iron control?" As he spoke, he slid his finger inside her.

She nodded, trembling wildly. "So much."

Bryce gripped her hips, holding her down, and Steffi held her breath. Softly, teasingly, he brought his mouth down to gently touch the core of her sex. She cried out, her body jerking violently, her hands grasping tightly onto the sheets at her sides as her toes curled. He brushed his tongue upward and she opened her legs wider, offering herself to him completely. As if from a distance, she heard him moan with his own desperate desire as he teased her again, tasting her flesh over and over. Then his tongue plunged deep and she lifted herself wildly, thrusting upward toward his mouth, her back arching off the bed. He used his thumbs to pull her outer lips apart, his tongue darting in and out, while his mouth returned again and again to suckle and taste.

Steffi felt like a stranger in her own body. She didn't know the trembling, gasping woman who lay spread wide-open, sheened with sweat, panting with desire as she handed over mastery to this man and let him drive her to the edge of madness. This was what she had always dreamed it would be like. This was the loss of control she had dreaded and longed for.

She was shaking all over, her body racked by violent shudders as she strained toward his mouth. She was so close…but then her mind began to work against her, whispering that she couldn't do this, she wasn't going to make it. She felt the waves of pleasure begin to dim and gave a moan of humiliation.

"Stop fighting me, Steffi." Bryce raised his head to growl the words. "We're on the same side."

So she did as he asked. She relaxed her limbs, cleared

her mind of everything but him. Focused on that magical tongue and let the boundaries inside her mind come tumbling down. She was panting with the pleasure, unable to do anything except cry out his name, poised on the edge of a sensation that felt like it was about to tear her in two.

"That's it." Bryce's words vibrated against her, stoking the pleasure even higher. "Just let it happen."

A final masterful thrust from his tongue tipped her over the looming precipice. A rasping cry escaped her as she thrashed and arched into the oncoming abyss. Nothing had prepared her for this. She screamed as she fell over the edge and into oblivion. Darkness crowded her vision, only to be filled with brilliant arcs of white light. Ecstasy stormed through her body, fizzing along her nerve endings and convulsing her over and over.

Bryce eased up the pressure gradually, allowing her to come back down slowly. When the spasms began to subside, he moved to her side and held her in his arms.

"You did it." Her eyes were wide and dazed as she gazed at him. Bryce rested his forehead against hers. "Now we're even."

"*We* did it." She pressed a kiss onto his collarbone, hiding the intensity of her feelings behind flippancy. "If they had coaches for this sort of thing, you would be major league." She almost groaned aloud. Was that the best she could do? He had just turned her world upside down and she was making a joke about it?

He grinned. "You could write a reference for my résumé."

Maybe laughter was the best way to deal with the force of the emotions powering through her. Because Bryce *was* major league at this, she reminded herself.

To him this was just another lighthearted encounter. No big deal. While to her it felt life-changing.

Of course my first orgasm is going to change my life, she told herself firmly. *Let's not overanalyze this.*

She had very little time to analyze anything as the smile faded from Bryce's eyes to be replaced with a purposeful look. As he moved over her, the stiff flesh of his erection pressed between her sensitive folds and a new hunger tore through her. There was nothing slow or gentle about what she felt, or what she needed from him. This was hot and furious and just about the most wonderful thing she had ever experienced. Second most wonderful, she decided. Nothing would match that first orgasm…

His thumbs found her nipples, and her back arched at the touch of his calloused flesh. His hardness nestled against her, driving her wild with wanting. She could barely keep from screaming as he shifted his hips, rubbing and caressing her still-sensitized clitoris.

Placing kisses across the mounds of her breasts, he moved lower to find her nipples. A moan burst from her as his lips covered one hard tip and surrounded it with liquid heat. His tongue rasped and licked, flicking over her nipple back and forth before he began to suck it hard. Steffi gripped his hair and held him to her, wanting to keep the sensations going on forever.

She lifted her hips and ground against the iron-hard shaft rubbing her while his tongue tormented her nipples. The twin flares of sensation that tore through her increased the mounting pleasure building in her core. How could she feel like this when she had climaxed just minutes earlier?

As Bryce moved away, she murmured a protest.

"Condom," he explained, reaching for the backpack he had left at the side of the bed.

"You packed condoms?" She didn't know whether to be relieved at his forward thinking or annoyed at his presumption. Although, considering the events of the last hour and the position they were in right now, wasn't his confidence justified?

"I always carry condoms." The comment acted like a shot of cold water. Of course he did. She'd forgotten that the women of West County were lining up to be where she was. To be stretched out on a bed with Bryce Delaney between their thighs. This forceful, beautiful man wasn't hers to hold on to.

"Hey." He placed a hand on either side of her face, gazing down at her with a question in his eyes. There was also such a blaze of passion there that her doubts flew away. Nothing mattered except here and now. That Bryce wanted her every bit as much as she wanted him. The scorching need consuming them both was the only message she was prepared to listen to. Her senses spun out of control each time he looked at her. Each touch sent a whiplash of sensation powering through her.

She lifted her hips to meet his sheathed length, signaling the end of any hesitation. As he pressed all the way into her, the pleasure was so intense it was painful. Shooting sparks of electricity tore through her whole body. Each pulsing, zinging surge rushed across her nerve endings, jerking her hips upward in sharp, staccato movements. Each slam of his pelvis against hers stoked the blazing fire inside her even higher.

He impaled her, his iron-hard length rasping over her sensitive nerve endings, driving the pleasure to new heights. It was hotter and stronger than anything she had ever known or imagined. A flame grew in her core and spread outward. She was going to climax again. So soon and so strong. The sensations were building and growing, driving her closer to release with each thrust.

Bryce gripped her buttocks, lifting her higher and opening her to him so she could feel the grinding of his pelvis against hers. She matched his rhythm with wild movements of her own, wrapping her legs around his waist and writhing against him. She didn't want slow and easy. She wanted this. Bryce. All of him. His power and dominance. The searing ecstasy, and the painful pleasure that only he could give her.

She jerked in his hold as the first explosion hit. Her internal muscles tightening on him, gripping him and throbbing around him as she gasped his name. Ecstasy tore through her, and a desperate cry left her lips as she heard Bryce whisper her name in response. His lips moved to hers, kissing her and heightening the sensations that shuddered through her.

She felt him throb with his own release as his hoarse male groan vibrated through her. Lying beneath him, Steffi could feel his heartbeat against her breast, and her throat tightened with an emotion she didn't recognize. She wanted to surrender to it. To wrap herself around him and stay close and safe, shutting out the rest of the world. This was why she didn't do relationships. This closeness was a step along the way to trust, and trust was a scary place.

Just in time, she was roused out of her warm bubble when Bryce eased away from her and dropped a kiss on her neck. "We should get ready and go out to your house."

* * *

Even though Steffi's house was empty, it was situated in one of the most closely guarded square miles in the world. Accessible through two guarded checkpoints, the surrounding properties had private security; the area was patrolled day and night, and the alarm systems were electronic works of art. Getting Steffi past her own front door was going to require skill, ingenuity and probably a hefty amount of luck.

Steffi explained that her own approach to Beverly Hills living was low-key. "I have a full-time housekeeper, Elsa, who has her own bungalow on the grounds, but I don't have any other live-in staff." She bit her lip. "Of course, I don't know what's been happening while I've been away. I hope my management company has maintained the house and continued to pay her salary."

"What about security?" Bryce forced himself to focus on the task ahead of them and not on the mindblowing events of the last few hours. It wasn't easy. Sex had always been one of his favorite pastimes. He didn't fool himself about why it had been such a necessary part of his life since Afghanistan, to the point where it had become almost an addiction. It didn't take any in-depth analysis to tell him he was using sex as a replacement for the part of his life he had lost. That he was trying to bolster his self-esteem between the sheets. He got all that. But wasn't there also an argument in favor of saying sex made him feel good, so why shouldn't he just go for it? It was a great way of relieving tension and taking his mind off the crap that went on inside his head a lot of the time.

But sex with Steffi? That had been a whole new experience. That had been about so much more than just feeling good. He almost laughed out loud. Good? It had felt amazing. But he had never felt the sort of connection he had experienced with Steffi. Sex had always been about giving and receiving pleasure. With Steffi, he had lost himself in her, completely and intimately. And while he wanted to explore that feeling further, it frightened the hell out of him at the same time. He didn't understand the new emotions that were tugging at him. Why did he suddenly want to sit Steffi down and analyze what had happened between them? Get her perspective on it? Talking about his feelings? That would be a first. He was fairly sure she'd enjoyed it, too. Why not leave it at that? Until now, he'd never experienced a need for reassurance about his performance. But he was fooling himself by pretending this was about the sex. It went deeper than that. He wanted to know what Steffi was *feeling*. Where this was going. In the past, if a partner wanted to walk away after one night, that was fine. More than fine. It suited him. He didn't want a commitment beyond a few hours. Now? Now he sensed he might be in deep trouble.

"I have an alarm system." Steffi responded to his question, bringing his mind back to the task ahead of them. He realized he was staring at her with an intensity that had brought a frown to her brow and he looked back along the street. "But I don't use a security firm. I like my privacy. My management company hires bodyguards when I need them."

They walked around the perimeter of the secure community. Bryce viewed the six-foot-high wall with its security cameras, before returning to view the gate from a distance.

"You live here. What's the easiest way in?"

Steffi blinked. "Pardon?"

"What do the residents complain about?"

"Oh." She appeared to give it some thought. "People sharing their security passes. Cars tailgating each other. Delivery trucks not being properly checked. That was a big one recently after a company selling flowers got through without being stopped by the guard."

He nodded. "I'll take a guy and a gate over a wall and a camera any day."

It was a long wait, but eventually a delivery truck pulled up at the checkpoint. The gate opened as the guard left his booth and approached the cab of the truck.

"Now."

Bryce caught Steffi's hand and propelled her through the gate on the opposite side of the truck to the guard and the driver. In their black clothing, and using the cover of the wall and the darkness, they were able to crouch low and sneak inside without detection. They walked stealthily past Steffi's house several times, checking it out until Bryce was as certain as he could be that no one was watching the property. He supposed that three months after the murders the police were reasonably sure that Anya Moretti wasn't coming back here. Probably they were unable to spare the man power to watch the house any longer. His biggest concern was whether Walter Sullivan had anyone on the lookout for them. Steffi had told Walter she knew where the cell phone was. It would be reasonable for Walter to make the assumption that it would be here. Bryce had expected Walter to have posted a couple of guys here at Steffi's house. If they were here, they were staying well out of sight.

Tucked away behind high hedges and wrought iron

gates, the Mediterranean-style villa was only just visible from the road. They had the advantage over other housebreakers. Not only did Steffi have a set of keys, she also knew the codes to the alarm system. As she led Bryce past the main gates, he caught a glimpse of an ornate fountain in the marble tiled courtyard. He resisted the impulse to give an appreciative whistle. He thought of his two-bedroom house on the edge of Stillwater with its view over the lake. With its fenced yard and decking that always seemed to need a coat of varnish, it was about as far from this miniature palace as it was possible to get. He had known that Steffi lived in a different world, but now the reality of that difference was thrust right under his nose.

"This is the way deliveries come in." Steffi punched in a code on a door next to the quadruple garage and it swung inward. After a swift glance around, they slipped through.

Bryce took a moment to get his bearings. They were at the side of the house, sheltered from view by the garage. He figured anyone watching from a distance would be looking at the front entrance and not in this direction.

"Can you get us in around the back?"

Steffi nodded. Clinging to the shadows, they made their way along the garage wall and across to the rear of the house. Bryce took a moment to appreciate the features of the graceful property. Stretching beyond the house itself, green lawn surrounded an elegantly curved swimming pool. Beyond that, he could see intricate gardens and a gazebo. They crossed a sun terrace with neatly arranged patio furniture.

"It's like I never went away." Steffi shook her head

in surprise. "The pool has been cleaned and the lawn is freshly cut."

"Do you live here alone?" Bryce looked up at the imposing facade. From its size, the house had to have at least seven bedrooms.

"Yes, although my adoptive parents visit—" she bit her lip as she corrected herself "—*visited* sometimes."

"Have you had any contact with them since Greg's death?" Bryce could sense her distress. Although she had mentioned the couple who had adopted her after the deaths of her parents a few times, she hadn't gone into any detail about them. This was the first time he had gotten any sense of her relationship with them.

Steffi took a steadying breath as she led him to a set of patio doors. "I called them once, the day I went on the run, just to reassure them that I was okay. They are very private people and I've always taken care to keep them out of the limelight." Her voice wobbled slightly. "I knew they'd be worried about me, but I didn't want to drag them further into this mess. I didn't give them any details about where I was, or what my plans were. At least that way, when the police spoke to them, they wouldn't be able to tell them anything. I didn't know it at that time, but it seems it also worked in my favor when Walter visited them."

Drawing the set of keys she'd brought with her from the pocket of her jeans, she inserted one of them into the patio door. It opened silently and they stepped inside.

"Wait here while I switch off the alarm." Steffi moved quickly through the darkened house. After a minute or two, Bryce heard a faint electronic beeping and her footsteps returning.

She gave a relieved smile. "I had a horrible feeling

that someone might have been in here and changed the codes."

Although they couldn't switch on the lights for fear of alerting the security guards who patrolled the other houses on the road, there was enough light from the streetlamps and the almost full moon for Bryce to appreciate the luxurious features of the house. As Steffi led him through a lounge with elegant, light-colored rugs and furnishings, he noticed several sculptures on stands and paintings on the walls. Something about the way they were displayed told him they were original pieces of art.

"This is my study," Steffi said as they stepped inside a smaller room, furnished with a desk and chair. One wall was lined with books. "Normally, Elsa would bring my mail in here and leave it on my desk for me to open each day. I haven't checked my mail since before I went away to Italy on location. If Greg sent the cell phone to me, I'd expect it to be in here."

"Unless the police went through your mail and took it," Bryce said.

"If they didn't know what they were looking for, why would they take it?" Steffi moved toward the desk. Sure enough, there were several neat piles stacked up on its surface. Even in the gloomy light cast by a streetlamp, it was easy to see that each item had already been opened.

"Even if Walter has been in the house during your absence, we know he didn't find the phone." Bryce eyed the piles of letters and packets. "If he had, he wouldn't have needed to ask you where it was. He would have just killed you as soon as he found you in Stillwater."

"We should still go through this mail. Greg might have sent me a note that wouldn't mean anything to someone else." Steffi glanced at the window. "If we close the drapes we can switch on this desk lamp."

Half an hour later they had been through every item on the desk and found nothing from Greg. Steffi, who was seated in the chair, slumped back in an attitude of despondency.

They had discussed the possibility of calling Greg's cell phone to see if they could hear its ringtone. But, as Bryce pointed out, after three months of not being charged, there would be no life in the battery.

"We didn't expect to find anything here," Bryce reminded her. "We just have to eliminate this place and Greg's apartment and hope to find something that might give us a clue."

She nodded gloomily, her whole body drooping in an attitude of defeat. "I guess just being here again brought it all back to me."

He drew her close, wrapping her in his arms and trying to instill some warmth into her trembling limbs. They stayed locked together like that until the sound of a footstep on the tiled floor of the hall disturbed them.

Chapter 10

Bryce pressed a finger to his lips. Steffi's heart was pounding so hard she thought it might give her away. Because she knew the layout of the house so well, she could tell the person who had come in had taken the same route as them. Coming in through the patio doors and cutting across the lounge area before heading into the marble tiled hall. He, or she, was heading their way.

"Who is there?" The voice was high-pitched, wavering and familiar.

"It's Elsa," Steffi whispered to Bryce. "My house-keeper."

The footsteps came closer to the study, then paused. "What are you doing here? This is private property." Elsa's tone was panicky now.

"Who is she talking to? She can't see us." Bryce whispered as he moved cautiously toward the door. Before he reached it, Elsa let out a scream. It was followed immediately by a thud. Steffi couldn't be sure, but it sounded a lot like a person falling to the floor.

Bryce moved quickly, pulling Steffi down with him behind the desk. Silently, Steffi slid open the bottom drawer. Twelve months ago an overenthusiastic fan had managed to get onto the grounds of the house. He hadn't been dangerous, quite the opposite—he had been harmless and friendly—wanting to talk to her about how much he enjoyed her movies. But the incident had troubled her. Not to the point where she was prepared to have live-in security—her privacy was too important to her for that—but enough to make her think about protection.

Steffi hated guns. It didn't take much imagination for her to work out why that might be. Every time she worked on a film that involved a shooting scene, she had flashbacks to the deaths of her parents. Nothing would have convinced her to get a gun. Instead, she had upgraded her alarm system and placed pepper spray in strategic positions around the house, including a canister in the bottom drawer of her desk. Now her hand closed eagerly around the comforting cylindrical shape.

The frame of the desk blocked their view, but she heard the footstep as someone entered the room. Her senses told her this wasn't Elsa. The person who had just come into the room was big, his or her movements dominating the small space. And he—she just knew somehow that it *was* a he—was light on his feet, as though sneaking around in the dark came naturally to him. If it had been a police officer, he would have announced his presence by now, and he wouldn't have harmed Elsa. No, Steffi was willing to bet that this person spoke with a Russian accent.

The lamp was still on and, as the footsteps approached the desk, Bryce sprang to his feet. Although he motioned for Steffi to stay down, she ignored him. Clutching the pepper spray in her hand, she faced the intruder side by side with Bryce. Her hunch had been right. Although the left side of his face was still a mess of cuts and bruises where she had smashed the quartz into him back at the lake house, Sergei managed a sneer.

"The Big Guy said you would come here sooner or later. You are wasting your time. We've searched every inch of this place and the phone isn't here." He reached into his inside pocket. "The Big Guy also said it's time to say goodbye to the boyfriend."

Steffi moved fast. Vaulting across the desk, she tried to remember the instructions she had been given when she purchased the pepper spray. *Aim for the eyes.* That was the most important one. Extending her arm, she shot a jet of the fiery liquid straight at the upper part of Sergei's face.

Letting out an enraged bellow, he dropped to his knees, rubbing wildly at his eyes. With a shaking hand, Steffi disarmed the canister and tucked it into her pocket. She turned to find Bryce looking at her with an expression of mingled exasperation and admiration.

"I was going to tell you to start trusting me and listen when I want you to stay back, but I guess it worked out okay this time. We'd better get going. Erik and Alexei won't be far behind."

As they passed Sergei, who was writhing on the floor and moaning, Bryce reached into the Russian's pocket and withdrew the gun he had been reaching for. Although Sergei tried to kick out at him, the temporary blindness induced by the pepper spray rendered his actions ineffective.

Steffi shuddered. "I hate guns."

"If we meet up with Walter again, I'll feel safer if I have this in my hand."

An image of Greg's dead body came into her mind and she bit her lip before nodding. "I guess you're right."

When they passed through the hall, Steffi gave a soft cry as she saw Elsa stretched out on the tile floor. Bryce dropped down on one knee, quickly checking the housekeeper's unconscious form. "She's alive. Looks like he hit her over the head. It's lucky for us she came into the house and interrupted him when she did. If she hadn't called out to him, he could have sneaked up on us."

"We can't just leave her here." Steffi couldn't bear the thought of the loyal, kindly woman who had worked for her for so many years lying injured and at the mercy of Walter's thugs.

"Let's get out of the house and through the gates. Then we'll call for help." Bryce's clasp on her hand was warm and reassuring. "We can tell the police they might want to take a look at the man in the study and his associates in connection with the murder of Greg Spence. Who knows? They may even listen."

On the drive back from her house, Steffi had made up her mind. As wonderful as sex with Bryce was, it would be a mistake to get too involved. She was going to tell him they should cool things down. That it should be a one-time-only thing. The situation they were in had gotten them all fired up and they had let the super-charged emotions go to their heads...and other parts of their bodies. They were adults; they could share a hotel room and deal with a little physical attraction without ripping each other's clothes off again.

Only now they were back in their hotel room, Bryce was moving toward her in a very determined way, and her carefully rehearsed speech had dried up. At that precise moment, Steffi couldn't remember why she had even prepared a speech. She was struggling to remember her own name. Her brain was thinking *Why not?* and her body was responding *very* enthusiastically to the purposeful look in his eye.

"Come here." A smile quirked one corner of his mouth.

"You're bossy." Although his forcefulness was one of the things she found most attractive about him, she felt she should at least try to make a stand about his high-handedness. While she could still think straight.

"And you are overdressed." The smile deepened. "So let me rephrase my earlier instruction. Take your clothes off and then come here."

It was as if he had her body on remote control, Steffi decided, as her fingers moved to the buttons of her shirt. The light in those brown eyes told her he knew her better than she knew herself. She couldn't even pretend she was able to fight this. A raw, primal hunger surged through her. She was acting on adrenaline and impulse. Rational thought was relegated to another time and place. Bryce had awakened something in her she had believed didn't exist.

Steffi had always thought she wasn't a very physical person. Had always put that down to her issues with trust and commitment. The rare sexual encounters she'd had in the past were brief and pleasant. Apart from not being able to climax, she had enjoyed them, but she had never understood the burning intensity that led other people to make fools of themselves over sex. Murder, war, infidelity? And for what? She lived in a world where excess was normality, but she just didn't get it. Sex wasn't that important to her. She could even—she'd admit in a whisper—live without it. Occasionally she had wondered if she was missing some vital part of her psyche. She had no close friends; no one she could ask. It wasn't the sort of question she could discuss with an acquaintance. *Is there something wrong with me? I just don't think sex is all that great.*

Now she wanted to laugh out loud at the memory of that time. Of the person she had been when she had those thoughts. *I just hadn't met Bryce Delaney back then.* Hadn't seen that look in his eye, experienced the dominance he could exert over her body or felt the sizzling, uncontrollable force that surged between them. He was like a tornado, sweeping past her puny defenses, tearing down any barriers she attempted to put up and leaving her breathless and longing. It didn't matter how much she told herself she shouldn't want this, shouldn't want *him*.

Common sense tried to intrude and remind her that they were living on a knife edge of danger. That she was on the run from the police, wanted for a double murder. That Walter Sullivan and his Russian bodyguards were breathing down their necks. That even if by some miracle they got out of this alive, they lived in different worlds, one in which she was an ice-queen movie star and he was a small-town super stud. None of it mattered. He only had to look at her to have her breath catching raggedly in her throat.

Bryce closed the distance between them, pulling her shirt the rest of the way off and tossing it to the floor.

"I thought you wanted me to undress myself?" She tipped her head back to look at him.

"You were overthinking again." His voice was a growl as he tugged down the lace of her bra, exposing her breast. Steffi shivered at the hunger in his gaze as he lowered his head to lick her nipple. "So pretty." The glittering look in his eyes as he raised his head almost brought her to her knees.

"Too small." She gave an embarrassed laugh. "And now I'm skinnier than ever..."

"You're perfect." His hands moved around to undo the clasp of her bra. Sliding the straps down her arms, he dropped it at her feet. His palms were warm as they covered her breasts. "Don't ever let me hear you say different."

His hand caught the back of her neck, holding her at the perfect angle as he brought his lips to hers. His kiss was melting, stealing her breath away at the first touch. Steffi tilted her head, her senses consumed by the taste of him. How had being in his arms suddenly become the most natural thing in the world? He was a living flame, lighting the darkest corners of a world she was only now recognizing had been desperately cold and lonely before she found his presence.

As he scooped her up and carried her to the bed, Steffi realized she had found something that had been missing from her life. Security. In Bryce's arms she felt safe for the first time ever.

He placed her on the bed, removing the rest of her clothes and shedding his own before lying next to her. "Your body is beautiful." His lips stroked the hollow of her throat before moving along her collarbone. "The most perfect thing I have ever seen." He probably said that to every woman he met, but in that moment, the heated, husky note in his voice was so potent, Steffi actually believed him.

A moan escaped her lips as his fingers circled her tight nipples. Caressing her neck with his mouth, he gripped one hard bud with his thumb and forefinger. The contrast between the soft touch of his mouth and the half pleasurable, half painful tug of his fingers pushed aside the last shreds of her control.

"Bryce…" His name was a ragged cry on her lips.

He lifted his head with a glinting smile. "I like it when you say my name that way. Sounds like you can't get enough of me."

He covered her breasts with his hands, his fingers returning to torment her nipples as she writhed against him. As he trailed them down her body, she lifted her hips, parting her thighs and arching to his touch. With tormenting delicacy, he teased her, lightly tracing the narrow slit with one fingertip. As he pressed his thumb inside her, his fingers circled the hard, aching bud of her clitoris, sending her into a frenzy of delight.

As he moved into position between her thighs, she heard the sound of a condom wrapper tearing and felt Bryce reach between their bodies. Then his thick length was nudging her, spreading her sensitized folds apart as she gazed at him in a haze of pure rapture.

When he was fully seated inside her, he held still for a moment, staring down at her. Placing a hand on each side of her face, he kissed her with a tenderness that stunned her. Then he began to move. Strong, steady thrusts sent tension powering through her. How had she lived without knowing what she needed was Bryce filling her, pumping into her, spreading molten heat out from her core to every part of her body?

"Bryce… Oh…" She jerked upward as he held her hips.

"You feel so good, Steffi." His strangled growl had her writhing against him, driving him deeper. "So hot and tight."

He caressed nerve endings she had never known existed. This wasn't just sex. Bryce was staking a claim to her and she was responding by giving him everything she had. She knew, with absolute certainty, that nothing would ever again feel as good as Bryce thrusting inside her, impaling her with his heat and strength, stealing away every thought except those of him.

As he powered her toward climax, his lips returned to cover hers and his hips moved in a rhythm that was almost brutal in its intensity. Sensations began to flame through her. Everything felt *more*. Realer. More intense. More perfect. The feel of her muscles tightening around him with a strong, rhythmic pulse heightened the feeling and she gripped his shoulders, calling out his name.

His kiss claimed her mouth as she felt him climax. He drove into her deep and hard, his groan echoing into the kiss as he shuddered in time with her. Her nails pierced his skin, and her legs tightened around his hips as she lost herself in him. To hell with the rest of the world. In that moment nothing mattered except Bryce and how he made her feel.

"Eat." Bryce pointed to the food with what he hoped was an authoritative expression.

The diner was almost empty and he had selected a

quiet booth from which he could watch the door. He didn't think they had been followed from the hotel, but he wasn't taking any chances. Sergei's gun was tucked into his jacket pocket and Steffi carried the pepper spray. This place advertised the best breakfast in town and Steffi was eyeing the huge plate in front of her with an expression of dismay.

She looked up at him with a smile. "Are you this forceful with every woman you—" she caught herself up with a gasp, clearly too embarrassed to finish the sentence.

"Every woman I what?" he asked, enjoying the look of delicious confusion on her face. "Have red-hot, toe-curling sex with?"

She speared a piece of bacon. "Something like that." Her face flushed to a deep rose color. Bryce decided he liked making her blush.

"I don't usually stick around for breakfast." He winced. What kind of creep did that make him sound like? *I sleep around, but don't worry... I run out on my partners before we get to share a meal together. Yeah, that's the kind of guy I am.* "That came out wrong."

Steffi studied him thoughtfully. "I think it came out truthful. And it's okay."

"What is?" He took a slug of coffee, wondering where this conversation was going.

"I understand that this doesn't mean anything." The blush was still there, but her gaze was steady on his.

"Do you?" *Because I sure as hell don't.*

She gave a soft laugh. "People think that because I'm a movie star I must be mega-experienced." She bent her head over her plate, toying with her food. "I'm sure you noticed that I'm not. But I'm not naive, either." She took a deep breath. "Sex with you is amazing, Bryce. But we both know sex is all it is."

"Do we?" He kept his voice neutral, trying not to make the question into a raging demand for more information.

She nodded, seeming to gain confidence from his words. "It would be silly to think anything else, wouldn't it? We live different lives. You don't do anything other than one-night stands. I don't even do that most of the time. So even if we get out of this alive, neither of us wants anything more than to get our toes curled." She scooped up a forkful of scrambled egg, concentrated on eating it, then looked back up at him. "Right?"

"I guess not." He maintained his noncommittal tone.

Her smile was mischievous. "My toes are enjoying themselves."

He hoped she couldn't see how much effort it took to return the smile. "Mine, too. Now eat."

What was his problem? He should be grateful to her. Wasn't she giving him his own speech? Making things easy for him? She hadn't said anything that wasn't true. And there was so much more to it. Relationships weren't for him. Until he was able to straighten his head out, they never would be for him. He had known that ever since he had come back from Afghanistan. He had returned from that nightmare alive, but changed in ways that only someone else who had been through it could understand. The only way he could describe it was that the best part of him had died that day. What was left was a shell. A shell that performed all the functions of his former self, but without being able to take any joy or pleasure in life.

But something had changed again since he had met Steffi. Last night he had watched her as she slept. Watching her soothed him. Her lashes had formed dark crescents on her pale cheeks. Her brows were twin black arches with a slight upward slant. He had studied her delicate features, taking each in turn. When he first met her, he had decided she wasn't beautiful. Now he thought she was the most stunning woman he had ever seen. As she slept, her glorious, generous mouth had curved into a slight smile and Bryce, recalling how that mouth felt on his, how it felt wrapped around his erection, had grown hard all over again at the memory.

Steffi was incredible. Her need for him matched his desire for her. What they had was unique, lighting up the air between them. He should accept this time together for what it was, a never-to-be-repeated erotic fantasy. So why, when she said this was a no-strings situation, did he suddenly want more? And why did what he wanted from her mean more than sex?

The problem was, Bryce was finding for the first time in his life that a one-off wasn't enough. Not with Steffi. But he couldn't commit to forever. He needed to get that simple truth through to his brain before things got messy. This fight against Walter Sullivan was a one-time-only deal. Once Steffi was free and clear, Bryce was walking away from this situation and anything like it. He was going back to Stillwater, back to routine, back to his small-town, easy life. So far he had coped with the pressure of what was happening to him and Steffi. More than coped. He had treated this like one of his missions in Afghanistan and gone about it with his old strength and determination. The panic attacks—pounding heart, tunnel vision, shaking hands, the inexplicable

feeling that he couldn't make even the simplest decision—had stayed away. Was that forever? He hoped so,
but there were no guarantees.

At first, he had worried about this challenge. Would
he cope face-to-face with a new assailant? Or would he
panic and remember the last time he had been in danger? Until he'd faced Walter Sullivan and his thugs, he
wouldn't have known the answer to that question. Now
he knew he could face Alexei, Sergei, Erik or any other
of the Russians and match them for skill and aggression.
His overriding ambition was to get his hands around
Walter's throat and not let go until the light was completely gone from those coldly smiling eyes.

Last night, after watching Steffi, he had drifted off
to sleep. He had a talent for panicking while asleep. His
dreams were usually horror-filled, turbo-charged nightmares of blood and gore with a soundtrack of explosions
and shouts of terror. Given a choice, Bryce preferred insomnia. Yet, with Steffi next to him, he had slept deeply
and his slumber had been undisturbed by dreams.

In his darkest moments, Bryce had thought about
ending it all. Drinking enough cheap whiskey so that
placing the barrel of his gun against his temple became
the easy option. Anything to end the sense of being
tainted by his experiences. To drive away the memories of the torn-apart bodies of his friends. At least a
bullet to the brain would take away the feeling that all
he would ever be from now on was a target. As he recalled that feeling, Steffi indicated her empty plate with
a glint of playfulness in her expression.

"See how obedient I am?"

The dark thoughts splintered into a thousand pieces.
Her smile reminded him that life was worth living. He

probed the impression further and realized with relief that the days of wanting to self-destruct were over.
When had that happened? Was this newfound appreciation of life Steffi-related? He had a feeling it was.
This seemed to be a morning for revelations. Maybe he
should just stop the angst, enjoy her company and worry
about what was going on inside his head and heart once
they found that damn cell phone.

It felt like a plan…another plan. "If Walter had his
guys watching your place, it's likely he has them watching Greg's apartment, as well."

"It may not be as easy for him to observe us going
into Greg's building," Steffi said. "Security in that
apartment block is really tight. It's the reason many
actors choose to live there."

"Walter got someone in there to kill Greg and the
girl he was with," Bryce reminded her.

"Yes, but they had to have gotten in and out again
real fast. Anyone hanging around Silverlight Towers
would be noticed by the security team. I've been stopped
a few times myself and Greg had me on his list of ap-
proved visitors."

"If that's the case, how easy will it be for us to get in
this time?" He watched her animated features, drinking
in the details of her face as she talked. He could watch
her forever. Last night it had been while she slept. Now
he found the same level of pleasure in watching her during wakefulness. He had never experienced this utter
fascination with another human being before. Perhaps
he was being drawn by the quality that had gotten her
to the top of her profession. It was hardly surprising
that one of the finest actresses of her day should be
fascinating.

"I think we should rethink our dress code for this one." He raised a brow at her, but she didn't elaborate.

"Are you absolutely sure that the apartment is still empty? I don't want to turn up only to find out that there is already a tenant."

"I called the leasing agency. The apartment is still empty." The corners of her mouth turned down. "The girl I spoke to told me the police only recently released it back to them, and now no one wants to rent the place where two people died."

Bryce took her hand and she glanced down with a brief look of surprise, before returning the clasp of his fingers. "Do you have a fob for the underground garage?" he asked.

"And my key to Greg's apartment, of course." The corners of her mouth turned down. "Although I don't think the cell phone will be there."

"Nor do I." Bryce got to his feet. "But it's another place to tick off our list."

"We have a list?" As Steffi followed him out to the car, he was pleased to see she was no longer limping. "Why didn't I know about that?"

"There is no list." He held open the passenger door so that she could get in. "It just sounds better than admitting we don't know what the hell to do next."

Chapter 11

"Bliss. The last message Greg sent me before he died was that single word followed by those numbers. 2713," Steffi said. "It must have meant something."

"Could the word *bliss* have been an expression about his state of mind?" Bryce maneuvered the car through the early-evening traffic toward Greg's apartment building.

It was something she had already considered. "For the sake of a few extra characters, why not just type 'I'm happy'? And given everything that was going on with him, he clearly *wasn't* happy. He was angry enough to push Walter into a meeting."

"Bliss wasn't a word you'd heard him use before in another context?" The streets were busy and Bryce kept his eyes on the traffic. "It didn't have a connection to something the two of you had in common? Something in your childhood, maybe? Or one of your movies?"

Steffi wrinkled her nose in an effort to remember, although she had already been over and over this. "It doesn't mean anything to me. At the time I thought it was a random word, a mistake. Possibly it was a message meant for someone else, or that Greg meant to send me a different message and got distracted halfway through. Because he died so soon after sending it, it's assumed a significance to me that might not have been his intention." She hunched one shoulder as she turned to view the familiar route. "I've spent way too much time thinking about it."

"Tell me about Greg." Bryce's voice was low and sympathetic.

She felt a smile tug at the corners of her mouth. "He was my big brother. Even though we hadn't seen each other for so long, he slipped back into that position very easily. Right away, I had someone who was there for me, unconditionally." Strangely, it didn't feel awkward opening up to Bryce this way. Normally, she'd have run a mile from a personal conversation of this kind. "Until it happened, I wasn't aware I needed that. I mean, I'd made my way in life, pretty successfully. It was safe to say my bank balance was healthy. I'd already learned the hard way how to see off the inevitable creeps who wanted to get to know me because of the movie star persona. I couldn't imagine why I'd need someone to have my back. But as soon as Greg was there, I didn't know how I'd ever gotten along without him. That sounds corny, I know."

"It's how being a brother works," Bryce said.

"Of course you have a brother, too." She turned her head to view his profile.

"I have two brothers. Vincente is my half brother. We

have the same father, but different mothers. Then there's Cameron—he's the middle brother. We have the same mother and father." There was something about the way he spoke of Cameron that was different. She sensed a deep affection for the brother she hadn't met, as though there was a wealth of untold memories when Bryce said his name. "For a long time, Vincente and I didn't have the best relationship. It's hard to say what went wrong. I guess it started during our childhood and neither of us ever did anything as we grew up to put things right. It took a nasty situation just recently, when Cameron and Laurie—who is now his wife—were in danger, to bring the three of us together. We finally saw that blood means more than any petty squabbles or jealousies."

"So we both know how it feels to find a brother we lost."

A corner of his mouth tilted up in the way she loved. *Loved?* Where did *that* come from?

"I guess so."

She returned to her memories. "Greg was clever and witty and he made me laugh. I mean, he could just look at me and make me crack up at totally the wrong moment. When we were on set together, he was lethal. He made me realize I didn't have much fun in my life before he came back into it. I'd been on this work treadmill. Trying to get to the top, then once I was there, being determined to dig in and stay there no matter what."

"Why was that?" Bryce asked. "What made you so driven?"

"Are you analyzing me?" She asked the question without heat, even with a trace of humor.

He shrugged. "Just curious about what makes the great Anya Moretti tick."

"The great Anya Moretti." She repeated the words slowly. "That's the whole point. She's a facade. She isn't me. I don't need anyone else to analyze me. I can do it myself. Anya Moretti is who I hide behind. Success is my sanctuary."

They had reached Silverlight Towers, the great, gleaming apartment block that had been Greg's home. Bryce used the fob Steffi had given him to the underground parking lot. While he waited for the doors to open, he flicked a glance her way. "Fame is the attic no one can drag you out of?"

As he turned away again, she gazed at the side view of his face, stunned that anyone, least of all Bryce, with his tough exterior, would understand. He couldn't know how powerful the words he had just spoken were. He had distilled her whole life into that sentence. All she had ever wanted to do was build a wall around herself, so she didn't have to let other people in. Her life could have gone in a totally different direction. She supposed she could have become the ultimate recluse. After the death of her parents, shutting out the world and living alone on a small farm with the animals she loved had been the fantasy world into which she had retreated. Although she had no pets as an adult, her love of animals had always been one of the strongest forces in her life. If she could, she'd have filled her home with as many as she could. Since her lifestyle didn't allow for that, she compensated by using her money to maintain an animal charity.

As she grew up, her desire for solitude often still seemed like an ideal world. Instead, her acting ability had shone through from an early age. She had been singled out at school, and her adoptive parents had sent her to a prestigious dramatic arts academy. How they had found the money, she never knew. But from that moment on, the barriers she built around herself had been those of stardom. She had made herself untouchable in her own way. Her remoteness hadn't been of the physical sort; it had been based on the power of celebrity.

Bryce pulled into a parking space and turned to look at her. The smile in his eyes warmed every part of her. She wanted to sit here in this car and, for the first time in her life, talk for hours about who she was and why she made the life choices she had. She wanted to dismantle the walls, brick by brick, and let the real Steffi emerge. Instead, she had to make her way upstairs and walk into the apartment where she had seen her brother's dead body.

"Can you do this?" Bryce must have somehow picked up on her thoughts.

"I have to do this." She clasped her hands tightly together. "It's for Greg."

"All Greg's things are gone." Steffi clutched Bryce's hand as they moved through the open-plan living space. "Someone must have already been through everything that was in here."

Her eyes were fixed on a spot in the middle of the floor. There was nothing there except a brightly colored rug, but Bryce was willing to bet good money that was where Steffi had seen Greg's body. And that of the girl. The girl bothered him. Why hadn't she been identified yet? Three months was a hell of a long time, even in LA with its transient population.

"The newspaper reports I read in your house said Greg and the girl he was with were in a compromising position. What did that mean?"

Steffi dragged her gaze from the center of the room and up to his face. She had pushed her dark glasses up on top of her head, so he could see the painful memories swirling in the amber depths of her eyes. "They were both naked. He was sitting in a chair—" she gestured to the place where the rug now lay "—there. His legs were apart and she was kneeling between them. They had both been shot through the head at close range. The press speculated that Anya Moretti, the jealous lover, had found them that way and killed them in a rage."

He was fascinated all over again by the way she spoke of Anya Moretti as a different person. She really had created another life for herself, one that allowed her to escape into a different world. Wasn't it similar to what he'd done since he'd left the army? Perhaps not in such a high profile way, but he'd done his best to keep the world at arm's length. Made a pretty good job of it, too.

"Did Greg have a girlfriend?" Bryce asked.

"No." She shook her head. "I know there had been someone special in his life for a long time. It was before he and I met up again. I don't know what happened between them, but she went away. Although he didn't talk about it much, I got the feeling he was having a hard time getting over her."

Bryce gave that statement some thought. "Well, he wasn't alone when he died." Steffi probably wasn't going to like his next question. "Do you know if he went with hookers?"

Although she frowned, he suspected Steffi had already considered the question. "If he did, it's not an aspect of his life he shared with me."

"Sorry." He held up a hand in apologetic gesture. "I shouldn't have asked that. He was unlikely to have told his sister if he did take comfort with a working girl every now and then."

"Even if she was a prostitute, why haven't the police found out her name by now?" Steffi unconsciously echoed his thoughts of minutes earlier. "She was a person. She had a life, a family, people who loved her. Someone must be missing her and wondering where she is."

"I guess that lifestyle makes it so much harder to trace someone." Bryce caught the glint of tears in Steffi's eyes for the unknown woman who had died here. He slid an arm around her shoulders. Her body slumped against him, and he took a moment to be amazed all over again by her. In spite of the danger surrounding her, she was able to feel for the suffering of someone she had never met. One of the richest women in Hollywood was moved by the plight of a nameless woman.

"They should try harder," she muttered before straightening determinedly. "I suppose we should look for his cell phone. Just in case?"

Bryce nodded. "Got to be worth a try." It probably wasn't.

Although he suspected it was a waste of time, it felt like this was a ritual they had to perform. If they didn't, they would always wonder if this might have been the place where Greg had left the cell phone with its incriminating recording. The phone was like the proverbial needle in a haystack, but Bryce was determined not to leave a single piece of hay unturned in their search. He would keep looking until the phone turned up…or the police or Walter caught up with them. He didn't like to dwell on which was most likely to happen first.

They had completed their search of the apartment, and found no sign of the phone when there was a knock on the apartment door. The fact that whoever it was took the trouble to knock made him cautiously optimistic. He didn't think Walter's men, or the police, would have bothered with the formalities.

The man who entered the apartment wore a security guard's uniform. Bryce sized him up quickly. Late thirties, early forties. No tattoo on his right hand. Something about him said "ex-military." He looked like he had been able to handle himself once, but maybe the beer and take-out pizza had come first for a while now. Bryce decided with a feeling of relief that he wasn't going to need the gun.

"No one told me anyone was due to look around this apartment today." The guard consulted a clipboard in an officious manner.

Before Bryce could respond, Steffi moved forward. He wasn't sure how she did it, but she instantly dominated the situation. Flicking back strands of the long, red wig she wore, she took on a whole new personality. He could only stand back and watch as one of Hollywood's greatest stars took center stage. So this was why she'd insisted on the change of clothing.

"I'm not surprised they didn't tell you." She jerked her head in Bryce's direction. "They never do."

The security guard cast a bemused look at Bryce before turning his attention back to Steffi. It was hard to look away from her. With those flowing red locks and the floating, embroidered dress adorned with scarves, she resembled a fortune teller from a 1950s movie. She had spent the morning dragging him around vintage clothing stores until they got the look just right. He was only thankful that his own costume of suit, shirt and tie was more conservative. The fact that he had no idea of his role was more of a problem.

"They?" The guard frowned at his clipboard, clearly hoping it might tell him how to handle this unfamiliar situation.

"You didn't tell him, did you?" Steffi turned on Bryce, her voice a combination of sadness and annoyance. "You couldn't bring yourself to tell this poor man the reason why we are here."

Sensing something other than silence was required of him, Bryce went for noncommittal. "I thought it was for the best."

Steffi gave a sigh that was worthy of an Oscar in its own right. Ignoring Bryce, she drew the guard to one side. "That's what they always say. The truth is, they're ashamed to admit that they've brought me in to help cleanse the place."

The guard frowned. "The manager already had the apartment thoroughly cleaned after the police handed it back."

Steffi gave a tinkling laugh. "Not cleaned—" she leaned closer to read the man's badge "—Bill. *Cleansed.* There is a good reason why this apartment still stands empty. I expect you can feel it." She placed a hand on his arm. "Ah, yes. You have an empathetic soul."

Bryce leaned against the counter, crossing his arms over his chest and hiding the smile that wanted to emerge. You had to hand it to Steffi. She was magnificent.

"I don't know what you mean." Bill was starting to look nervous.

"Oh, Bill." Steffi shook her head. "Those poor souls who died here are still in torment. They haven't been able to leave. They aren't at peace. You and I know that because we have empathy. The people who come to view the apartment, they don't know it. They just don't like the feel of the place. Mr. Studworth, here—" she gestured to Bryce "—in his real estate agent's office, all he wants is to rent this apartment. But sometimes he has to call me in to help put the souls of the dead to rest."

Bill cast a pleading glance in Bryce's direction. "You do?"

"I do. But you can understand how I don't like to advertise it. It's not great for business." Bryce attempted to look hard-nosed and unempathetic.

"Business." Steffi's expression was sad. "You and I know there are more important things, don't we, Bill?"

"How do you…uh, get rid of them? Is it like exorcism?" Bill asked.

Steffi laughed again and Bryce noticed she had introduced a new, slightly manic note into her laughter. "Exorcism? That's for amateurs. I invite the poor souls that have no resting place to enter my body, to live within me. They need to find a place to rest, Bill. An empathetic home. Of course, with you here, they have two empathetic people to choose from…" She closed her eyes and began to sway, humming lightly under her breath.

"You know what?" Bill spoke directly to Bryce. "I may just leave you to it. I need to finish my rounds."

With a quick look at the air around Steffi, he hurried out, closing the door carefully behind him.

"Steffi, you are a witch," Bryce said appreciatively.

She pushed her glasses up, opening her eyes wide. "Not a witch, Bryce, a *cleanser*. Weren't you listening?"

His lips twitched. "And Mr. *Studworth*? What was that all about?"

She studied him with her head on one side. "Oh, I don't know. I thought the name suited you."

"Unfortunately, I think Bill is likely to be watching on his monitors, waiting for us to leave this apartment, so you'll have to flutter around continuing your performance for a few minutes." He smiled. "But when I get you alone, I intend to show you exactly how much it suits me."

Steffi closed her eyes and resumed her swaying and humming. "I'll look forward to it."

Chapter 12

"We have nothing." Steffi slumped back against the pillows. "A big, fat zero."

"I wouldn't say that," Bryce said. "We have pizza, beer—" he tilted his half-empty bottle in her direction "—and I'm enjoying the company."

Wow. He probably had no idea of the knee-weakening effect of a comment like that. She assured herself that she was doing a good job of maintaining the facade that Bryce had not touched her feelings in any way. The effect he had on her body couldn't have escaped his attention. Not when he could reduce her to a mass of screaming, pleading ecstasy within seconds. But she was trying to play it cool on the emotions front. It wasn't what she wanted. Every time she looked at Bryce, she wanted to crawl all over him like an out of control kitten and demand to know what he was thinking. More important, she wanted to know what he was thinking and feeling about *her*. Her head and heart were at war over him. Every time her head told her not to get too close, her heart started to do wild somersaults.

As soon as I get near him, I turn into a needy teenager. I hate and love it at the same time. Hate because I don't want to hand control of my body over to another person when I don't know where this is leading. Love because I never knew it was possible to be swept along on such a magical tide of pure sensation.

"But you're right. We have nothing when it comes to the cell phone."

Bryce leaned back with his hands behind his head, allowing Steffi to feast her eyes on his muscular torso. The bruises inflicted by Erik back at Steffi's cabin were starting to fade both on his face and his body. Whatever mayhem might be going on around them, there were definite compensations to this situation. Being in bed with a gorgeous man was one of them. The other was a surprising sense of liberation. Steffi hadn't realized how restrictive her life had been until she broke free of it. Other people might imagine she had the money and power to do pretty much anything she wanted. The reality was that the opposite was true. Her work schedule had been so punishing that she never had time to draw breath. Never really had a second to enjoy the wealth she had earned. Sitting naked in bed in the middle of the afternoon, drinking beer and eating pizza? She'd have had to pencil that in for a date about eighteen months in advance.

"There is one thing that bothers me more than anything else. With that recording, Greg had the evidence he needed to prove Walter killed your parents. Walter himself admitted it." Frustration echoed in Bryce's voice. "So why the hell didn't Greg go straight to the police?"

"Maybe he wanted Walter to suffer?"

"I thought about that, but I just don't buy it as an explanation," Bryce said. "Greg knew how dangerous Walter was. Holding on to that recording? Taunting Walter with its existence? Giving him a chance to mobilize his tattooed assassination squad against him? Why would anyone do that?"

Steffi thought about what he was saying. Bryce was right. It didn't make sense. "Unless..." She was thinking aloud now, voicing her ideas as they came to her. "We don't know what was in the recording, do we? What if there was something Greg didn't want to make public?"

"You mean the information about who your father was?"

Steffi shook her head. "I don't think that would have stopped him going to the police. We'd talked about it. While we wouldn't have gone public with that information for no reason, if we could have pinned the murders on Walter, we agreed we'd have revealed our father's identity to do it."

"So what sort of information would have stopped Greg from going to the police with the recording?"

Steffi shrugged. "I don't know, and, until we find the cell phone and listen to the recording, it's speculation."

"Is there anyone else Greg might have trusted enough to give them that recording?" Bryce asked.

"I didn't know all his friends, obviously. We'd only recently become close again. But there wasn't anyone he talked about. I think, like me, he was scarred by the events of his early life. That's why it was so amazing for us to reconnect. Neither of us had anyone else. Except our adoptive parents." She turned troubled eyes to Bryce. "You don't suppose…?"

"That he might have given the cell phone to his parents? You were away, he had no one else to turn to. We can't rule it out." He scanned her face as though trying to gauge how much his next words would affect her. "Which means we have to add them to our list."

Steffi tried out a smile. Her lips trembled in the middle of it, but she persevered and got there in the end. "Our nonexistent list?"

"Tell me why the thought of contacting them bothers you so much." Bryce's voice was soft and persuasive. Damn him for noticing her distress. He was getting way too good at reading her. Now he was using the sort of tone that made her want to lay her head on his shoulder and place her cares in his hands. But Steffi didn't surrender to those sort of impulses. She couldn't. She had learned early how to be strong and fight her own battles. She had never let other people do those things for her. Now was not the time to start. If she let Bryce take over, what would happen when he walked away? She would crumble, that was what. *Not going to happen.*

"Because they—Nancy and Tanner, Greg's parents— will have spent the last three months thinking Anya Moretti killed him." She turned anguished eyes to Bryce's face. "So how can I turn up out of the blue? How do I start that conversation? 'Oh, hey, guys, remember me…yes, I'm Steffi, the kid you knew, but I'm also *that* woman, the one the newspapers say shot your son through the head…'" She felt tears threatening to spill over and blinked them furiously away.

"But when you explain that Steffi, his sister, and Anya Moretti are the same person, they'll know you didn't kill him. The whole police case against Anya is that she was the jealous lover. Once you take that away, because you—Steffi—are his sister, not his lover, that case falls apart."

"If they had the cell phone, wouldn't they have handed it over to the police?" Steffi asked.

"Not if they didn't know what they had." Bryce ran a fingertip gently down the frown line between her brows as though attempting to smooth it away. "Where do they live?"

"They live here in California. In Leucadia, in Encinitas." She smiled at the memory of visiting Greg's parents as a child. "Tanner has a boat and he takes tourists out on tours. Not fishing, because that would be against his principles. Nancy has a health food store. They were hippies in the true sense of the word. They never bought anything new if they could avoid it. Greg grew up wearing the weirdest hand-me-downs you've ever seen. He hated it, and I envied him every minute."

Bryce gave her one of those strange looks he did every now and then, as though she had surprised him. "For someone who has a lot of it, you don't seem to like money."

"I've seen close-up how much damage it can do," she said quietly.

"Ah, hell, Steffi. I'm sorry. I wasn't thinking." He tossed the empty pizza box onto the floor and moved closer to draw her into the circle of his arms. "Walter killed your parents over money."

She nodded, enjoying the rasp of his chest hair against her cheek. Enjoying him against her. "But I've seen money at its worst in other ways. The celebrity lifestyle can be horribly destructive. I don't want to come across like the poor little rich girl. I've led a hugely privileged lifestyle over the last few years and I've enjoyed the benefits it's brought my way. I've also learned that fame can be used as a force for good."

"I get the feeling you've used yours that way."

"I try." She didn't elaborate. The charity foundation she had set up for rescued animals was something she didn't care to talk about too much. She just hoped it was continuing in her absence. "My ultimate ambition is to run an animal sanctuary." Why had she said that? She had never said that out loud. It made her sound weird.

"Why don't you?" There it was again, that probing note in his voice that said he had figured out way too much about her for Steffi's liking.

"Oh, you know." She decided it was time to lighten the mood. Deflect attention away from this analyze-Steffi thing that Bryce was getting so good at. "Commitments. And now there's this whole on-the-run, wanted-for-murder thing getting in the way of any future plans. What's a girl to do?"

Bryce shook his head. "I thought I was good at being armor-plated, but you have it down to a fine art."

She took his hand and placed it on her breast. "No armor plating here."

Flames ignited in the dark depths of his eyes. "Nice move, Steffi." He bent his head and kissed her thoroughly. "That's one way to bring the confidences to an end." His hand edged downward from her breast with agonizing slowness. "Just so you know, I'm onto you. I know exactly what lies beneath the tough exterior you show the world." As his fingertips reached the apex of her thighs, Steffi arched toward him with a soft moan. "And it's as soft and tender as the sweetest petals of a new blossoming flower."

* * *

June and Todd Grantham had been unable to have children of their own. They had been kind and understanding toward the adopted daughter who had shared their life. Because they knew about her background, they had understood about the nightmares and the intense shyness that had gradually developed into a need to adopt different roles. When her acting talent had been obvious from an early age, they had done their best to nurture and encourage it.

They had sent Steffi to Russian school on the weekends so she continued to speak her home language and understood her culture. They had even done their best to stay in contact with Greg's new family, although distance had been a problem, particularly as Greg's free-spirited parents used their telephone infrequently and tended to be indifferent letter-writers.

It wasn't her adoptive parents' fault that Steffi had always been… She searched for the right word—*distant* was probably too severe. *Composed* was about the best she could come up with. They had wanted to be able to help her. She hadn't given them anything to work with.

It wasn't that she didn't love them, or that she wasn't grateful to them. It was just that she felt something in her, that part of her that was able to express love and gratitude, whether verbally or through gestures, was broken. It had died along with her biological parents. She was an actress, so she should be able to act the part of the loving daughter, right? It didn't work like that. She couldn't slip into a role when it came to her family. She wouldn't sell them short that way. If she couldn't give them genuine, she wouldn't give them anything.

Now her heart was breaking because she'd let them

down. The whole world believed she'd killed Greg, but the whole world paled into insignificance compared to what June and Todd thought. They knew, of course, that she hadn't killed him. They would know for certain that Steffi could not have killed her brother.

What June and Todd would never be able to understand, and what Steffi couldn't explain to them, was why she had gone on the run. There were no gray areas in her parents' lives. Steffi envied them their ability to see the world in black-and-white, but she couldn't subscribe to it. June worked part-time in a diner, and Todd was a legal assistant in the Sheridan district court. Their lives were all about routine, reliability and duty. When she had called them on that first day of panic after Greg's murder, she had hoped for reassurance. With hindsight, she should have expected the response she got. June had taken the call and listened to what she told her before calmly and carefully explaining why Steffi had to go to the police. The only thing she could do, her mother had explained, was give herself up.

Even Todd, when he came to the phone, had reiterated the same commonsense argument, although he had offered to meet her and support her. At the time, she had been too distressed to notice his bizarre choice of meeting place, and it was only later that it had struck her as odd. Todd's voice had been calm and persuasive. She was making it look worse for herself; innocent people didn't hide from the law. The longer she left it, the more lurid the stories about her in the press would become. Todd had finally uttered the words Steffi had been dreading: What if the story got out about who her real father was? By going on the run, wasn't she proving that the genes she had inherited from Aleksander meant she was unable to function as a law-abiding citizen? They were all things she had already told herself, but hearing them spoken aloud by Todd made them sound so much worse.

She hadn't been able to bring herself to tell them about the man she had seen in the elevator of Greg's apartment. The one with the tattoo that linked him to the murders of her biological parents. Saying it out loud would make it too real, too nightmarish. Although her parents repeatedly asked where she was and what her plans were, Steffi decided they would be safer if they didn't know. They had ended the call without either June or Todd asking how she was doing. Not because they didn't care, just because they didn't do that level of emotional engagement.

And I guess that's to do with who I am and the relationship we have...or don't have. Steffi was under no illusions about where the issues lay. She was the one who didn't do trust and openness. Even at five years of age, she hadn't been able to open her heart to this gentle, kind couple. She was the immovable object in this equation. Even so, if at any point she'd opened her heart, she wasn't sure June and Todd would have been able to respond. *We're well matched. Just not emotional people.*

"You have to do this." Steffi looked up from the cell phone in her hand to find Bryce's eyes on her face. She had no idea how long she had been sitting on the hotel bed, staring at the blank screen, trying to summon the courage to make the call.

They had discussed this at length the night before. Although Steffi had a vague idea of where Greg's parents lived, she didn't have an actual address. And there was a possibility that they could have moved. Steffi knew that June painstakingly sent a card every Christmas. She even occasionally got one in return. Steffi's own parents were the only link they had with Greg's. She got the feeling from Bryce's intent expression that his insistence that she should make this call was about more than finding Nancy and Tanner Spence. He wanted her to be comforted, and assumed the people who could give her the reassurance she needed would be her parents.

Taking a deep breath, she tapped in the landline number she knew by heart. After a few rings, the call was answered by June. At the first sound of her firm, capable voice, Steffi experienced a rush of regret. When she had first arrived in their home, June and Todd had explained that they knew she already had her own mom and dad. They had offered her a choice about what she would like to call them. Steffi had always used their first names.

"Hi, June, it's Steffi." Sadly, it was twenty-two years too late to change her mind and do things differently.

Bryce wandered aimlessly around the bland retail units surrounding the hotel, leaving Steffi to finish her call in private. Her face and voice when she had spoken to her adoptive mother had done something to him that had left him feeling restless in a way he didn't understand. But that was how Steffi affected him. She awakened emotions in him he'd never felt before, shook him up and left him feeling wrung out and confused.

His own childhood had been filled with love and laughter, the only flaw being his stormy relationship with Vincente. Bryce couldn't imagine what Steffi's early life must have been like. To have experienced something as violent as the execution of her parents—even if she hadn't witnessed the actual murders—at such a young age was horrific. To have then been separated from the brother she loved had only compounded the trauma. Bryce wondered why the authorities hadn't done more to keep them together. Admittedly he knew little about such things, but surely there were families out there who would be willing to take a brother and sister who had been through so much?

Bryce thought of his own mother. Sandy Delaney had raised her own two sons and her husband's son from his first marriage with all the love her big heart could hold. At the same time, she had managed to find plenty of tenderness for every other child she came across. A smile crossed his lips as he remembered the comfortable, family kitchen with his, Cameron's and Vincente's friends, all gathered around to enjoy the results of one of Sandy's marathon baking sessions. Would his mother have turned her back if she had heard of a plight like that endured by Steffi and Greg? He could just picture her now, confronting his father, hands on her hips and that militant, maternal light in her eyes. Clearly, there had been no Sandy Delaney available to step forward for Steffi and Greg.

In the face of everything she had endured, Steffi amazed him. She wasn't untouched by her experiences, but she had emerged from them with an inner strength and goodness that was remarkable. Even in the early days of knowing her, he had been drawn by her humor and feistiness. Now he knew her better and was able to appreciate the many other layers to her personality.

He wanted to find Greg's cell phone and hand the recording it contained over to the police so that he could

get both their lives back on track. He craved the famil-
iarity of his daily routine in Stillwater. His military career had given him enough danger and uncertainty for
one lifetime. But did his desire for normality mean he
wanted Steffi out of his life? For the time being Steffi
was in his life. She had made her way in there by unconventional means. Snapping and snarling at first,
then fighting at his side before melting in his arms.
He didn't know what role she had in his future, even
if there was one for her there. But having nothing to
do with her when this was over? The thought left him
cold, but it was hard to see past the different lives they
led and whether this intense physical bond they shared
would work long distance or long-term. He guessed it
wouldn't, but the thought left him feeling unaccountably
bereft. Steffi had never openly acknowledged that she
knew about his PTSD, but he felt she understood. More
importantly, she made a difference, helped him keep
things in perspective. That wasn't the only reason he
wanted to keep her in his life, but it sure as hell helped.

What bothered him more than anything else right
now was that, if Greg's parents couldn't help them tomorrow, they had no idea where to go next in their
search for that damn phone. Secretly, he thought Steffi
was right. If Nancy and Tanner Spence had the phone,
they would have handed it over to the police when Greg
died. Unless they didn't know what it contained.

Bryce tried to work out the timescales. The last time
they knew for sure Greg had used his phone was the
night before his death when he had sent a message to
Steffi containing that single, cryptic word and four
numbers. *Bliss 2713.* Sometime between that message
and the time of his death, the phone had gone missing.

Bryce could only think of a few scenarios for what had happened to the cell phone in the hours between the sending of the message and the murders. The first was that Greg had hidden it in a place where he knew it would be safe. Steffi had been out that night at an awards ceremony and Greg had a key to her house, so the most likely places to have hidden it were his apartment or at her place. They had drawn a blank at both of those locations and, although they were three months late in their search, they knew that neither the police nor Walter had found the cell phone during that time. If the police had discovered the recording, Walter would be in custody. If Walter had it, he would have no reason to ask Steffi where it was. No reason to keep Steffi alive.

The second possibility was that, in the hours before his death, Greg had mailed the phone to someone he trusted. Bryce had some reservations about that option. It meant Greg must have known he was in immediate danger. Greg had placed himself in danger anyway, by meeting the man who killed his parents and telling him he knew the truth, but perhaps he thought the recording would be his insurance policy. How would Greg have learned of Walter's intentions toward him? Walter hadn't advertised the fact that he intended to kill Greg. And, since Greg was with the girl who died alongside him, he'd clearly had plans for what to do with his time that night. If Greg had taken this option, Steffi was the most obvious person to whom he would send the phone. But it had not been in the mail they had searched at her house. That meant that, if this was what had happened to the phone, Greg had to have mailed, or hidden, it elsewhere. If he had sent it to his parents, he must surely have put a note inside it informing them of its significance. Bryce supposed that the contents of that note would dictate their actions.

There were some other possibilities. Greg could have sent, or given, the phone to someone else or put it in a safety deposit box. He could even have emailed the audio file to another person. Someone Steffi knew nothing about. Even, possibly, to an attorney for safe-keeping. Once again, Bryce struggled to picture this outcome. Once Greg died, the need for secrecy was at an end…unless that person knew Steffi was in danger. But why hadn't the mystery person who had the record-ing come forward and given it to the police? Or tried to contact Steffi?

Unless they had, and the police hadn't discovered the recording or understood its importance. That would have to be a special kind of irony. That he and Steffi were busting their asses running around trying to find the damn recording when it could be in the right place all the time…but of no use.

Which led him on to a third alternative. There was the possibility that the cell phone was either lost or sto-len. That someone cleaning out Greg's apartment had thrown it out with the trash, or slipped it into his or her pocket. In which case, the recording was gone forever.

Bryce wasn't going to allow himself to think that way. For the first time since he had returned from Af-ghanistan, he was going to let optimism play a part in his life. If Greg had even a particle of the same strength and courage as his sister, then that cell phone was going to turn up. And when it did, it would bring down Wal-ter Sullivan.

If they drew a blank with Greg's parents tomorrow, the only option Bryce could see was to take everything they had and present it to the police. He knew how hard that would be on Steffi. He didn't want her to have to tell her story to an impersonal, suited detective in a bland, downtown Los Angeles office, or jail cell. His thoughts went to Stillwater and his sister-in-law, Laurie. Thinking of home triggered a reminder...

Damn. He needed to call Vincente, but Steffi had his cell phone.

There was a lanky teenager sweeping up trash outside a fast-food joint. He didn't even glance up from his task when Bryce sprinted up to him. "Is there a pay phone nearby?"

"Gas station." The kid pointed without breaking the rhythm of his brush strokes.

When Bryce reached the pay phone, he was pleased to find it worked. Hoping that he remembered the number correctly, Bryce fumbled coins into the slot and waited for Vincente to answer.

"You okay?" It wasn't so long ago that Bryce had avoided speaking to his half brother. Now the sound of Vincente's voice, with its note of concern for his welfare, sent a warm rush of comfort straight to his veins.

"Fine. It's just frustrating not to get anywhere." He briefly outlined the events of the day, making Vincente laugh with an account of Steffi's acting ability. "What are you doing tonight?"

"Laurie is here and Cam is on his way. They are going to endure my attempts at Italian cooking." That was another new development. There was a time when Cameron would never have stepped foot over the threshold of Vincente's apartment. Mainly because he would never have been invited.

"Put Laurie on."

"Hey, stranger." His sister-in-law's voice was teasing as she came on the line. "Where did you disappear off to without saying goodbye?"

"Much needed vacation." Bryce was aware that the words came out too gruff. "I need to ask you something. Some advice, for a friend."

"Okay." He could tell by the changed note in her voice, just in that one word, that she knew things were serious. "Ask away."

"If a crime has been committed, and someone, an innocent person, went on the run because they were scared, can they turn themselves in to any police officer? It doesn't have to be within the jurisdiction where the crime was committed?"

"Bryce, if you are in trouble…"

"Please, Laurie. I don't have any more coins."

"Yes, they can turn themselves in to any police officer." He heard her draw in a deep breath in Stillwater, felt her concern for him in his ear in San Diego. "Bryce…"

"Thanks, Laurie. Say hi to Cam for me. I love you both." He replaced the receiver.

Chapter 13

Leucadia was a small, beachfront community located within the coastal city of Encinitas. Unchanged by time, it looked exactly the way Steffi remembered it. The community was vibrant, active and diverse, working hard to maintain its funky reputation. Art galleries, a variety of restaurants, quaint coffee shops, and an abundance of surf and craft shops dotted the streets, but the serious focus was the water and the beach. Surfing was the main activity, with fishing, swimming, sailing and sunbathing also proving popular pastimes.

Steffi felt curiously rejuvenated after her conversation with her parents the night before. It hadn't been soul-purging and it hadn't involved tears or deep analysis, but it had been more open than any talk she'd had with them before. It felt like a turning point, like she had finally accepted who she was and who they were. There was no such thing as the perfect family, but they hadn't done too badly over the years. As strange as it seemed, she felt she had Bryce to thank for setting her straight on that. He had a knack for getting her feelings in perspective, although she wasn't quite sure how he did it. It was something to do with that no-nonsense aura of his. After the years she had spent living in a world of high-stakes narcissism, his down-to-earth approach made a refreshing change.

At the end of the call June had given her the address she had for Nancy and Tanner Spence. Although now they were driving along the main street in Leucadia, Steffi realized she didn't need it. Her memory would have guided her to the yellow-and-black-painted shop front with its sign that read Simply Bee. To one side, there was a swinging sign shaped like a giant bee.

"Oh, I remember now. It hasn't changed a bit." She turned to Bryce with a smile. "The bee wasn't fixed on properly and it kept falling off. One time when we came to visit, it had hit a tourist on the head and he was threatening to sue."

"He should have just let it *bee*." Bryce kept his face straight. "I can't believe he would make much money *stinging* a health food store."

Steffi rolled her eyes. "Oh, you are so funny."

"*Honey*, I haven't even started yet."

She snorted with laughter. This was how a day at the beach should be. Laughing and enjoying the sunshine and scenery. The dark undercurrents that accompanied them shouldn't be part of their lives.

As Bryce found a parking space alongside an odd assortment of vehicles, Steffi schooled her face back into a semblance of normality. She was going to see Greg's parents for the first time since she had been a child. More important than that, she was going to speak to them about the man they had all loved and lost. It was important, for all their sakes, to get this right.

Her nerves reached stratospheric levels as they walked along the sidewalk toward the store. As she stepped over the threshold into the shaded interior, the familiar aroma hit her and she couldn't stifle the exclamation that rose to her lips. Whenever she went into a health food store, it reminded her of this place, but it was never quite right. There were some things that all similar stores had in common, but there always seemed to be a missing ingredient, or one smell would be overpowering at the expense of others.

Now she realized that this was what she had always been searching for. In her head, this was the perfect health food store scent. This clean, malty, herbal smell with strong lavender and lemon notes. And honey. Lots of honey.

"Oh!"

A tall woman behind the counter turned at the sound of her voice, pausing in the act of dusting the array of glass jars that filled the pine shelves. Her long gray hair was pulled back in a ponytail and her sharp blue eyes looked exactly the way Steffi remembered.

"Steffi? Is that you?" Nancy Spence came around from the other side of the counter with her arms outstretched.

Steffi was drawn into an embrace that threatened to rob her of the ability to breathe. She'd forgotten that Nancy was a hugger. Steffi wasn't really comfortable with hugs. It was like a language she didn't speak. It never felt enjoyable because she was always wondering what she was meant to do, and how she was supposed to feel. Pull away now and risk causing offense? Keep hugging too long and come across as weird? Hand placement? Kiss or not? It was a minefield of protocols other people seemed to understand. *No one told me the rules.*

"How did you know me?" Steffi asked. The last time she had seen Nancy, Steffi had been a child with waist-length auburn curls.

"I would know you anywhere. You look just like Greg." Nancy drew away, her expression clouding over.

Her eyes flicked to Bryce's face, clearly expecting an introduction, and Steffi reached for his hand. "This is Bryce Delaney."

As Nancy's eyes took in their entwined fingers, she nodded without comment. "Can I get you a drink? I have some homemade lemonade in the fridge."

They took their drinks onto the patio at the rear of the store and sat in mismatched deck chairs. "Tanner will be home soon. He had a charter. A group of tourists who wanted to see the coastline from the ocean." Nancy sipped her drink in silence for a few minutes before turning those bright eyes to Steffi's face. "We've been expecting you. Ever since we heard that it was Anya Moretti who killed Greg, we knew you would come to see us."

Steffi felt sharp tears sting her eyelids. "You knew I was Anya Moretti?"

"Greg told us. But Tanner had already guessed when we saw you together on film." Nancy's smile was sad. "Like I said, you look like your brother."

"You know I didn't kill him?" Steffi felt the words catch in her throat as though they were scared to come out. Which, in a way, was true. Once she had spoken them, there was no going back. She had to hear the answer.

Nancy's brows drew together sharply. Before she could answer, a man's voice spoke for her. "You have to ask that?"

Tanner Spence was tall and tanned, and his bald head shone in the sunlight. He wore faded khaki shorts and a T-shirt of an indeterminate color. They could have been the ones he was wearing the last time Steffi saw him.

Steffi swallowed hard. "I have to ask. It matters."

"Of course we know. Whatever happened to Greg, we know you had no part in it." Tanner eased his long frame into one of the deck chairs. It creaked alarmingly. "What we couldn't understand was why you went on the run."

"Tell them." Bryce leaned forward and placed a hand on Steffi's wrist. "They need to know…and you need to tell it."

"More butternut squash and apple casserole, Bryce?" Nancy stood over him, holding her ladle in her hand like a weapon.

Before today, Bryce would have scorned vegan food. He was a true son of Stillwater, a town where steak and burgers were the favorite meals on the menu at Dino's. Tonight he had surprised himself by eating two helpings of casserole and several pieces of delicious home-made corn bread.

He shook his head, patting his stomach regretfully. "I wish I could, but you've achieved what many would consider the impossible, Nancy. You've filled me up."

Tanner had poured them all a glass of his homemade wine, but after a few sips of the lethal brew, Bryce had switched to water. Although Nancy had offered them a bed for the night, he preferred to drive back to the hotel. He wanted to be in full possession of all his senses, particularly his sight, when he made the journey.

"I wish we could help you." Nancy's voice was filled with regret. "But Greg never mentioned this recording to us."

"We don't have much time for technology," Tanner explained. "Neither Nancy nor I own a cell phone, and we rarely use our landline. Greg never called us. He just turned up when he wanted to see us."

"We wondered if he might have sent you a package just before he died," Bryce said. "If he knew he was in danger, he could have decided to dispose of the phone by hiding it or sending it to someone he trusted. It wasn't at Steffi's house or his apartment, so we wondered if he sent it here."

"No." Nancy shook her head. "Obviously, we would have remembered if anything had come from Greg before his death. There was nothing."

Bryce did his best to contain his disappointment. Although this was what he had expected, his heart sank and he avoided looking in Steffi's direction, knowing that she would be devastated.

"So this politician, this Walter Sullivan, he's the one who killed our son?" Tanner asked. "And he is also the one who murdered your parents?"

Steffi nodded. "When Greg recognized him, he confronted him and recorded the conversation."

"Why on earth didn't he go straight to the police?" Nancy's voice was incredulous.

There it was again. The question that was the key to this whole damn case. If Greg had only taken that recording to the police, none of this would have happened. From everything Steffi had told Bryce about her brother, holding on to the recording was out of character. Yet it was the question they kept coming back to. At that pivotal moment in his life, Greg had behaved in a way that was unfamiliar. As soon as he recorded Walter's guilt, the obvious thing to do would have been to walk into a police station. So why had he kept that recording? What had he been thinking?

Bryce's thought process was interrupted by Steffi. "When did you last see Greg?"

"He came down here the day before he died. I'll always be glad we got to see him." Nancy's smile was sad. "Although he did seem distracted. I remember asking him if everything was okay. He said he had a lot on his mind." She dabbed at her eyes with a handkerchief. "I thought he meant work."

Tanner laughed. "I don't think we can flatter ourselves it was us he came to see."

Bryce felt a stirring of interest. "What makes you say that?"

Tanner and Nancy exchanged an amused glance. "As soon as Bliss came home, we were just waiting for Greg to return. Her presence has always been like a magnet to him."

Bryce and Steffi jerked upright in unison. He could see out of the corner of his eye that Steffi's expression of shock perfectly reflected his own feelings. "Bliss?"

"Bliss Burton," Nancy said, regarding their reaction with surprise. "She and Greg had been sweethearts since high school. They were inseparable until about a year ago. I don't know what happened, but when they broke up, Bliss went away. She's a nurse, and she was doing relief work in Africa."

"This was the first time she had returned home," Tanner said. "But we knew—just knew—that as soon as she did get back, Greg would be here. There was too much history between them."

"Have you seen Bliss since Greg was murdered?" Bryce asked.

"No. I called around at her apartment a few days after he died. I knew it would hit her just as hard as any of us. She loved him. But she wasn't there. Her neighbor told me Bliss was due to go back to Africa the day Greg died. Even though she probably heard it on the news, I got the neighbor to give me the address of the place where she works out in Nigeria. I wrote a letter, but she didn't reply," Nancy said. "I expect it was too painful."

"I don't suppose you have any pictures of Bliss?" Bryce managed to keep his voice relaxed, even though tension was beginning to coil through him. Could this be it? The breakthrough they had been waiting for?

"We have plenty." Nancy's laughter was tinged with sadness. "When Greg was younger, we used to say the only way we could pry the two of them apart was with one of the oars from Tanner's old rowboat."

While Nancy went inside to search for a picture, Tanner looked from Bryce to Steffi with a bemused expression. "What's going on?"

"The night before he died, Greg sent me a message. It was just one word. *Bliss*," Steffi said. "There were also four digits. Two-seven-one-three."

Tanner's whole body jerked as though in reflex to a sudden pain. "Nancy's birthday is June 27 and mine is January 13. Greg always used those numbers as his password."

"We haven't been able to figure out what the message meant until now." Bryce drew a deep breath. "Maybe the message was sent to Steffi by mistake. Possibly Greg intended to send it to Bliss herself. Or maybe it was the clue we've been looking for. Perhaps he gave the missing cell phone to Bliss."

"You think the cell phone you're looking for could be in Nigeria?" Tanner's tone was incredulous.

Bryce laughed. "I'm hoping it's a little closer to home. Hopefully in Bliss's apartment."

Nancy emerged from the house carrying a carved wooden trinket box. She cleared a space on the food-laden table and placed the box in the middle, opening it as if it was some sort of ritual. Which it clearly was, Bryce decided as he observed her face when she shuffled through the photographs and mementos it contained. He felt bad for intruding on their grief, but a horrible certainty was beginning to gnaw at his gut. He could see it in Steffi's face, as well. She had pushed her dark glasses up onto her head, and her eyes were strained, her face pale as she watched Nancy.

"This is a good one. It was taken at the beach a few years ago." Nancy held out the picture and they saw a laughing Greg with his arm around a slender girl. She was pushing the strands of her hair out of her face. It was hair that drew the eyes as it curled wildly in brilliant gold corkscrews. "Although I don't know why you would want to see her picture when she's all the way across the other side of the world."

As she spoke, realization hit her and she raised a hand to her mouth. Tanner rose and placed an arm around her shoulders as the picture fluttered to the floor. "You think Bliss is the girl who was killed with Greg, don't you?"

Bryce stooped to retrieve the picture. "I hope I'm wrong, I really do. But it's a possibility."

Steffi felt the knot of tension in her stomach growing tighter as she studied the picture of Greg and Bliss. They looked so relaxed and happy. So in love. There was no doubt in her mind that the person in this picture was the one she had seen in Greg's apartment. Although she had only glimpsed her briefly and she hadn't seen her face, that mane of hair was unmistakable. Together with the message Greg had sent before his death, it seemed to be conclusive.

This picture added another piece to the mystery of what had happened just before her brother was murdered. It looked like Greg had canceled his plans with Steffi so he could spend a few precious hours with Bliss, who had been leaving for Africa the next day. When Walter's killer had arrived at Greg's apartment, he had found them together and murdered Bliss, as well.

"No one has been looking for Bliss." Steffi murmured the words as she ran her fingertip sadly over the picture. She remembered the suitcases that had been in the hall of Greg's apartment. Steffi had almost fallen over them in her panic as she ran out the door. They must have belonged to Bliss. Probably she was planning to go straight from Greg's apartment to the airport. "She is supposed to be in Africa."

Nancy nodded, tears brightening her eyes. "Her parents are both dead and I don't think she has any other close family."

"What about her employer in Nigeria? Surely they would have been concerned when she didn't turn up?" Tanner asked.

"They probably tried to get in touch with Bliss herself," Bryce said. "But it's a lot to ask that anyone would make the connection with a missing person here in America. Clearly no one did."

"We need to go to her apartment." Steffi got to her feet, turning to Bryce. "That's where Greg's cell phone will be. I'm sure of it."

"Okay." He held out his hand to Nancy and then Tanner. "Thank you for everything."

Nancy glanced nervously at them as she reached into the pocket of her apron. Withdrawing a pen and a slip of paper, she scribbled down the address to Bliss's apartment. "You will be careful, won't you?"

Bryce grinned as he tucked the address into his shirt pocket. The expression made Steffi's stomach flip over. How did he do that? Right in the middle of the most stressful time of her life, he could make her feel safe, happy and turned on…just with a smile.

"I may not be careful, but I will be successful." Coming from Bryce's lips, the words didn't sound arrogant. It was a promise, not a boast.

Steffi held the picture out to Nancy, but the other woman shook her head. "Keep it as a reminder of what this is about. Do this for them. Both of them."

She held out her arms to Steffi, folding her into a hug. This time Steffi returned the embrace with real warmth. Physical contact wasn't usually her thing. It never had been. Back in preschool other girls were always hand-holding or playing with each other's hair. In middle school they had progressed to linking arms and hugging, while Steffi stood to one side and watched, wanting to understand how to be part of it, but not knowing where to begin. All day-to-day touches had always caused her intense discomfort. If she couldn't escape the contact, she would freeze inside, embarrassed and unyielding until she could get it over with.

Shy. That was how June used to explain it to other people. Steffi had known what she really meant. *Damaged.*

Now she was instantly soothed and grounded. The fear and anger didn't go away, but those emotions temporarily took a back seat. Nancy pressed her cheek against Steffi's so only she could hear. "I remember how uncomfortable you were with hugs when you were a child. Learning to relax can be incredibly hard, especially for someone whose trust has been broken."

The words brought the sting of tears to Steffi's eyes. There was acceptance and understanding in Nancy's voice. For the first time ever, Steffi felt like it was okay to stop fighting. *I can accept who I am. The scars and the damage are part of me, but I'm still okay.* She drew back and looked into Nancy's smiling blue eyes. It was such an inconvenient time to have a lightbulb moment.

"Come back and see me when this is over," Nancy said. "I want to know you put it right for him." Her eyes flickered from Steffi's face to Bryce. "I want to hear all of it."

They made their way inside. The shop was in darkness and Nancy was just about to reach for the light switch when Bryce placed his hand on her arm. Pointing to the front window, he indicated a figure on the sidewalk outside. With a sinking heart, Steffi followed the direction of his finger. As he paced up and down, the man outside was in silhouette against the streetlight, but that bulky outline was unmistakable. It was Erik.

"Is there another way out?" Bryce whispered.

"Yes." Tanner kept his own voice low. "Out the back, where we just ate dinner. You'll have to climb the wall, and it's quite a drop on the other side, but you can get out that way."

"Are you okay with that?" Bryce asked Steffi. "Will your ankle take it?"

She nodded. "It's almost healed and I'd rather take my chances with a wall than with the biggest of Walter's bully boys."

"What can we do to help?" Nancy clasped her hands together as they made their way back out into the tiny yard.

"Two things. You can lend us a flashlight. And once we're gone, you can blow the dust off that landline of yours and call the police," Bryce said. "Tell them there's a guy outside acting suspiciously."

Tanner provided the flashlight and Bryce tucked it into the waistband of his jeans before hauling himself up the wall. When he reached the top, he swung himself over. Steffi listened until she heard him dropping down the other side. Tanner placed his hands around her waist and boosted her up until she was able to catch hold of the top of the wall. Once she was there, she hoisted herself up. Clinging on with both hands, she looked down at Bryce. He had his arms outstretched.

"Let go. I'll catch you." Suddenly, it seemed a long way down. "Trust me, Steffi."

Why did he have to say that? Why did he have to make this about trust? She had been fine until then, but as soon as Bryce said *that* word, she froze. Her rational mind and her emotions became disconnected from each other. Her brain was telling her she could do this, that jumping from this height wasn't a problem. At the same time, her body was displaying all the signs of terror. Clinging to the wall as if her life depended on it, refusing to let go, unable to relinquish control and put her trust in the man below her. Even though she knew Bryce wouldn't let her down. *How can you know that?* She groaned. This was not the time for that doubting voice to creep in.

"We have to go." Bryce's whisper was urgent. "Erik might decide to check out the rear of the property anytime now."

He was right, and she was being foolish. She remembered the picture in the back pocket of her jeans. This was for Greg. Taking a deep breath, Steffi let go of the wall and slithered down into Bryce's waiting arms. She caught a glimpse of the tension on his features.

"When are you going to trust me without having to think about it?"

He set her on her feet, and, without waiting for an answer to his question, led her back toward the car.

Chapter 14

Bryce drove away from the coast toward the San Diego Botanic Garden. The rental car's GPS led them to a quiet road and he pulled over, eyeing the apartment block across the street. The building was mostly in darkness, with only one or two windows lit up. He consulted the piece of paper on which Nancy had written the address.

"This is it."

Steffi didn't reply. She had been silent since they had left Nancy and Tanner's place. Huddled down in her seat, she appeared to be wrapped in her own emotions. Bryce assumed it was because she had been unable to trust him at first about jumping from the wall. That bothered him more than he wanted to admit. He understood why she was so vulnerable and insecure. Witnessing the murder of her parents at such an early age, and by a man she had thought of as an uncle, had destroyed her ability to trust. He got that. As a consequence of what she had been through, Steffi had erected huge barriers between herself and the rest of the world. She lived behind them, in her own protected space. If she ever left that safe haven, it was on her terms and she quickly retreated back behind the barricades when things got tough. He suspected that, until three months ago, *tough* had meant something as simple as an inappropriate touch or an unkind word.

When he had seen her relax and hug Nancy, he knew it was a momentous moment for her. He just wished she could open up in the same way with him.

Greg's and Bliss's murders might have forced Steffi to leave her safe place physically, but emotionally those barriers were as strong as ever. Increasingly, Bryce found himself wanting to tear them down, to show her what life could be like. That a little danger could be fun and exhilarating. Only he didn't know where to start. They had a physical bond that went beyond anything he had ever known, but they had a tacit agreement not to go past that. Talking? Sharing feelings? Not going there. It wasn't just Bryce keeping his distance. Steffi had made it clear. Their relationship was about sex. Nothing more. Hot sex with a Hollywood superstar and no strings. It was every man's fantasy. It should make his blood sing, right? He shouldn't get this weird feeling of *incompleteness* every time he thought about it. He shouldn't want to take her by the shoulders right now and try to convince her that, even if she never trusted anyone else in her life ever again, she could trust him.

None of this fit with his own feelings of detachment. He was being shaken up and forced to confront a side of himself he had kept hidden. While Steffi had been building her walls, Bryce had been dealing with his own issues in a different way. If he refused to acknowledge he had feelings, he didn't have to deal with them. It was a principle he had clung to ever since his return from Afghanistan, and it had worked just fine. Was he about to abandon it now? Let Steffi get under his skin? For what? When this was over and Walter was behind bars, they'd both look back on this time with an incredulous shake of the head and a smile… Bryce behind his desk in Stillwater and Steffi on a film shoot in some glamorous location. Their worlds may have collided briefly and dramatically for these brief moments, but nothing had changed. They lived totally different lives.

Bryce huffed out an impatient breath. He should probably concentrate on how he was going to break into that apartment without getting caught, rather than on his wounded male pride.

"Steffi?" She seemed to rouse herself from a trance. "This is Bliss's apartment building."

He made a move to get out of the car, but Steffi placed a hand on his arm. "Wait." When Bryce turned back to her, he could see by the golden glow of a nearby streetlight that her expression was troubled. "How did Erik know we were at Nancy and Tanner's place?"

Bryce sat back in his seat, considering the question. He glanced around the deserted street and in the rearview mirror. "You think we're being followed?"

She shook her head. "You made sure we're not. But Erik knew we were going to be at Simply Bee *tonight*."

He frowned. "Walter can't be monitoring our calls. Vincente is the only person who knows I have this number."

"And we didn't call Nancy and Tanner to tell them we were coming." Steffi hitched in a breath. "The only people who knew we were going there tonight were my parents."

Bryce took a moment to process what she was saying. "You think Walter has been to your parents' place? That he coerced them into giving him that information?" No wonder she was so quiet.

"How coincidental would that be?" Her hand was shaking as she raised it to her throat in a panicky gesture. "No, either Walter has had someone at their house or has been monitoring their calls the whole time since I went on the run—which would be crazy, even for Walter—or my parents let him know we would be at Nancy and Tanner's place tonight."

"What makes you think your parents told Walter we would be at Nancy and Tanner's place tonight?" Steffi saw the concern in Bryce's eyes as he asked the question. Was he wondering if she had finally become unhinged? If the stress had gotten too much for her? She wouldn't blame him if that was the way he was thinking. "Why does that have to be the solution instead of a coincidence, or Walter somehow watching us, or monitoring their calls?"

"It's not just the fact that Erik knew we would be at Simply Bee tonight. That could be explained away by the things you've just said. But I remember the way Walter spoke about my adoptive parents when we were in his house in Stillwater." She twisted her hands in her lap as she spoke. This was not something she wanted to say out loud. It wasn't even a suspicion she wanted inside her head. "I thought it was strange at the time, but

I was so caught up in everything else that was going on that I didn't have time to stop and think about it. I was too busy focusing on the existence of Greg's cell phone."

Bryce frowned as if he was trying to recall exactly what Walter had said. "I know he said he didn't hurt your adoptive parents, but I don't remember much else."

"When he talked about searching for me, Walter said he already had their address. Not that he *found* their address. Not that he tracked them down. He said he already had it." Steffi recalled how much those words had bothered her, even though she had pushed them to the back of her mind.

"Are you sure?" Bryce asked.

"Absolutely." That word brought with it a renewed certainty in what she was saying. "And that's not all he said that was odd. That whole conversation stuck in my mind because it was so strange. When I said my parents were good people, Walter agreed with me. He said he knew they were. And he knew my real name was Steffi Grantham. But that's not all. He called them by their first names. He called them June and Todd." The words were tumbling out in a frantic rush now as if they were in a desperate hurry to be heard before they slipped away and were lost. "As if he knew them."

"How could he know them?" The gentle note in Bryce's voice incensed her. How dare he humor her?

"I did not imagine those things!" She turned around in her seat to glare at him.

"Steffi, I'm not suggesting that you did. I'm asking a serious question. What do you suppose the things Walter said to you actually meant?" Bryce took her hands in his. "Do you really think Walter knows your parents? And that they would tell him where you are? Is that what you are saying? Because, if Walter knew where you—a witness to the murder of your parents—lived all these years, why wouldn't he just have killed you?"

His touch had the effect of causing the anger and tension to ooze out of her and she slouched back in her seat, the fight going out of her. "They raised me. They gave me everything. Yet I'm suspecting them of doing something that would harm me. What sort of person does that make me?"

"One who is under immense pressure." Bryce slid an arm around her shoulders, drawing her closer. "We don't know how Erik found out where we were tonight, and right now it's not worth speculating about it." He tilted his head to scan her face. "Do you want to call your parents and speak to them before we go into Bliss's apartment?"

"No, it's late, and I don't want to worry them over something that's probably just my imagination. I'll call them in the morning."

"Talking of calling people—" he gave an apologetic grimace as he took out his cell phone "—I need to check in with Vincente."

Steffi watched his profile as he called his brother's number, letting her eyes roam over his strong features. She was only half listening to his conversation with Vincente. There was something about the quality of Bryce's voice that soothed her. Idly, she wondered what had come first—attraction or being tuned in to that frequency in his voice that massaged her psyche. She couldn't remember. Their first meeting seemed so long ago. Was it possible for a person's character to show in their voice? If so, then Bryce's deep, warm tones would represent his finest qualities. They indicated that he was a good person.

The thought took her back again to that troubling conversation with Walter about her parents. The floodgates of doubt had been opened in Steffi's mind. Other memories began to surface, insidious things that bothered her. Once she began to dwell on them, she couldn't shake off her misgivings.

Bryce, with that knack he had for knowing when something was worrying her, ended his call and turned to look at her. "What is it?"

She gave a shaky laugh. "Now I really am being foolish. It's just—" She might as well say it. It didn't sound any more irrational than the things she'd already told him. "When I called my parents to tell them Greg was dead, they didn't seem surprised, even though it hadn't hit the news."

"That does seem strange." Bryce spoke slowly as though he was carefully absorbing her words.

"And at the start of the conversation, June tried to get me to go straight to the police and give myself up. But when I spoke to Todd, he tried to persuade me to meet him in San Francisco. He said he wanted to be with me to support me when I gave myself up."

"Well, that would make sense," Bryce said. "I can imagine how he would want you in their home so they could be with you when you talked to the police."

"You'd think that, wouldn't you? And because I had no intention of giving myself up, I didn't think too much of it. Until now. But June and Todd don't live in San Francisco. As far as I know, it's a town that means nothing to them. It certainly means nothing to me. Their home is in Sheridan. Like you, I grew up in Wyoming."

"So why, when their home is in another state, did Todd ask you to meet him in San Francisco?" Bryce was starting to look as bewildered as Steffi felt.

"I don't know. But Walter Sullivan is meticulous about detailing his movements on social media, so it will be easy to find out where *he* was that day. If Walter was in San Francisco, I guess we'll have the answer to the question about whether my parents know him or not, won't we?"

The apartment complex comprised four buildings arranged in a square around a central garden. Each building was two floors high. Bliss had the corner apartment on the second floor, farthest from the road. From Bryce's perspective, the location was ideal. While Steffi held the flashlight, he was able to get a good look at the front of the apartment without risking being seen.

There was no alarm, which was a bonus. There were only two possible ways of getting in from this level. One was through the front door, which, since it was solid wood with a substantial lock, didn't appear promising. The other was through a small window to the left of the door. Bryce figured if he could pry it open, he could just about fit through it…but that would mean damaging the window.

"The apartment would be left wide-open after we've gone," he explained. "If we're wrong, and Bliss is alive, I don't want her to get back from Africa to find the place has been stripped bare while she's been away."

"We're not wrong," Steffi said quietly.

"Even so, it doesn't feel right to leave her stuff exposed to looters."

He signaled to Steffi to switch off the flashlight

and, keeping to the shadows, they followed the wall of the building around to the rear of the apartment block. Looking up at Bliss's home, Bryce could see a small balcony. French windows opened from the apartment onto it.

"That's the way in." His voice was low as he pointed upward.

"How will you get up there?" Steffi whispered back.

"I'll have to drop down from the roof."

"How do you plan on doing that?" The words started out as a squeak, but she managed to get her voice back under control.

It was a good question and one to which there was no immediate answer. Bryce took a moment to study the garden. It was an unimaginative layout, with a few low-level shrubs, some tired-looking palm trees and two large maples. He studied the closest of these thoughtfully.

"That's how," he said at last.

Steffi followed his gaze. The tree was a few feet shorter than the building itself, and Bryce figured if he climbed it, he would be able to scramble across from the highest branches and onto the roof. That was his plan. Since it was the only one he had, he turned a confident face to Steffi.

"You're serious, aren't you?"

He slid down the wall into a sitting position, slipping off his boots and socks and rolling his jeans up to midcalf. "As a kid I was the champion tree climber of Stillwater."

"I hate to break this to you, but you are not a kid anymore. And we didn't come here so you could relive old times."

He handed her his boots, the flashlight and his cell phone. "Once I'm on the roof, go up and wait for me by the front door. I'll let you in that way."

"Okay. And if you don't make it to the roof, it was nice knowing you." Although she attempted a quiet laugh, he could hear the nervous note in her voice.

"Do you trust me, Steffi?" He took her face between his hands, dropping a kiss onto the tip of her nose.

"I want to." The whispered words tugged at his heartstrings. Although her inability to trust him was frustrating, he was beginning to understand how much it defined her.

Making his way swiftly across the open stretch of garden, Bryce launched himself at the tree, grappling his way onto the lowest branch. He soon discovered there wasn't much dignity involved in climbing trees as an adult. It was a case of groping and clawing his way up, testing out and finding the branches that would hold his weight. He also had to make sure he did it in silence. Any grunting, groaning, creaking of branches—crashing to the ground—would alert the residents to his activities. Choking back the occasional curse that rose to his lips when his hands or feet slipped, he managed to reach the higher branches and was able to contemplate the sloping roof.

From this angle, his plan appeared more ambitious than it had from the ground. The distance between the tree and the roof was greater than he'd calculated and he would have to reach up higher than he'd expected to catch hold of the edge of the roof tiles. If he missed? He looked down through the leaves, catching a glimpse of Steffi's upturned face in the moonlight. That was a hell of a long way to fall.

He waited for a few minutes, expecting it to come crowding in on him. He anticipated the familiar tightening in his chest and the prickling sensation up and down his spine. Next would come the feeling that giant, invisible hands were pressing down on his chest, forcing the air from his lungs so he couldn't take a complete breath. Then he would get the urge to run, to hide, to curl up in a ball. To do nothing because he was worthless, hopeless. And that would be it. Paralyzing, illogical fear would have him in a death grip.

But it didn't happen. He could breathe normally. He felt nervous, but so would anyone who was about to throw himself from the top of a tree onto a roof. He even felt a little bit of the old adrenaline rush he used to get before a mission or a cage fight. Looking down, he gave Steffi a thumbs-up. She probably couldn't see him, and it didn't matter. The gesture was more for himself than for her anyway.

He guessed on some level his PTSD would always be with him. It was woven into his psyche. But every time he fought those demons and won, it was worth a celebration.

Bryce stood on the thickest of the high branches with his back against the tree trunk. The leaves were thinner here and he was able to shift his body until he was at the best angle. No time like the present. Pushing back against the trunk, he launched himself toward the roof. Relief flooded through him as his hands caught and held the rim of the gutter at the edge of the roof tiles, holding the weight of his body. His bare feet scrabbled against the brick, seeking a foothold. It was no good. There wasn't one.

It was a few years since Bryce had done any rock

climbing out on the peaks around Stillwater, but he remembered Cameron teaching him how to heel hook.
In some of the trickier situations they'd been in, this
move had involved getting his heel above his hand to
get a grip on the rock. Pain flared through his fingers
as he used them to hoist his body higher and swing his
right leg out. Bringing his foot up, he managed to get
his heel into the gutter. The effort it took and the pain
that screamed through his muscles was a reminder that
he'd been a lot younger and lighter the last time he'd
performed that movement.

Slowly, he hoisted himself onto the roof. Taking a
few moments to sit with his knees bent and his head
lowered, he caught his breath. His fingers were burning and every muscle felt like it was on fire. Now all
he had to do was slide down the roof, drop onto the
balcony and break into Bliss's apartment through the
French doors… That damn cell phone had better be in
her apartment.

When Bryce opened the apartment door and let Steffi
in, she couldn't decide whether to be furious with him
for placing himself in so much danger or elated that
he'd managed to survive his escapades. In the end, she
settled for feeling relieved that they were inside Bliss's
home.

"I saw you get onto the roof, but how did you get in?"

"That was the easy part." He closed the door behind
her and Steffi switched on the flashlight. "Once I'd slid
down the roof and dropped onto the balcony, I just had
to figure out how to open the French doors. Luckily,
they were the old-fashioned kind with no dead bolts.
That old credit card trick really does work."

"I can't believe we actually had some luck on our side at last."

Bryce grimaced as he flexed his fingers. "I'm not sure my joints would consider they've been lucky."

By the narrow beam of the flashlight, Steffi could see that Bliss had an eclectic approach to interior decoration. The small space was a mix of bold color, old and new, quirky and elegant. It was clear the occupant of the apartment chose the pieces because she liked them, rather than with any overall design in mind. The end result was cluttered but comfortable. Steffi experienced a pang of regret that she would never get to know the woman her brother had loved.

Nothing that had gone before had prepared Steffi for this moment. She had experienced stage fright many times in her life. Had known what it was like to suffer the nerves that went with public appearances, speaking at a podium, facing a crowd of thousands. None of those things could compare to the fear that assailed her now. Her heart was pounding wildly, her palms were sweating and her breathing was uneven.

"It's here." She choked back a sob. "I just know Greg's phone is going to be in this room."

Bryce nodded. "I only wish Bliss had been a minimalist. It would have made searching so much easier."

The search took a long time. They were careful to move and replace Bliss's many possessions. Finally, while Steffi was crawling under a side table, Bryce removed a pile of cushions from an armchair.

"Here." He slid his hand under the throw that covered the chair and brought it out, holding it up to show Steffi the cell phone.

"The charger is here, as well. I was wondering what

we were going to do about the dead battery, but Greg seems to have thought of that."

She went to him and wrapped her arms around his waist. Had she actually ever believed this moment would come? She had set out on this mad chase because the alternative was to hand herself over to Walter—or the softer option of the police—and give up the fight. But had she really been convinced they would find Greg's cell phone? There had always been doubts at the back of her mind, but it was only now that she realized how many. She had envisaged lots of different endings to this madness, but never this one. And she couldn't have done this alone. Without Bryce, she wouldn't have been able to reach this point.

"It's not over yet." Bryce had that uncanny knack of following her thoughts. "Let's get out of here. I want to listen to that recording."

Chapter 15

"I guess this is the moment when we find out if 2713 is the access code Greg used for this phone." Bryce sat on the hotel room bed with his knees drawn up and his forearms resting on them. The cell phone, its charger plugged into the socket at the bedside, was in his right hand. Steffi rested her chin on his shoulder and he could feel the tension thrumming through her.

He held the cell phone out to her, but she shook her head. "Shaking fingers." She held her hand up to show him. "I'd make a mistake and get us locked out of the damn thing before we even started."

Bryce wasn't sure he was going to be much better. His own nerves were sky-high. The phone's home screen was a picture of a Leucadia Beach at sunset, and the beautiful image was at odds with the horror its owner had endured. Carefully, Bryce tapped the access code onto the on-screen keyboard. To his amazement and relief, it took him straight in.

Steffi hissed out a breath that told its own story about how she felt. This cell phone was the same popular model as the one Bryce had ditched in the fountain at Walter's Stillwater home. It meant Bryce was easily able to navigate his way around its features. Accessing the folder in which Greg stored his voice recordings, he offered up a brief thank-you to Steffi's brother for his organizational skills. Greg labeled his files neatly, and the one they were looking for was unambiguous.

Walter Sullivan—Confession. The label was followed by the date. It couldn't have been clearer.

"Ready?"

He would never get tired of looking into Steffi's eyes. It was nothing to do with how unusual they were. It was because they were a window to her emotions. He loved watching for the moment they began to sparkle with mischief or joy. When she was concentrating, her gaze would become fixed and refuse to shift until she had pursued the thought that had her in its grip. Then, when she was troubled, as she was now, her eyes became stormy and Bryce could see the darker, amber flecks in their golden depths. That was when he wanted to smooth his fingers over her brow and absorb her cares into his own body. But right now nothing he did was going to take away the darkness he could see in her eyes. Listening to Greg's recording was either going to make things better…or it wasn't. Either way, Bryce wanted to let her know he would be there for her.

Steffi slid her hand into his. "Maybe *ready* is the wrong word. I don't know if I'll ever feel ready to listen to this. But I have to do it."

"We'll do it together."

She nodded and he could see gratitude in the change in her expression. Bryce pressed the red play button on the screen. The recording started with some background noise, then Walter Sullivan's voice was in the room with them and Steffi jerked as though she'd been on the receiving end of an electric shock.

"Some people might think your persistence is commendable. I find it annoying. Being dragged along to a meeting because you profess to have evidence of my involvement in a murder is a waste of my time."

"You don't know who I am, do you?" Greg's astonishment could be heard in his voice.

"Should I?"

"Arrogant bastard," Steffi whispered, and Bryce pressed a finger to her lips.

"I'm Gregori Anton." There was silence. "My parents were Aleksander and Ekaterina. You used to come to our home when I was a child."

"I remember." Walter's voice was harsh.

"You and my father were business associates." There was a tremor in Greg's voice that betrayed his nervousness, but he plowed on. Bryce spared a moment to admire his courage. "I remember your men. The ones with the tattoos on their hands. You know the ones I'm talking about, don't you, Walter Sullivan? The ones that look like a bloodshot eye. They were the men who were with you on the night you killed my parents."

Walter's laughter was like a whiplash. "What do you want from me? A confession? The men with the tattoos were your father's gang members, until they switched their allegiance to me. Aleksander double-crossed me. He cut me in on one of his drug deals, but I found out from Alexei Ivanov that he was paying me a fraction of what his Russian partners were getting. Alexei came to me with a proposal. If Aleksander was dead, there would be a lot more money for me…and your father got what he deserved. No one cheats me. Ekaterina—" Bryce heard Walter's indrawn breath. Even on the recording, he sounded like a man who was battling for control. "It was her fault things reached that point. She knew what Aleksander was doing. If she had shown me more loyalty—"

"Shown *you* more loyalty?" Greg cut across him incredulously. "Her loyalty was to my father, her husband."

"Ultimately that was the decision she made." Walter seemed to have regained some of his composure. "So what next? How much do you want from me?"

"I should have known you'd think this was about money." The nervousness was gone from Greg's tone now. It had been replaced by contempt. "It isn't. I wanted to look you in the eye and see if you felt any remorse for what you did."

This time there seemed to be genuine amusement to Walter's laughter. "And what about Stefanya? Doesn't she want to look me in the eye? But I should call her Anya these days, shouldn't I? Anya Moretti. Little Stefanya Anton has done very well for herself."

Bryce felt Steffi freeze at the words. Her hand in his twitched convulsively.

"You didn't know me, but you do know who my sister is?" Greg's voice on the recording was suspicious.

"Know her? I *made* her. Anya Moretti wouldn't exist if it wasn't for me." Walter laughed again, and Steffi's grip on Bryce's hand had tightened to the point where it became painful.

"What are you talking about?" Greg asked.

There was a moment or two of silence. Then Greg uttered a startled exclamation. "No!"

"Next time you see Stefanya, tell her Uncle Waltz said hi." The microphone had picked up the sound of footsteps and then a door closing. And that was where the recording ended.

"That's why Greg didn't go to the police." Steffi paced the small hotel room restlessly. "He wanted to speak to me first about what Walter said. He was waiting for me to get back from Italy."

Bryce went to her, catching hold of her and drawing her into his arms. "It could have been an idle boast. Walter must have known anything he said about you would hurt Greg."

Steffi rested her forehead against his chest, breathing deeply. "No. Don't you see? Walter knew who I was. He knew Stefanya Anton and Anya Moretti were the same person." She lifted her head to look at him. The remnants of tears shimmered on the ends of her lashes, a consequence of what she had heard her brother endure. "A handful of people know my real name. I try to keep it hidden so that June and Todd can stay out of the limelight. But anyone who does know my real name knows me as Steffi Grantham. No one knows I'm Stefanya Anton…because I'm not." She clutched the front of Bryce's shirt as though he was the only thing holding her upright. "I haven't been Stefanya Anton since I was five years old."

"So you think Walter has been following your progress since your parents died?" Bryce asked. As crazy as it seemed, what Steffi was saying must be right. It was the only way Walter could have known what had happened in her life.

"He must have." Steffi's expression became even more distraught. "Which means I was correct when I said Walter knows my adoptive parents."

Bryce ran a hand through his hair as he struggled to come to grips with the implications of what she was saying. "But why would Walter want to know what was going on in your life? Why didn't he just kill you? You knew who he was. You could have given the police valuable information about him. Could he have been feeling guilty because he killed your parents?"

"He didn't look very remorseful when he turned away from my father's dead body. And, if that was the case, why didn't he know what had happened to Greg since our parents died? He had no idea who Greg was. He said so at the start of that recording. If he felt guilty about what he'd done, why did that guilt only extend as far as me?"

"Favoritism? Maybe he preferred you over Greg?" Bryce was trying to find rational explanations for Walter's behavior, but he wasn't finding it easy.

"He did. He brought me toys and books, and left Greg out. Greg was jealous. But there is a world of difference between that and watching over me at a distance after he slaughtered my parents." The look in Steffi's eyes was anguished. "And what happened at the end of the recording? It went quiet, and then Greg cried out. He said 'no.' Then it sounded like Walter left. What did that mean?"

"We'll probably never know." Bryce kept his voice

gentle. "Only two people were in the room when that recording was made. Greg is dead, and we're not going to see Walter again. Not until the trial." Steffi's chin came up sharply at that. The troubled look in her eyes was replaced by a militant sparkle, and Bryce got a glimpse of her thoughts. He didn't like what he was seeing. "Steffi…"

"You said it yourself. Only two people know what happened, and we can't ask Greg."

"And we sure as hell aren't going to ask Walter." When she didn't respond, he ground out a frustrated groan. "You can't seriously intend to confront him again. That recording is a cast-iron confession. All we have to do is hand it over to the police and Walter is history. They have him for the murder of your parents, and for Greg and Bliss. You will be cleared of any involvement."

"I might be cleared, but I wouldn't have the answers to my questions. Walter said he *made* me, Bryce." Steffi's eyes glittered dangerously. "I need to know what he meant by that. Did he make me into a successful movie star? I've always wondered where my parents got the money to send me to the best performing arts school in the country. They didn't earn much, but I always had the best of everything."

"Don't parents always try to give their kids the best they can? I know mine did." Bryce felt like a man who was attempting to fight an unstoppable force. He got the feeling Steffi was determined to confront Walter, with or without him. He might not like the direction in which this was heading, but she sure as hell wasn't going to do it alone.

"You don't understand. June and Todd gave me things that were way out of their league. When I was a child, I got the most expensive toys. Then, when I was in my teens, it was designer clothes. I was the kid everyone envied, even though I wasn't into labels. On my seventeenth birthday, I got the keys to a sports car that would have cost my father several years' salary."

"Didn't you ever question it?"

"I tried once or twice." Steffi bit her lip. "But we didn't really do heart-to-heart conversations."

A family in which talking to each other didn't come easy was something Bryce didn't recognize. He could have told his own parents anything and asked them any questions. Now, if he needed to, he could take his problems to either of his brothers. Even when things were tough between him and Vincente, hadn't he always known deep down that his brother would be there for him? And it worked both ways. There had been a time, not so long ago, when Vincente had infuriated Bryce beyond reason. Even so, if his half brother had asked him for help, Bryce would have dropped everything and gone to his aid.

Yet you've shut them out of the most important conversation of all. That annoying little voice spoke up at the back of his mind, refusing to be silenced. *They know you have been hurting since Afghanistan, but you won't let them in. You haven't allowed them to be there to support you.*

He silenced that voice. This wasn't about him; it was about Steffi. He tried one final attempt at talking her out of a confrontation with Walter. "It sounds to me like the people you need answers from are your adoptive parents."

"I was planning to call on them on my way to visit Walter." She regarded the cell phone he had placed on the locker next to the bed as if it was a coiled snake.

"Why do you suppose Greg hid the cell phone that night?"

The abrupt change of subject caught Bryce off guard. "What do you mean?"

"Why *that* night? Why not as soon as he made the recording?" Steffi picked up the cell phone. "Did Greg know Walter was coming after him? Was that why he sent me the message and left the cell phone in Bliss's apartment?" She raised troubled eyes to Bryce's face. "There were two suitcases in Greg's apartment the day he was killed. Maybe Bliss wasn't the only one going to Africa. Greg said he had something to tell me. We've assumed it was about the recording. What if he also wanted to let me know he was going away?"

"There may be some clues in his phone," Bryce said. "We know he sent Walter a copy of the recording. Maybe there were other communications between them."

Steffi automatically handed the phone to him. It was as if she felt the device might scald her if she held on to it for too long. Accessing a dead man's messages didn't feel comfortable, but Bryce decided the need to find out what had happened took precedence over the protection of Greg's privacy.

"The last message he sent from this phone was to you. *Bliss 2713.* Your reply asking him what he meant is here, but he never read it." He held up the screen to show Steffi. "It looks like he sent you that message and then immediately hid the phone in Bliss's apartment."

Steffi wrapped her arms around herself as if she was cold. "Are there any messages to Walter?"

Bryce continued scrolling. "Greg made a number of phone calls to Walter in the days prior to their meeting. That must have been to set the meeting up. Then there

is a message the day after the meeting sending Walter
a copy of the recording. Ah, here we have it. Just before Greg messaged you, he sent Walter a message."
Bryce read the words on the screen. "'Tell your goons
to leave Bliss Burton alone.' There was an attachment."

He opened the photograph that had been attached
to the message. Although it was grainy, it showed two
men standing in the shade of a large tree. Erik's bulk
and Alexei's bald head were unmistakable. Bryce also
recognized the tree. He had climbed it earlier that day.
Greg had taken the picture from the balcony of Bliss's
apartment.

"Walter replied to that message."

"What did he say?" Steffi looked like she wasn't sure
she wanted to know.

"'Hand over the cell phone or you are both dead.'"

Bryce could see it all. Greg must have done exactly
what Bryce would have done. He had called Steffi telling her to meet him the next day, then sent her a cryptic
message telling her where the cell phone was. He didn't
need to be too specific; he would be seeing her the next
morning…or so he thought. He had hidden the phone
in Bliss's apartment and taken his girlfriend to his own
apartment building where the security was better. With
their bags packed, ready to leave for Nigeria the next
day, Greg must have believed he'd outwitted Walter.

Did anyone ever outwit Walter?

"We do this my way or not at all." From that stubborn
expression on his face, Steffi could tell Bryce wasn't
planning on backing down.

Although her initial instinct was to rebel against his
high-handedness, she kept it in check. She really didn't

want to do this alone. In a flash of searing honesty, she realized she didn't ever again want to do anything without him at her side. This was turning out to be a day of life-changing revelations.

Keeping her turbulent emotions under wraps, she sat on the edge of the bed. "What are your terms?"

Bryce leaned a shoulder against the wall and grinned down at her appreciatively. "You are not fooling anybody with that passive act, Steffi. We both know you want to kick my ass up and down this room for daring to tell you this is going my way from now on."

"You're the boss." She kept her jaw clenched.

He laughed. "How come I never heard those words from you when you worked for me? I could get used to this new, docile Steffi...although I think the other drivers at Delaney Transportation may be wondering what I've done with their coworker."

"Oh, just get on with it." She huffed out an impatient breath.

His expression became serious again. "First, I'm sending a copy of that recording to Vincente right now."

Steffi considered the suggestion. Vincente knew about their plight, and he knew of the existence of the recording. He was already their insurance policy if anything went wrong. It made sense to include him as backup. The hoops they'd had to jump through to track down the cell phone highlighted the issue of having only one copy in existence. And Vincente was someone they could trust. He would follow Bryce's instructions when it came to how to use the recording.

"Okay." As soon as she said the word, Bryce got to work sending a message containing the recording to Vincente's cell phone.

"I've told him not to do anything with it until he hears from me," he said as he pressed Send. "Second, when we meet with your parents, we won't go to their home."

"Why not?" Steffi was surprised at the request.

"Because there's a possibility that either Walter or the police will be watching their place. You'll call them in advance and arrange to meet them somewhere very public. A fast-food joint or a coffee shop," Bryce said.

"But if I'm right about them, they'll alert Walter. He'll know where we'll be." Steffi pointed out the flaw in the plan.

"Exactly. But if we're in a crowded, public place, he won't be able to make a move on you. He might try—" Bryce's face tightened "—but he won't succeed."

"Okay. Do you have any more conditions?" Maybe a little advance planning wasn't such a bad thing. Whereas Steffi would have gone storming out into the night, Bryce had thought this through.

"Plenty. But I'll keep those on hold until the time comes to confront Walter." He stretched his arms above his head. "Right now it's after midnight and I don't have a single muscle that isn't aching. If we're going to travel to Wyoming tomorrow, I need some rest."

"Rest?" Steffi quirked an eyebrow at him as she got to her feet and moved closer.

He gave her one of his stomach-flipping smiles. "Did you have other plans?"

"One or two, but if you need to sleep..."

"Sleep can wait." He caught her up in his arms and, with his lips on hers, walked her backward until her knees hit the bed.

Steffi's whole body was instantly electrified by his

touch. As he raised his head, the look in his eyes melted her. Anticipation thrilled through her at the unspoken message she read in their depths. Her hands gripped his shoulders, moving over the fabric of his shirt before pulling frantically at the buttons. Obediently, Bryce removed the offending garment. The rest of their clothing quickly followed and he tipped her back onto the bed.

He kissed her again, his tongue twining with hers, one hand tilting her head so he could deepen the kiss. Steffi wound her fingers into his hair, gripping the thick strands tightly as she fought to get even closer to him. Too close would never be close enough.

His roughened hands roamed over her body, his fingers rasping deliciously against the sensitive flesh of her breasts. One finger moved down her body, sliding into her depths, stretching her, opening her tight muscles. The sensation made her gasp and she clawed at the taut muscles of Bryce's back, already so aroused that a muffled scream escaped her lips. She slammed her hips up and down in response to the quick-fire movements of his finger, taking a brief instant to marvel at the way her body instantly responded to his touch. Then thought was no longer possible as she was lost in a swirling vortex of sensation.

"I can't wait to be inside you."

Steffi shivered as his touch was withdrawn, but the welcome sound of foil ripping tipped her senses into overdrive. Immediately, the mattress shifted as Bryce moved his weight over her and her thighs were pressed apart by his hips. His breathing was harsh as one hand moved beneath her, lifting her to him. Desperate to feel him inside her, Steffi tilted her hips, gasping at the whiplash of pleasure that streaked through her at the fiery heat of his intrusion into her body.

Bryce pushed into her, caressing her sensitized nerve endings with his steel-hard flesh. Hunger, raw and pulsing, clawed at her. Bryce commenced a rhythm of slow, even strokes, teasing her, keeping her at the peak of torment, taking her to the point of cataclysmic explosion and retreating. Over and over.

"More, Bryce. Please, I can't wait." Her hands beat at his shoulders. Slow and steady was a delicious torture, reducing her to pleading, near sobbing, desperation.

In response, he began to pump his pelvis harder and faster. Steffi's hips slammed up from the bed, meeting his thrusts, matching his speed and passion. Her body was dissolving around him, becoming liquid fire; heat bubbled up from her core and spread through her veins, touching every part of her. As her climax hit, she shattered into a thousand tiny pieces. Helpless, she clung to Bryce, her body becoming part of his, merging with him, connecting to him on a level that took her to new heights of ecstasy. She was dimly aware of Bryce gasping her name as she felt him jerk out his own release, before he collapsed onto her.

After a moment or two Bryce shifted his weight to her side before going to the bathroom to take care of the condom. When he returned, Steffi curled into his arms. The action felt right. Scarily so. This was her favorite place to be. She didn't want to stop and examine that thought, because if she did, she would have to start unpicking her feelings. She wasn't sure where they were going to lead her.

"Have you always been so resolute?" she asked.

"Pardon?" Bryce tilted his head to look at her face

by the light of the bedside lamp. She got the feeling her question had shocked him, but she didn't understand why.

"You always know what to do, and you have real belief in your decisions," Steffi explained. "I wondered if it came naturally to you. Or was it something they taught you in the military?"

To her surprise, Bryce started to laugh. There was some genuine humor in the sound, but there was also a trace of bitterness. "You think I'm decisive? Oh, Steffi. You have no idea."

His self-mocking tone intrigued her and she leaned on her elbow, looking down at him. "Tell me."

He was lying on his back with his hands behind his head and his eyes half closed. He remained silent for several minutes and she thought he wasn't going to respond at all. When he did speak, his voice was low and husky. "Maybe I was sure of myself once. Possibly it was one of the qualities that got me into a leadership position in the army. I certainly wouldn't have considered myself weak. Not until the day I led my unit out on patrol in Afghanistan." He sat up abruptly, scrubbing a hand over his face. "I'm sorry. I've never talked about it. I thought perhaps I could do it now…to you. But I can't."

Steffi sat up next to him, drawing him into her arms and pressing her lips against his temple. His whole body shook as though racked by some terrible fever. Acting on instinct, she held him until the shivers finally subsided. "You don't have to talk about it."

Bryce lifted his head, and she was shocked at what she saw in his eyes. Twin pools of torment stared back at her. "I do. I've fought it for too long. And I can do it." He clasped her hand. "With you here with me."

"I'm here." She returned the grip of his fingers.

"I was an explosive ordnance disposal expert. My unit worked in the badlands of Helmand province. On this occasion we were on patrol near the airport, working alongside Special Forces on a major operation. We discovered a number of improvised explosive devices, or IEDs. They are commonly used as roadside bombs and they're difficult to disarm because each one is different. The insurgents don't leave a step-by-step guide." The words were coming out fast now, as though, having decided to talk, he wanted to get it done in case fear overcame him again. "I gave the order and we set to work on them. All my men were highly qualified, but some had more experience than others. It was my job to assess the situation and allocate the task of disarming the IEDs to the most suitable person. This time—when it mattered more than ever—I got it wrong."

Watching him, Steffi realized he was barely there in that hotel room with her. His expression was intent, his eyes fixed on the distant desert horizon in his memory. "It must have been incredibly hard to face those sort of challenges every day."

Bryce nodded. "We faced death every day. Mentally, physically, emotionally…it drained us. But we had to keep going for the sake of our colleagues. They were running out of superlatives for my team. Legends. Best of the best. Phenomenal. We'd heard every accolade, been given every award. It all ended that day in the dust." He gripped her hand tighter. "I'd disarmed two IEDs and was moving onto a third when it happened. I'd allocated the most innocuous-looking mine to the most junior officer—still a highly skilled bomb disposal expert—but it was booby-trapped. It blew sky-high. Out of a team of eight, three of my men were killed, and the other five, including me, were injured."

"Bryce, you didn't do anything wrong. You made your decision based on the information you had available at the time." On the surface he was so strong, yet underneath he was harboring a secret of such magnitude. It explained a lot about the enigma that was Bryce Delaney. She could see how the guilt he lived with every day was eating him up. She wanted to find a way to convince him it was misplaced. But how could she show him that? How could she judge what he'd been through? She hadn't been there.

"I try to tell myself that. Then I remember the torn-apart bodies of my friends. Guys I worked alongside every day. Men I laughed with, drank with, trusted with my life. Men who trusted *me* with their lives." He shook his head. "It was my call. You ask if I've always been resolute? Since that day, most mornings I can't make up my mind which side of bed to get out of."

"The operational side of Delaney Transportation runs like clockwork because of you," she reminded him.

"You have no idea how hard it is some days to make the easy decisions." His smile was lopsided and Steffi reached up to kiss the corner of his mouth.

"None of the decisions you've made since you found me on the floor of my cabin have been easy." She took his face between her hands. "If it wasn't for you, I'd be in a prison cell awaiting trial for murder, or dead in a ditch in Stillwater. You are a hero, Bryce Delaney. You were then and you are now."

Chapter 16

They left the hotel early the next morning. Bryce asked the desk clerk to recommend a cyber café nearby. He had to cut short what looked likely to be a lengthy conversation, and possibly a promising friendship, centering on the latest combat and car chase video games.

"Coffee and a Byte?" Steffi, who was still suffering the effects of what they had learned the previous day, viewed the glowing neon sign glumly. "Do I want to eat breakfast in this place?"

"Stop being a Beverly Hills diva." Bryce propelled her over the doorstep with a hand in the small of her back. "Welcome to the real world."

She made a rude gesture at him as they took their seats in a corner booth that was dominated by a huge computer screen. Bryce ordered coffee and pancakes and paid for an hour's internet access.

"Okay." He slid the mouse to Steffi. "Let's stalk Walter Sullivan."

When Vincente had bought a cheap, prepaid cell phone for Bryce, he had purchased a call and messaging deal. He hadn't included a data package. Bryce would have done the same. Why would anyone who was on a wild hunt for a dead man's cell phone have time to stop and check email or the internet? Only it turned out he and Steffi wanted to do just that. They needed to know where Walter had been when Todd Grantham asked Steffi to meet him the day after Greg was murdered. And, since Steffi had left her cell phone in her cabin in Stillwater, and Bryce had no data, Coffee and a Byte was the solution to their problems. Even if the lurid decor made Steffi wrinkle her nose.

While Steffi clicked her way through Walter's social media accounts, Bryce watched her profile. Although she had woken in a dejected mood, she was dealing well with what was going on. He had no doubt that her fighting spirit would soon kick in again. He felt fiercely proud of her and alongside that pride came a pang of sadness. *I don't have the right to feel that way.*

"You've done this before." He nodded at the screen.

The lighting in the café was gloomy and the other customers were focused on their own screens. Steffi risked removing her glasses. "More times than I can count. The smartphone I left in my cabin had these pages bookmarked." She pointed at the screen. "This is the day Greg met with Walter." There was a picture of a smiling, tuxedo-clad Walter standing on a red carpet. On his arm was a famous actress, and behind him the facade of a well-known Los Angeles movie theater could be glimpsed. Walter had shared the information with his followers that he was attending a long-awaited premiere. A few hours later he had posted pictures from the after-party. "From the timing of the recording, we know he met with Greg after the movie and before the party."

As Steffi scrolled down, Bryce gave a soft whistle. "You were right. Walter likes to let the world know what he's doing."

"He's a narcissist." Steffi's jaw was tight as she looked at the pictures. Walter smiling at the camera. Walter meeting and greeting lunch guests. Walter stepping into a limousine. Walter out jogging. "He loves the attention."

Bryce followed the information on the screen. "He stuck around. He was in Los Angeles the night before Greg died." Walter had shared a picture of himself attending a party on a friend's yacht.

"But the next day he'd moved on." Steffi tapped a finger on the screen. "He had a meeting at the headquarters of one of his retail groups." She slumped back in her seat. "He flew in his private jet. He says here it was a beautiful day and he wasn't traveling too far up the coast. Only as far as San Francisco."

Bryce shook his head in an attempt to clear it of the sudden fog that had descended upon it. What had appeared to be a wild hunch on Steffi's part now looked to be true. Todd Grantham had been trying to lure his daughter into Walter's clutches.

"My whole life has been a lie." There was a catch in Steffi's voice that felt like rusty wire ripping into his heart. "But I thought there was one part that was real." She raised a shaking hand and dashed it across her eyes, brushing away tears in its wake. "I thought June and

Todd were real. We might not have subscribed to the ideal of the perfect family, but we did okay."

"Steffi—" Bryce caught hold of her, drawing her to him with an arm around her shoulders "—you don't know yet that they weren't real. There could be a dozen explanations for this." But however hard he tried, right at that moment Bryce couldn't come up with one.

Her whole body quivered as she subsided against him. "Or there could be one very obvious one. They didn't adopt me because they wanted me. They took me in as a favor to their friend Walter."

The pain in her voice caused that wire to rip deeper into Bryce's heart. How had he ever believed the connection between them was just physical? Seeing her hurting like this tore him apart. He would do anything in his power to make this better, but he couldn't think of a single thing. All he could do was try to ease some of the heartache by holding her, by using his body to show her he was there and he cared.

After a while, the trembling in Steffi's limbs subsided and she straightened. Remaining within the circle of Bryce's arms, her gaze was fixed on the screen as she began an internet search.

"What are you looking for?" Bryce asked as her fingers flew over the keyboard.

"Just a hunch. Todd works as a legal assistant, but I know he has a law degree. I once asked him why he didn't practice law, but he never gave me a straight answer."

Bryce watched in silence as she searched. She had that intent, determined look she got when she wasn't going to let something go. Stubborn Steffi had returned.

He bit back a smile. After about ten minutes she sat back with a little huff of satisfaction.

"There." She pointed triumphantly to a black-and-white picture on the screen. It looked like it had been cropped from a newspaper. A much younger Walter Sullivan stood on the steps of a courthouse with his fists raised in a triumphant salute above his head. The caption above the picture read Sullivan's Legal Team Achieves the Impossible.

The article, which was twenty-five years old, went on to recount how Walter had been prosecuted following a major accident at one of his factories in which twelve employees had died and twenty more were left seriously injured. Despite a damning report by health and safety officers criticizing every aspect of Walter's approach to employee safety, he had walked out of the courtroom without a fine.

"See the man standing in the background?" Steffi indicated a figure to one side of Walter. While the rest of the people in the picture had joined Walter in celebration, this person's stance was more subdued. "That's Todd Grantham."

They had agreed that Bryce would drive the rental car from Los Angeles to Sheridan. Although Vincente had retrieved Steffi's driver's license from her locker at Delaney Transportation before they embarked on their quest, she was still wanted for murder. Walter had been scathing about the fact that the police were looking for Anya Moretti instead of Steffi Grantham. Both Steffi and Bryce had more faith in the forces of law and order. The police hadn't released her real name to the press, but it was unlikely—strike that; it was *impossible*—

that they didn't know it. If Steffi took the wheel and they were pulled over, there was a chance, probably a good one, that her ID would be checked and she would be arrested.

The burden had fallen to Bryce. Having traveled across California and into Nevada, they had left I-80 in Utah and cut across and up through Wyoming. Frequent stops for food and strong coffee had broken the journey and kept Bryce from dozing at the wheel. He explained that early in his army career he had been trained to drive in different conditions, including the demanding environments he would face on operations. During that time, he had acquired the knack of being able to pull over at the side of the road and nap in his seat.

Steffi, who found it impossible to do anything more than doze lightly, had spent a lot of time watching him and coming to terms with a new and profoundly disturbing revelation.

In the middle of all the action, heartache and shock, she had managed to fall in love with Bryce without noticing what was happening to her. *Or maybe I did notice, but I pretended not to.*

Because it was easier to fool herself that it had sneaked up on her. That way, she didn't feel quite so naive. She wasn't really that much of a cliché…the woman who had fallen for a beautiful face, a perfect body and a man's ability to drive her wild in bed.

As soon as that thought struck, she knew she was being unfair, to herself, and to Bryce. She was a Hollywood actress. If she was going to fall for superficial things, she'd have done it long ago. But Bryce was about so much more than his looks, and that was why she knew this was real. She'd called him a hero, and that was what he was. Her damaged hero. Steffi had fallen in love with who he was, not what he looked like. And now she had to deal with that.

So this was what being in love felt like. It wasn't all the things the poets said it would be. It wasn't stomach-swooping and starry-eye inducing. It was scary and lonely. Maybe that was because, for Steffi, it was one-sided. She and Bryce were destined to be a short story instead of an epic romance. She snorted at her own analogy. *At least we get to be an erotic story. With the start we had, we could so easily have been a comedy or a work of horror.*

The noise made Bryce glance briefly away from the road and in her direction. "Everything okay?"

How was she supposed to answer that? If she was going to be truthful, where would she start? *Let me see... No, everything is very far from okay. We have been in this car for a day and a half. These clothes feel like they are molded to my body, and I need a shower. I'm still on the run from the police. The man who killed my parents, my brother and my brother's girlfriend is still bragging on social media about what a great senator he's going to make. I don't know what Walter Sullivan meant when he said he* made *me, but I have a feeling I'm not going to like the explanation when I hear it. And it looks like my adoptive parents have been keeping secrets from me.*

And, as if that wasn't enough, guess what? I've fallen in love with you, Bryce. Totally, head over heels, point-of-no-return in love...and I have no idea how I'm supposed to deal with that feeling. No matter how much it frightened her, there was a part of her that wondered if Bryce didn't deserve to know how she felt. Not because she expected anything in return, but because it felt sad that he would never know how wonderful she thought he was. That, whatever the outcome of this mad, dangerous adventure of theirs, he would walk away from it never knowing that Steffi had looked his way and seen magic and beauty.

She would never do it, of course. Never open up and make herself vulnerable in that way. She couldn't bear to see the look of admiration and arousal in his eyes fade, only to be replaced with embarrassment or, even worse, with pity.

"Fine." She kept her voice light. All those years of acting classes came in useful. And earned her millions, of course. She really shouldn't forget that. "I just wish I could share the driving."

During the journey they had talked endlessly, on just about every subject under the sun. Now, when they were just a few hours from Sheridan, Bryce threw a sidelong glance Steffi's way. "What causes your eye condition?"

She sensed something in his manner, possibly a slight hesitation, as he asked the question. Having lived with it all her life, she didn't have a problem with being asked about it, but she was used to other people's reluctance to approach the subject. At the same time, she knew it aroused curiosity. There was something almost mystical about the way her eyes looked. Even Steffi, who saw them every day in the mirror, had to acknowledge it.

"Coloboma? The word itself means 'defect.' It can affect different parts of the eye, and it happens when that part doesn't form properly in the womb. I have coloboma of both irises, but it can also affect the lens or the eyelid. There can be complications, but my only problem is some light sensitivity. To be honest, I wear dark glasses more to hide my eyes than to protect them."

"Is it hereditary?" Bryce asked. It was an unusual question. Most people wanted to know how it affected her sight.

"It's something I've wondered about. But there never seemed to be any clear answer to that question, so I consulted a geneticist a few years ago." She bit her lip, wondering whether her reason sounded foolish, given her single status. "A doctor once told me that males can experience more severe symptoms than females. I wanted to know what it would mean if I ever had children."

"And what did you find out?"

"It's a condition that is usually not hereditary. Whether it's passed down in families or not can be a complex subject. Since Aleksander did not have it, it is impossible that I inherited it from him. Apparently, I could only inherit this disorder from a father who had coloboma himself. It is possible that I inherited from Ekaterina, if she was a carrier, although I remember her saying to a doctor when I was a child that there were no other cases in her family. So it seems likely that I'm an isolated case." Steffi recalled the detailed, complicated and very expensive report produced by the geneticist. "Unfortunately, it is possible that I could pass it on to my own child."

"Would you let that stop you from having children?" Bryce took his eyes off the quiet road briefly to look at her.

"I don't think so." It was something she had already thought long and hard about. "Coloboma has never caused me a problem. It's a minor inconvenience, not even a disability."

Even after hours spent talking about favorite books, just as long arguing the merits of rival pizza toppings and then drifting into a nighttime analysis of their own childhood fears, this conversation felt uncomfortable. Talking about the children she might have in the future with the man with whom she was currently having red-hot, no-strings-attached sex seemed all wrong. Particularly as he was the reason she might never have children. Loving Bryce was going to be a powerful impediment to prospective future relationships.

Steffi turned her head to look out the window at the landscape. It comforted her to be back in her home state, even though each mile took her closer to the confrontation she was dreading. During the drive, they had seen everything Wyoming had to offer. Ranch land and rodeo country, isolated mountain ranges and vast empty spaces. Small towns and abundant wildlife. Wyoming had welcomed them home in style.

They had been traveling for so long, she barely knew what time of day it was. Even so, she was aware enough of her surroundings to notice that something was wrong. This was not the route she had expected them to take. "We're not going to Sheridan, are we?"

"No." Bryce cast another sidelong glance in her direction. "I thought it would be better if you called your adoptive parents and asked them to meet you in Stillwater."

"Walter is in Stillwater." Since they had last seen him, Walter had been campaigning in earnest. Her internet searches had shown her his recent activity. Finally based at his Stillwater home, he had been getting out and about among the voters of Wyoming. "As soon as I arrange to meet my parents there, he'll know about it."

"Wherever you arrange to meet them, he'll know," Bryce said. "Walter probably feels safe right now in his hometown. But Stillwater is my hometown, too. If we're taking this fight to him, that's where I want to do it."

Steffi nodded. "Then let's finish this in Stillwater."

As they approached Stillwater, Bryce experienced a pang of sadness. They were close and that was a cause for happiness. Getting out of this car, stretching his limbs, showering, changing out of these clothes…all would be welcome. But he and Steffi had been wrapped in their own world for almost forty-eight hours, and he would miss that. Speaking in low voices—sometimes talking complete nonsense—laughing together, drifting into companionable silences, sharing confidences and silly jokes. Over the past few days he had spent more time in her company than he had with anyone other than his brothers and his army colleagues, and she was the only person who had never bored him. He knew she never would.

Steffi had the opposite effect on him. The more he was with her, the more she fascinated him. It had gotten to the point where he thought she must be conscious of it. When he was driving it was easier to hide the fact that he wanted to gaze at her. All the time. As soon as they'd leave the car to get a snack or a coffee, she had to be aware of him staring at her like a moonstruck kid. Or maybe that was how everyone in Steffi's life looked at her? Perhaps it was all part of being a movie star.

He longed to just keep on driving. To say to hell with the rest of the world and find somewhere he could take

Steffi and hide away with her forever. *There are laws against abducting people*, he reminded himself. Now and then he liked to think that Steffi wouldn't mind locking herself away with him and throwing away the key. Occasionally, he thought he saw a glimpse of his own feelings reflected back at him in her expression. The same raw emotional need. He bit back a laugh. How had he gone from flat-out despair to extreme arrogance in the space of a few days? *We Delaney boys don't do things by halves*. Even so, that had to be the biggest mood swing ever.

Steffi had been quiet ever since the call she had made to her adoptive parents. They had to know something was up, but they had agreed to meet her at Dino's. They had assured Steffi they would be leaving right away. Bryce figured it would take them about three hours from that moment to reach Stillwater. And if what they believed of June and Todd Grantham was right, at some point they would need to let Walter know what was happening. Would they call him or stop by his house? *Doesn't matter. The end result will be the same.*

"Walter will have worked out who I am by now."

Steffi wrinkled her nose. "How would he do that?"

"My story to Walter was that we were workmates who had a one-night stand, but his guys found us at the lake house…a house owned by Mayor Delaney. He knows you worked for Delaney Transportation. A little snooping around is going to get him the news that Bryce Delaney hasn't been around for a few days."

A glance at her profile confirmed his suspicion that she was gnawing her lip. "Do you think he may have gone after your family?"

"I doubt it. Walter has presented himself as a legitimate businessman for many years, remember? He's running for the Senate, possibly with even higher ambitions in the future. My brother is the mayor of Stillwater and his wife is a police detective." Bryce was doing his best to convince himself as much as Steffi. "Walter won't go there. Not unless he has to. And we can use that to our advantage."

"How?" Steffi turned in her seat to stare at him.

"We are only in danger when we're alone. Until we want to be in private with Walter, all we have to do is surround ourselves with people."

"So we call the shots?"

Bryce laughed. "I wouldn't go that far. Let's say Walter isn't as powerful as he thinks he is."

They were driving into Stillwater now, and his heart lifted at the sight of the beautiful old town with its historic buildings and backdrop of mountain scenery. Given what he'd just said, he had discarded his original plan to continue on through town and straight to his own house. They would be isolated there and at risk from Walter's men. Instead, he drove to Lakeside Drive and pulled into the parking lot in front of Stillwater City Hall. This majestic structure housed both the mayor's office and the police department, among other municipal services.

Steffi eyed him warily. "What are you planning?"

"I think it's time you met my other brother."

"Bryce, I have been in this car for two days. I've barely slept. I haven't showered or brushed my teeth. I'm disguised as a teenage boy, one who has possibly the worst hairstyle in history—" with her huge cat's eyes and her spiky hair standing on end, Steffi reminded him of an outraged kitten "—and you want to take me in there to meet the mayor?"

"Look on the bright side, Steffi."

"There's a bright side?" She pulled on her hat and donned her shades.

"At least no one will look at you and think 'beautiful movie star.'" He was still laughing at her expression as they grabbed their backpacks from the trunk, went across to the building and entered the lobby.

Bryce led the way through a set of double doors to the left of the central reception desk. From there they climbed a flight of stairs up to the second floor and went through another set of double doors leading to an outer office. Here, Cameron's secretary, Alberta Finch, guarded her boss's privacy like a tiger protecting her cub. She gave Bryce her usual frosty look over the top of her glasses before casting a disapproving eye over his grungy companion. He knew from experience that she wouldn't lower her guard for family.

"He's busy." Alberta was a woman of few words.

"In-a-meeting busy, or paperwork busy?" Bryce asked.

"I really don't think that's any of your—"

Bryce didn't wait to hear any more. Stalking past her desk and dragging Steffi with him, he made his way to the door of Cameron's office. Ignoring Alberta's outraged protests, he marched in.

Cameron was seated at his desk. Another man was opposite him with his back to the door. At the interruption, Cameron looked up from his conversation with a frown. Bryce paused on the threshold, the words of apology for interrupting his brother's meeting dying on his lips.

When the door opened, Cameron's companion had turned his head to see who had come into the room. As he recognized Bryce, a smile touched his lips. It widened when his eyes moved on to take in Steffi.

"I'm sorry," Cameron said. "I gave my secretary instructions I wasn't to be disturbed."

"It's not a problem." Walter Sullivan was charm personified. "Please introduce me to your visitors."

Chapter 17

In looks, Bryce and Cameron were very alike. And right now they wore matching frowns. The only person who looked remotely at ease was Walter. It was a situation that infuriated Steffi, and it stiffened her spine. *You killed my family. You've turned my life upside down... twice. You don't get to sneer at me, as well.*

"We've met. I'm surprised you've forgotten the circumstances of our last meeting already, Mr. Sullivan." Cameron regarded her in surprise as she strode into his office. She paused in front of his desk and held out her hand. "It's nice to meet you, Mayor Delaney. I'm Steffi Grantham."

She was aware of a silent communication taking place between the two brothers. It was something she had never witnessed between two people before. The bond between them must be truly remarkable. Whatever he saw in Bryce's eyes must have convinced Cameron to go along with Steffi. Looking away from his brother, he shook her hand.

"It's nice to meet you, Miss Grantham. Won't you take a seat? Mr. Sullivan and I are just finalizing the details of a charity fund-raising gala that's being held in the memorial hall in this building tomorrow night."

"We're not staying." Bryce intervened before she could speak. "We have some people we need to meet. But I guess you—" he kept his eyes on Walter's face "—already know that."

"Didn't you have something for me?" Some of the smoothness had gone from Walter's tone. He appeared bewildered by Steffi's unruffled manner. *Unruffled on the outside. You have no idea of the ruffles going on inside me.* "You can hand it over right now."

"No." She looked him in the eye. Those disconcertingly dark eyes. "We need to talk before I hand anything over."

"That was not our deal."

Although his expression hardened, his voice remained conversational. Steffi guessed she had the presence of Stillwater's mayor to thank for that. Bryce had been right. Walter wasn't going to risk showing his true colors in front of other people. Not unless he was pushed to his limits. Steffi had no idea what Walter's limits were, but he clearly hadn't reached them yet. She wanted to test his boundaries. Wanted him to feel some of the things he had put her and Greg through. To experience a fear so intense it actually felt like it was flowing alongside the blood in his veins. She wanted to force him to survive on adrenaline and instinct, glancing over his shoulder every few minutes just to check who was there and what was happening. She would never be able to make Walter pay for what he had done to her family, and she knew that seeking revenge would damage her as much as him, but he didn't need to know that.

She leaned closer. "You were quick to claim you *made* me, Walter. Be proud of your creation."

Bryce caught hold of her hand. "Cam, we'll be at Dino's. When you finish up here, meet us there." He nodded at Walter. "We'll talk soon."

His voice was cordial, but his eyes conveyed the threat he had been looking forward to issuing. Walter's color rose and Bryce smiled. Walter was an arrogant bully. It must be hell sitting there, keeping his temper in check, when last time they'd met, Bryce had knocked him out and set fire to his elegant dining room.

When he answered, Walter's jaw was rigid. "You can count on it."

They left Cameron's office and, dodging the outraged secretary, made their way down the stairs, through the double doors and into the central lobby. Because there were a number of services located within the building, this area was busy. Putting into practice his plan to make sure they weren't alone and vulnerable, Bryce moved up close to the central reception desk.

"What next?" Steffi pulled her hat down lower and adjusted her dark glasses as she cast a nervous glance around. She was reassured when she observed that no one was looking their way.

"As soon as Walter leaves Cameron's office, he'll call Alexei. For all we know, he already has." Bryce withdrew his cell phone from his pocket. "We need to get to Dino's without any problems from the tattooed gorillas."

"Who are you calling?" Steffi's gaze remained fixed

on the staircase they had come down. Her heart was in her mouth as she waited for the moment when Walter would emerge.

"Vincente." Bryce held up a finger to indicate that his brother had answered the call. "Are you in your office?" Bryce didn't have time for pleasantries. "Good. Get into one of the trucks and come down to city hall. No, I haven't finally gone crazy. Just do it as fast as you can."

As Bryce ended the call a woman's voice hailed him. Watching his face as he turned to greet the woman with an attempt at an "everything's normal" smile, Steffi could tell he was experiencing a feeling of dread. Whoever this woman was, her sharp blue eyes scanned him behind a bright smile. They took in his crumpled clothing, two-day-old stubble and bloodshot eyes before moving on to study Steffi. A slight crease pulled her brows together.

"When did you get back from your—" those searching eyes seemed to let Bryce know she wasn't going to be fobbed off "—what did you call it? *Much needed vacation?* I hate to say this, but you don't look very refreshed."

Behind her glasses Steffi's gaze fastened on one thing. Bryce's companion was dressed smartly in black pants and a matching blazer over a crisp white blouse. And her Stillwater Police Department badge was prominently displayed on one lapel.

"Oh, you know. Traveling can be hell. And we just got back."

The woman turned her attention to Steffi. "I don't think we've met. I'm Laurie Delaney… Bryce's sister-in-law."

Steffi didn't answer. Her thoughts were working

overtime. If she told Laurie her name and Bryce's suspicious sister-in-law checked her out—which she was likely to do—then Steffi's cover was blown.

At that moment Walter came through the double doors at the bottom of the stairs. He paused as he took in the scene. From where he stood, only one thing was obvious. Bryce and Steffi were talking to a police officer. His expression was a mask of fury as he stared across the lobby at them. Then he stalked out of the building.

Steffi followed his progress, watching through the glass doors as Walter made his way down the steps and into a waiting car. She caught a glimpse of the driver's bald head before the vehicle pulled away. Seconds later a black truck emblazoned with the red Delaney Transportation logo drew up in its place.

"We can't stay and chat." Bryce turned to Laurie, who had been watching the brief exchange of glances closely. "Our ride has just arrived."

During the three months she had lived in Stillwater, Steffi had learned that Dino's was the place to eat. The place for everything, really. Meeting friends, hanging out, hearing the gossip. The restaurant in the center of Main Street was the essence of Stillwater.

Her need for privacy meant she had never tried it herself, of course. Now she was arriving in the least private manner possible. In the cab of a huge truck, sandwiched between two of the Delaney brothers.

Vincente's initial incredulity had turned to anger when, on the drive over from city hall, Bryce had given him an abbreviated version of the events of the past few days. Now, as he brought the truck to a halt in front of

Dino's, there was a glint of amusement in his expression.

"So, until you can confront Walter Sullivan and get the answers to your questions, your plan is to stay highly visible?"

Bryce nodded. "That about sums it up. We're vulnerable if his goons can get us alone. As long as we make sure we have people around us or we draw attention to ourselves, we stay safe." He gripped Steffi's hand. "It won't be for long."

"Isn't that dangerous, given that Steffi needs to hide her identity?" Vincente asked.

"Since everyone is searching for a beautiful actress, I'm doing my best to look different." Steffi grimaced as she tugged at her two-day-old T-shirt.

"And what's my role in this part of the story?" Vincente followed them into the restaurant.

"When the guys with the tattooed hands show up, you make it clear you're watching their every move," Bryce said.

Even in the middle of the afternoon, Dino's was busy. The restaurant had captured everything that was best about Stillwater. With windows that provided panoramic views of the mountains, it was laid-back and comfortable, hinting at the town's cowboy history and Western charm without being tacky. Bryce and Vincente, who were regular customers, were greeted with smiles by the hostess.

"We need two tables." Bryce pointed out which ones, in full view of the door and the rest of the restaurant. They needed privacy so he and Steffi could talk to June and Todd without being overheard, but he also wanted

Vincente—and Cameron, when he arrived—close enough so Walter's men would see they were together.

They had taken their seats and ordered coffee when a voice behind her startled Steffi. "Bryce Delaney. I thought you'd died…or found somewhere else to eat."

"I've been out of town, Dino." Although Bryce smiled, his jaw was tight, betraying his nerves. "You know I can never stay away from your steaks for long."

Dino moved into view, casting an interested glance over Steffi. She could almost read his thoughts. What was the legendary Stillwater stud doing with this sorry specimen? She wondered how many other women Bryce had been here with and was annoyed at the thought. It should hardly be uppermost in her mind right now.

With a touch of resignation, Bryce said, "Dino, this is my friend Steffi."

"Always happy to welcome a new customer. Although why you've chosen to eat in such poor company is beyond me." Dino looked across at the table where Vincente was seated alone. "You two fallen out again?" At that moment Cameron entered the restaurant and made his way toward them. "What is this? A Delaney brothers' reunion?"

"Dino, stop searching for gossip at this table. Go find yourself some other customers to insult."

"See what I mean?" Dino turned to Steffi with a sorrowful shake of his head. "Poor company."

He walked away, pausing to talk to other diners as he made his way toward the kitchen. "Is he always like that?" Steffi asked.

"That was mild," Bryce assured her. "His rudeness is legendary." He looked up as Cameron approached, and she thought again how alike, and how close, the two brothers were. "Thank you for coming."

"Do I get to find out what this is all about?" Cameron's expression held a hint of exasperation and a lot of concern. "Walter Sullivan was not a happy man when he left my office, and now I find one of our trucks out front taking up most of the parking lot."

"Vincente will fill you in on what he knows, and we'll talk more at your place tonight." Bryce looked at Steffi. "Okay?"

She nodded. "Okay." He was right. One way or another, they had to bring this to an end. Speaking of which… "June and Todd have just walked in."

June Grantham must once have been very pretty. Now her looks had faded, and she had a nervous manner that left her with the air of a frightened bird. Bryce didn't know, of course, whether that was always the case or if the circumstances of this meeting had increased her anxiety. Her husband appeared seriously on edge. Todd Grantham was tall and so thin he appeared skeletal. Bryce would not have been surprised to learn he was suffering from a life-threatening illness. Todd's graying skin was stretched tight across his cheekbones, and his whole body was coiled tight with tension.

Whatever was going on with Steffi's adoptive parents, they were not people who were at ease. That might be explained by the fact that their daughter was on the run from the law, wanted for a double murder. Bryce got the feeling that, from their physical appearance, their troubles might be more long-standing than Steffi's recent problems. But what did he know? Psychoanalysis in seconds? It was hardly his strong point.

"Steffi, you look awful." June slid into the seat next to her daughter.

"That's sort of the idea." Steffi's mouth lifted into what looked like a smile. Bryce wondered if June and Todd were fooled. He wasn't. No one could see her eyes behind her glasses, and her mouth did a passable curve. But he noticed the faint tremor in the muscles along her jawline, and knew the effort it was taking her to stay in control of her emotions. He wanted to haul her up out of her chair and hold her until he had injected some of his own strength into her. "I'm in disguise."

"Why did we need to come here?" Todd looked around him as though Dino's was the worst kind of hellhole. "Why *this* town?"

"Because this is where your friend Walter Sullivan lives. He killed Greg and the girl he was with, and now he's threatening me." Even Bryce was taken aback by the way Steffi just went for it. No gentle lead-in, no background information. Straight to the point.

Todd swallowed so hard Bryce heard the noise even above the sounds of the busy restaurant. Twin spots of color flared on his cheeks. "I don't know what you're talking about."

June leaned over the table and took his hand. "It's time to tell her the truth, honey."

Before Todd could say any more, the waiter came to their table and normality took over for a few minutes as they ordered drinks and, in Bryce's case, food. He almost felt the need to apologize that his appetite had resurfaced with a vengeance during such a crucial moment. Figuring he would need his strength to deal with any Walter-related confrontations, he quashed his guilt and requested a sandwich.

A glance around showed him there was no sign of Walter's men. At his brothers' table, Cameron and Vincente were deep in conversation. From Cameron's stunned expression, he guessed Vincente was doing a pretty good job of recounting the story so far.

"Let me make this easier for you." When the waiter had gone, Steffi spoke quietly to Todd. "I know you were part of the legal team that got Walter off when he faced huge fines because workers died in one of his factories twenty-five years ago."

"That was the worst day of my life." Todd's attempt at a smile was even less successful than Steffi's. "But I guess we don't know which way this one is going to turn out yet, do we?"

The worst day of his life? There was still a lot of explaining to do, but so far Todd wasn't sounding like Walter's biggest fan.

"Before we continue, I want to introduce you to Bryce Delaney. If it wasn't for him, I wouldn't be alive to meet with you today," Steffi said.

"Don't talk that way." June shuddered.

"Mrs. Grantham, it's the truth. Don't underestimate what Walter Sullivan is capable of." Bryce spoke gently but firmly. "Twenty-two years ago he killed Steffi's parents. Three months ago he had her brother and his girlfriend murdered. He wouldn't hesitate to kill any one of us if we stood in his way."

"I'm not sure that's true." Todd's voice was more resolute this time. "But let me tell the whole story before I explain my reasons for saying that."

Bryce had been keeping one eye on the restaurant door the whole time. As Todd was speaking, he caught a glimpse of two new arrivals. Alexei cast a swift glance around as he was waiting to be seated. When he caught sight of Bryce, he nudged his companion. Erik's trapezius muscles were so huge, they didn't allow him to turn his neck easily. Instead, he swiveled his upper body in the direction Alexei indicated. A grim smile crossed Erik's face as he caught sight of Bryce.

At the same time, Cameron called Dino over. Bryce didn't know what his brother said to the restaurant owner, who was one of Cameron's oldest friends, but the exchange was brief. Just as the hostess was about to escort Alexei and Erik to a table, Dino made his way to the greeting station. Although he couldn't hear the conversation, Dino's message was clear. Removing the menus the hostess had been about to hand Alexei and Erik, Dino shook his head and held open the door. Alexei's expression was instantly outraged. He pointed to several empty tables. Dino shrugged, crossing his arms over his chest. Erik took a step forward, but Alexei placed a hand on his arm and jerked a thumb toward the door.

As they left, Alexei cast a glance over his shoulder in Bryce's direction. His expression told its own story. *The Big Guy isn't going to be happy.*

He turned his attention back to what Todd was saying. "The death of those workers was not straightforward negligence. In my opinion, it was murder. Walter was repeatedly warned that conditions were unsafe. There were memos dating back several years from managers in his company, and the health and safety records were abysmal. I worked for the legal firm Walter used. When the case came to court, there was a mountain of evidence to plow through. I was responsible for taking depositions from witnesses. I couldn't see any way we could win this one. Although the fines imposed were unlikely to ruin him, the subsequent awards to the families of those killed, and of the injured workers who could no longer work, could do so." Todd's expression tightened. "When I read what happened that day, and how it could have been avoided, I wanted those families to take Walter for every dime he had."

"But you defended him anyway?" Bryce asked.

"That was my job." Todd turned to look at him. "There aren't too many law firms in Sheridan. I couldn't afford to throw away a job on a principle."

"That's not all of it." June's voice was quietly dignified. "I had just found out I had cervical cancer. We had medical bills to pay."

Todd gripped her hand across the table. "By the time we got to court, I realized we weren't dealing with an ordinary client. The depositions I had taken had been altered beyond recognition after I submitted them. Key witnesses had either changed their stories or gone missing. Those memos expressing concerns about worker safety? Not one of them could be found. Walter walked into that courtroom looking like a paragon of health and safety. He walked out with a mild rebuke from the judge. The incident was written off as an accident that could never have been foreseen."

Although Bryce didn't know this man, he could see the effect the memories were having on him. Todd's emotions were close to the surface, churning up inside him, ready to explode at any moment. Had it been this way for the last twenty-five years? Was this the legacy Walter had left him?

"I knew my bosses had to be complicit in the cover-up. For a few weeks I didn't do anything. I'm not proud of that, but like I said, I needed that job. Then one day I decided I couldn't live with it any longer. The thought of those twelve dead workers—and the others who could no longer work because of their injuries—was keeping me awake at night. I went to see my boss, one of the partners in the firm. I told him I had some concerns about what had happened in the Walter Sullivan case."

Todd's initial acceptance of the outcome of the court case had made him appear weak. This new revelation reversed Bryce's first view of him. He looked across at Steffi, who had been sitting still as a statue as she listened to Todd's story and saw his own surprise reflected back at him. "I'm guessing your visit wasn't a welcome one?"

Todd's smile dwelt on a memory. "Hardly. He told me I was imagining things. Said I was overworked and suffering from stress. Suggested I take a few days off to recover. That night we got a visit from Walter at home."

Steffi lifted a hand to her lips as she looked first at Todd and then at June. "Did he hurt you?"

"No. He oozed charm. All the threats he made were subtle. June was recovering from an operation, and he inquired after her health, said how sorry he was that she was unwell. He hoped she wouldn't suffer a relapse."

"Oh, that bastard." Steffi's voice shook with outrage.

"Nothing he said was explicit. There were just little hints about how powerful he was. Once or twice he mentioned my hands and my eyes, how important they were to a lawyer. I should look after them, he said. How terrible would it be if I had an accident and couldn't use my hands, or I couldn't see? He knew June's medical history, knew we couldn't have children and we were struggling for money." Todd closed his eyes briefly. "By the time he left, I had caved. Walter offered to help, and I accepted. That was it. From that day on, I was in Walter Sullivan's pocket."

"You mean you worked for him?" Bryce asked.

"No, I never did any legal jobs for him. I left the firm I had been employed at soon after and took a lower paying job at the district court. At least I could look myself in the face each day I was there. But I'd taken handouts from Walter. He owned me."

"And that's why you adopted me?" Bryce would have given anything to have been able to take away the note of anguish from Steffi's voice. "Because it was what Walter wanted?"

"My God, Steffi." June turned to face her, tears beginning a slow progress down her cheeks. "How can you think that? You were the most precious thing in the world to us…"

"But the circumstances of your adoption were controlled by Walter." Todd's voice was contrite. It was as if, now he had started this purge, he needed to confess every part of his past dealings with Walter. "We had only recently begun the adoption process, had barely finished completing the forms, when he came to see us and told us about you. He said you were the daughter of a friend of his who had died in tragic circumstances and, while he couldn't take care of you himself, he wanted to be sure you went to a family he could trust. We explained that we would be well down the adoption agency's waiting list, but Walter told us to leave it all to him. Within weeks a family who had planned to adopt both you and Greg together had dropped out and you were to come to us."

"There was someone who wanted both Greg and

me?" Steffi's voice cracked in the middle of the question. "We could have stayed together?"

"We told Walter we would take you both." June's tears flowed faster. "He said no."

"Even though we knew Walter had used bribery or coercion, we wanted you so badly, we ignored that. We thought we could put it behind us for the sake of a child of our own." Todd's lips twisted into a bitter, little smile. "But guilt has a way of prodding at you when you least expect it."

"Walter didn't interfere in your life, but he did send presents and money. And when we knew acting was in your blood, he paid your tuition fees. It was too much, really. We always thought you'd wonder where it all came from," June said.

"I did. I just never knew how to ask you about it." Steffi toyed with her coffee cup, her hands not quite steady. She took a breath before lifting her head to look at Todd. "But all this talk of a child of your own didn't matter just lately. When Walter asked you to get me to come to San Francisco, you were ready to hand me over to him, weren't you?"

"God, no!" There was no mistaking the genuine revulsion her words provoked. Todd's already pale face blanched and his jaw went slack. "Is that what you thought? Walter did get in touch with us and he told us what had happened. We knew before you called us that Greg and the girl he was with had been killed and that you had gone on the run. Walter suggested I should get you to meet me in San Francisco. He said he could arrange for us to be private and spend some time together without there being any danger that the police would find you. But I wasn't going to meet you with *him*. You're my daughter. I would never do anything to hurt you."

Bryce felt sorry for Todd in that moment. The man genuinely believed what he was saying. Even though he had been on the receiving end of Walter's manipulation for the last twenty-five years, he still thought he could hold out against him. Bryce wasn't sure whether that made Todd weak or strong, smart or stupid. All he did know was he could picture how things would have worked out if Steffi had agreed to meet Todd in San Francisco. He was willing to bet Walter would have been in control of that meeting. Would Todd even have lived through the encounter? Bryce guessed Steffi's adoptive parents had always been disposable, surviving only so long as they were useful to Walter.

Steffi's next words were almost an exact echo of Bryce's thoughts. "Okay. I'll believe you were naive enough to think Walter would let us meet alone, but how did he know we were going to Nancy and Tanner's house on the day I asked you for their address?"

Todd looked stunned. "Did you know anything about that, June?"

His wife hung her head. "Walter has been calling every day, asking how we're holding up, if we've heard from you, how you are. That day he called just after you did and I said he should stop worrying—at least that day you would be with people who would look after you. He asked what I meant and I said you were going to visit Greg's parents. But I never would have given away your whereabouts if I thought he was going to harm you. You have to believe me."

Todd turned to Bryce. "When you said Walter would kill any one of us if we stood in his way, I said I wasn't sure that was true. I believe the only exception to that is Steffi." He took Steffi's hand carefully as though he was scared she would snatch it away. "For some reason Walter cares about you. I don't know what it is, but I don't believe he would harm you."

"He has threatened to kill me and sent his thugs chasing after me," Steffi said.

"Walter likes to make threats. It's what he does best. Would he act on them where you are concerned? I'm not so sure. But what happens now?" Todd looked from Steffi to Bryce. "Walter is a dangerous man."

"We kind of figured that out already," Bryce said. "As for what happens now—" he looked at Steffi "—we get a good night's sleep before we confront Walter."

A faint smile touched her lips. "And maybe a shower and a change of clothes?"

"How can you talk about this so calmly?" June asked. "After everything that man has done…all the lives he has ruined?"

"Easy." Bryce drained his coffee cup and got to his feet. "The only life being ruined from now on will be Walter's. And he can't bribe or coerce his way out of it this time."

Chapter 18

"Take my advice. Don't go home." Bryce's voice left June and Todd in no doubt of the seriousness of the message he was giving them. "Get in your car now, drive somewhere you've never been before and stay there for a few days. We'll call you when this is over."

"You think he would come after us?" June looked nervously over her shoulder as though she expected to see Walter lurking there.

"I think he would do anything it takes to get Steffi to hand over the cell phone," Bryce said. Steffi had told them about the recording. In this new, no-secrets relationship, it seemed important that June and Todd should know everything. "If that includes threatening you, he'll do it."

June turned to Steffi, taking her hands. "Can you forgive us?"

Listening to the story of how the people who had raised her had been Walter's puppets hadn't been easy, but Steffi couldn't blame June and Todd for what had happened. They were weak and misguided, but they weren't bad people. There was only one person in this whole sorry story who was evil. Walter Sullivan. Bryce was right; it was time to cut the puppet master's strings.

"There is nothing to forgive." After twenty-two years, she was finally able to say the word she knew June had always longed to hear. "Mom."

June gave a convulsive sob and closed the distance between them in a hug. Coming around the table, Todd placed an arm around each of them and held them close. Maybe there was no such thing as too late, Steffi decided. Sometimes the perfect family was the one you had…and you just didn't know it.

"We'll talk soon." Her voice was husky as she broke free of their embrace.

She watched with Bryce from the window as Todd drove his familiar Ford car away from the restaurant. There was no sign of Alexei and Erik and she guessed that, following their expulsion from the restaurant, they had gone to report back to Walter. It meant her parents were able to drive away without being followed.

"You okay?" Bryce took her hands.

"I'm stunned, tired, smelly—" she grinned "—but you know what? I *am* okay, and I'm ready to kick Walter's ass." Something had happened during that hug with her parents. Like the first stretch of the morning, a tightness deep inside her had eased. And Bryce was part of that. He had paved the way for her to open up to her feelings. Without him, she would still have those barriers around her heart. She only wished she could tell him what he had done for her. *Heroes don't just fight bad guys, burn drapes, climb trees and throw themselves onto roofs. Sometimes they also make you look at yourself differently.* Bryce had done all those things for her.

He returned the smile. "Let the ass-kicking commence."

Cameron and Vincente had to have dozens of questions as they accompanied them out into the parking lot, but they managed to keep them to themselves.

"My place?" Cameron asked.

"Yes, but—" Steffi knew Bryce hesitated because he was thinking of Laurie. It would be unfair to expect a police officer to tolerate the presence of a wanted murderer in her home.

"We'll deal with the Laurie issue once we get there," Cameron said.

Steffi joined Bryce and Vincente in the cab of the truck while Cameron followed in his car. It would be too much to say that she felt safe, but having the three Delaney brothers watching out for her was about as close to that sensation as she was able to come, given the circumstances. It felt, for the first time, like the balance of power was shifting in their favor. Having Bryce on her side had been a huge relief, but it had still felt like the odds were stacked against them. Now it really did feel like they were taking this fight to Walter. They had already gotten under his skin. But this wasn't just about prodding the rattlesnake; they had to step into its nest and destroy it.

Cameron and Laurie were renovating an old ranch on the road that led out of Stillwater toward Park County. Vincente pulled off the main highway and down a quiet track. As they approached the property, Steffi could see exactly why they had chosen to make their home here. Encircled by majestic mountains, the natural stone and golden wood ranch house lay within a circle of verdant green. From the front porch, the view was breathtaking, with grass and wildflowers in the near ground rising up to meet a pine-topped ridge and snowcapped mountains in the distance.

Laurie was waiting on the porch as they pulled up. Her first words made it clear that Cameron had called ahead. "I'm going to fix dinner while you shower and change." She spoke directly to Bryce. "Don't talk in front of me. If I don't hear what you say, I don't know anything."

"Thank you." His voice was filled with genuine gratitude.

Cameron led Steffi and Bryce to a large guest bedroom. The thing that interested Steffi most was the bathroom and, as soon as Cameron had closed the door, she was tugging off her clothes and heading for the shower. Hot water had never felt so good. And Laurie had great taste in toiletries. Steffi returned to the bedroom clean, scented, moisturized and wrapped in a huge, fluffy towel.

Bryce regarded her with a smile. "You are incredible."

She laughed. "What prompted that?"

He came to her, gripping her upper arms and drawing her close. "After the day you've just had, most people would have crumbled. But you've kept going, kept fighting." The light in his eyes warmed every part of her. "Walter doesn't know what he's up against."

Steffi rose on the tips of her toes to press a kiss onto his lips. "We'll show him."

"We need to talk to my brothers, plan how we're going to do this." He slid a hand down her spine. "And I need to shower. Much as I want you right now, I'm not going to inflict my sweaty body on you."

"You can inflict your body on me anytime." Steffi gave him a mischievous look.

"Stop it," he groaned, pressing his forehead to hers. "I need to be able to think straight."

She sensed his reluctance as he let her go and made his way to the bathroom. He was right, of course. It was tempting to stay holed up in this cozy room, but they had too much to discuss. Tugging the last clean outfit from her backpack, she regarded the items with displeasure. Jeans and shirt were both equally creased. She shrugged. Wrinkled or not, it felt like heaven to be clean again after that epic car journey. Who would have thought that, after the privileged lifestyle she had once enjoyed, her idea of luxury would be the day when she didn't have to wash her underwear in a hotel bathroom?

Once Bryce had also donned fresh clothing, they went through to the large family room that overlooked the mountain view Steffi had seen on their arrival. Cameron and Vincente were awaiting them there. They both held half-empty bottles of beer and Cameron raised his in Bryce's direction without speaking.

Bryce nodded. "And keep them coming."

"Steffi? What can I get you to drink?" Cameron asked as he rose to get Bryce a beer.

"Just soda, please." She was so tired she knew the first sip of alcohol would knock her out.

When Cameron returned with the drinks, the four

of them sat on two large, squishy sofas that had been placed to make the most of the views. While Bryce drained half his beer in one long, grateful swallow, Steffi sank back against the cushions. She was enjoying the feel of being in a proper home for the first time in many months. *Don't get too comfortable.* That little warning voice inside her head spoke up. *This fight isn't over. The hardest part is yet to come.*

"I'll admit I had a hard time believing what Vincente was telling me," Cameron said. "But while you were freshening up, he played me the recording. It's pretty conclusive."

"How are you going to get close enough to Walter to find out what you need to know without placing yourselves in danger?" Vincente asked.

Bryce looked at Cameron. "For our plan to work, we're going to need your help."

Steffi sat up straighter. *Whoa.* They had a plan? She thought they were going to march up to Walter's front door and fire questions at him. Now it sounded like there was a strategy involved.

"Whatever you need." Cameron's voice was reassuring.

Steffi could see why people voted for him. He had been Stillwater's youngest-ever mayor, and he had just been returned to office with a hugely increased majority. Aside from his good looks, he was charismatic, but he also conveyed a strong sense of knowing what he was doing. Although Bryce had similar qualities, he had an edge his older brother lacked. Bryce liked to bend the rules, even break them. Politics would never be for him. He was a maverick who would never be able to conform for long enough to work within someone else's restrictions.

"Tomorrow night's fund-raiser. That's the place where we'll confront him." Bryce waited while the impact of what he was saying sank in. He took both Steffi's hands in his. "Do you trust me?"

Her heart rate kicked up a notch. There was no hiding from the look in his eyes. He had asked her that question so many times, and she had never been able to give him a straight answer. This time there was no hesitation. Only truth. "I trust you with my life."

"Good. Because I think it's time for Anya Moretti to come out of hiding."

"I told you, I don't want to hear anything," Laurie grumbled as Cameron escorted her into the family room. "If you tell me something and I think you're breaking the law, I'm going to have to report it."

"Laurie, please sit down and listen to what we have to say." Bryce patted the seat at right angles to him and Steffi.

She regarded him with a trace of stubbornness, but did as he asked. "Dinner will be ready in ten minutes." It was one final attempt to get herself out of the situation.

"This won't take long," Bryce said. "I didn't introduce you to my companion this afternoon for a reason."

Steffi had removed her glasses and Laurie regarded her thoughtfully. Even as Steffi began to speak, she could see the other woman trying to process where she had seen her before. It had happened to her many times. People had seen her face so often on-screen they thought they knew her. "My name is Steffi Grantham, but you may know me better by my stage name… Anya Moretti."

Laurie remained silent for a moment or two, still studying Steffi's face. Then she nodded. "I can see it now. Your hair is different, of course, and I think you've lost weight since your last movie." She looked around the group, her expression regretful. "You know I can't ignore this, don't you?"

"I'm giving myself up." Steffi smiled, and the words felt like a huge weight being lifted off her shoulders. "To you. But I want to ask you a big favor. Please don't arrest me until after the charity fund-raiser tomorrow night."

"I'm not sure I can agree to that—"

"Why don't I help you serve dinner? While we eat, we can explain why the fund-raiser is so important." Cameron stood and held out a hand to his wife. Reluctantly, Laurie allowed him to pull her to her feet.

As they left the room, Steffi heard her whisper, "I only cooked chili. If I'd known we had a Hollywood superstar staying with us, I'd have fixed something fancier."

Steffi gnawed her lip before turning to Bryce. "She didn't say yes."

"She didn't say no."

"When you get to know Laurie, you'll know that counts for a lot," Vincente assured her.

They sat around a big farmhouse table in the kitchen and ate Laurie's delicious chili. Steffi was amazed at how hungry she was, even though she was still waiting to learn her fate. Would she end the night sleeping in Bryce's arms in that big, cozy bed she'd seen in the guest bedroom? Or would Laurie slap the cuffs on her and drag her off to a cell?

As she and Bryce recounted their adventures one more time, Laurie's blue eyes grew increasingly rounder. She remained mostly silent, only interjecting an occasional question when the story became too entangled for her to follow. When they played her the recording, she covered her mouth with one hand.

"I sat next to Walter Sullivan at a political dinner a few months ago." Her voice was filled with loathing. "If I'd known then what I know now, I'd have stabbed him with my steak knife."

"Does that mean you'll help us?" Bryce asked.

Laurie nodded. "But I can only do what you've asked." Her voice was sad. "You're wanted for murder, Steffi. Even though that recording should clear you, once the fund-raiser is over, I'll have to do this properly. I will have to take you into police custody."

"That's more than I ever hoped for." Steffi smiled.

"I have the perfect dress for you to wear tomorrow night." The speed of Laurie's switch from discussing police protocols to party clothes made Steffi blink. "I ordered it online for a party Cameron and I were due to attend when he was reelected, but it was so revealing I thought it might give the Stillwater gossips a heart attack."

"Hold on a minute," Cameron said. "Why haven't I seen this revealing dress?"

Laurie rolled her eyes in Steffi's direction. The look was an invitation to camaraderie. Female friendship was something that had bypassed Steffi. Her ingrained shyness had made forming childhood attachments difficult. Now she was an adult, everyone assumed the Hollywood star had all the friends she needed. The truth was she had none. Laurie's look offered fun. In spite of everything, it made Steffi want to giggle. If she had to stay cooped up in this house until the following night, waiting for the moment when she could confront Walter, she might as well enjoy herself.

"The dress will be perfect for the sort of statement you want to make," Laurie assured her. She cast a critical eye over Steffi's appearance. "If you don't mind me asking, who styled your hair?"

"Bryce."

Laurie looked alarmed. "Never let him do that again."

Bryce opened his eyes as the dawn light began to steal through a crack in the drapes. Steffi was spread across his chest. Her knee was pressed between his thighs, which explained his raging, early-morning hard-on. When he attempted to ease away from her, she murmured a sleepy protest and snuggled closer. Resigning himself to his enjoyable predicament, Bryce lay back with his hands behind his head.

It felt like the cruelest twist of fate that he'd finally found everything he ever wanted. And there was no great mystery to it. All he wanted was Steffi. In his arms, in his bed, in his life. Forever. He loved her with a certainty and fierceness that hurt.

Whatever happened next, this was the last time they would wake up this way. Their adventure was coming to an end. They'd been living in an artificial world, wrapped in each other, fighting the enemy. Although he wanted the danger to be gone, Bryce wished the closeness and the sense of the two of them shutting out the rest of the world could continue.

Steffi stretched and opened her eyes, smiling up at him almost shyly. Leaning down, Bryce captured her

mouth, and her lips melted beneath his like a sugar
cube dropped into hot coffee. He groaned as his erection hardened even further. Coaxing her mouth open,
he used his tongue to simulate the action he planned to
use in other, more sensual ways. Steffi looped her arms
around his neck and pulled him closer. The soft coo-
ing sound she made almost tipped him over the edge.
His hands roamed over her body, exulting in the silken
feel of her skin and her slender curves. He cupped her
breasts, enjoying the way his large hands completely
covered the delicate mounds.

When he slid his hand between her thighs, she was
wet and ready. Steffi pressed into him as he slid a finger between her folds and circled it slowly.

"Bryce," she gasped, arching up to him again. He
loved that he could make her feel like this as soon as he
touched her. She gave a soft moan as her legs opened
farther and she matched his pumping rhythm. Inserting
another finger, he continued to massage her slick heat.

The pressure built, driving both of them toward gasping delirium. Bryce withdrew his fingers and gripped
Steffi's hips, turning her so she was on her hands and
knees. Reaching for a condom, he quickly slipped it on.

Lifting her bottom in the air, Steffi stretched back toward him. Bryce got in position behind her, gripping her
hips and holding himself steady against her entrance.
Her skin was smooth and tender beneath his fingertips.

She glanced back at him over her shoulder, her eyes
glazed and pleading. As he entered her, ecstasy swept
through him, sending tendrils of fire along his nerve
endings. She was incredibly tight, her muscles clinging
to him. He gritted his teeth to keep himself from surg-
ing violently forward. Slowly, inch by inch, he pushed

into her. Finally, he was fully seated and he paused to allow her to adjust to this angle. Steffi bowed her head, going down on her elbows, the action taking him even deeper, and he groaned, caressing the smooth globes of her ass in appreciation.

She stretched back against him. Bryce slid out and back in. Perfection. Pure and simple. He thrust freely. Wildly. Pounding out a rhythm that drove him to the edge of insanity. From the mewling sounds she was making, Steffi was experiencing a similar reaction.

She cried out and clenched around him. Bryce hardened and tightened. Leaning over her, he braced one hand around her waist, lifting her higher against him while he thrust into her. When she came, she bucked wildly beneath him and cried out his name. Shaking uncontrollably, Bryce took the full hit of his own climax. It took every ounce of his strength to stop himself from collapsing on top of Steffi.

When his trembling subsided, he trailed tiny kisses across her shoulders as he slipped out of her and rolled her over to face him. Her eyes were half-closed and a dreamy smile played across her lips. "That was wonderful, and it's early. We still have plenty of time to say our goodbyes."

Goodbye. The word caused the warmth and comfort of loving her to ebb away. The future stretched ahead, aching and empty. How was he ever going to let Steffi go?

Chapter 19

Laurie was right. The dress was perfect. Steffi was a fraction taller than Laurie and, after losing weight, she was slimmer, but the gunmetal-gray silk clung to her figure perfectly. Ending just above the knee, the dress was a high-necked, backless sheath. Luckily the two women wore the same shoe size and Laurie lent Steffi a pair of strappy silver heels that accentuated the length of her legs. The outfit might be a strange choice for someone who was planning to take down a dangerous murderer, but Bryce's plan was an unusual one.

"I can't do much with your hair." Laurie shook her head sadly. "But I might be able to neaten it up a bit."

For the second time in a week, Steffi allowed an unqualified person to approach her wielding a pair of scissors. Her stylist would never forgive her. Laurie was less brutal than Bryce and the end result wasn't unpleasant. The harsh, black spikes were softened and Laurie managed to neaten the hair at her nape and over her ears. The new style still took some getting used to, but she no longer resembled an escaped urchin from a Victorian Christmas movie.

Because she preferred subtlety, Steffi had always applied her own makeup. Her eyes needed very little enhancement, just a touch of eyeliner and mascara. This time she did it with a sense of surrealism. The past three months had changed her and, no matter how this night ended, there could be no going back. Staring at her face in the mirror when she had finished, she no longer recognized the person staring back at her. Anya Moretti was back for one final appearance, but in reality she had died that day along with Greg and Bliss. Steffi didn't know what that meant for the future, and now wasn't the time to make plans. All she knew for sure was that her movie-making days were over.

"You look amazing." Laurie didn't look too bad herself, in a fitted scarlet dress that emphasized her curves.

They made their way down the stairs to where the men were waiting. Cameron and Vincente had been to Bryce's house to pick up his suit, and Steffi's eyes were drawn straight to him. She thought she would hate seeing him dressed-up. He was her jean-clad hero. But he looked gorgeous. The dark blue jacket emphasized the width of his shoulders, and the matching trousers hugged his muscular thighs. A white shirt accentuated his tan. Steffi wanted to know she was the lucky woman who would get to undo those buttons and peel that crisp material from his torso tonight. Instead, the best outcome she could hope for was that she would be leaving the party in a police car.

He glanced up as she approached and his jaw dropped. He looked so dumbstruck and adorable, she wanted to walk into the circle of his arms and stay there. They were on their way to an encounter with a murderer. How she looked shouldn't matter. But it buoyed her spirits to see the flare in Bryce's eyes when he looked at her.

"Steffi, you look incredible."

"Tonight I'm Anya."

He moved closer, gripping her waist and sliding his thumbs over her jutting hip bones as though he was testing the slippery silk. "You will never be Anya to me." He looked over her shoulder at Vincente. "Did you check out the sound system?"

Vincente, who had spent the afternoon at the memorial hall carrying out Bryce's meticulous instructions, nodded. "It's all organized."

"And who else will be there?"

"Dino and Toby Murray."

Bryce nodded, apparently satisfied with that information. "Did you get in touch with Leon Sinclair?"

Steffi remembered that name. "Wasn't he the doctor who came to my cabin when I had the stomach flu?"

"I wanted to make sure we have a few people in the room we can trust one hundred percent," Bryce said. Steffi shivered slightly. His explanation made it seem real. This was happening. "Do you have the cell phone?"

She patted the purse Laurie had lent her. "In here."

"You're going to hand it over to Walter? Just like that?" Vincente asked.

"We have copies of the recording, and the cell phone is our reason to get him alone."

Steffi and Bryce were riding in Vincente's car with

him, while Cameron and Laurie were driving in their own vehicle. Once they reached city hall, Steffi would need to remain hidden until it was time to make her entrance.

"Are you nervous?" Bryce took her hand, spreading her fingers over his thigh.

She turned her head to smile at him. "I've made a few tricky appearances in my time, but I'd be lying if I pretended this was just one more."

When they arrived in downtown Stillwater, there was already a line of cars at the front entrance of the building, and the place was lit up like a Fourth of July celebration. Vincente bypassed the queue and drove around to where Cameron was waiting for them. Ushering them in through a side entrance, he escorted them upstairs to his office.

"Walter is already here," he told them. "Just give me the word, and I'll tell him there is someone who wishes to meet with him in private in my office. Since there are a number of big name contributors to his campaign attending tonight, he's likely to believe it will be one of them."

"Are you ready to do this now?" Bryce turned to Steffi.

"Let's get it over with." Her jaw was rigid with tension, but she was determined to see it through. Getting some answers from Walter was just the start of the evening. There was more to come.

"Once I've brought Walter up here, I'll have to go down to the party," Cameron said. "But Vincente and Toby will be outside."

"Who is Toby?" Steffi asked as Cameron went out.

"Toby Murray is a music producer. He and Cameron

became friends in tragic circumstances. Before Cameron and Laurie met, he was dating Laurie's cousin Carla. Carla was murdered by the same serial killer who also killed Toby's girlfriend, Marie."

Steffi shivered. "I heard about the case when I was working for you. The Red Rose Killer, is that right?"

Bryce nodded. "Laurie was the undercover cop who solved the case."

Although the words instilled Steffi with a new respect for Laurie, it was hardly the most mood-enhancing conversation. She moved to take a seat on one side of Cameron's desk, and Bryce sat next to her. That left Walter with the chair behind the desk. Was that the arrangement she wanted? It would look like Walter was calling the shots.

"You take Cameron's seat." How did Bryce always seem to know what she was thinking?

She threw him a grateful glance and had just changed places when Cameron walked in with Walter. Pretending not to notice Walter's look of surprise, Cameron closed the door behind him. "I don't think we need any introductions here."

Walter nodded curtly. "I suppose not."

"Then I'll leave you to it." Cameron went out.

"I hope this means you've decided to see sense and hand over that cell phone, Stefanya," Walter said as soon as the door closed behind him.

"Have a seat, Walter." Steffi indicated the chair she had just vacated.

"I'll stand."

"Have it your way." Now he was here, she was able to slip into a role. The nerves were gone. Crossing one leg over the other, she leaned back in the big leather chair. "I have a few questions for you before I hand over the phone."

"You may have questions, but I don't intend to provide answers."

"No answers, no phone." Bryce joined the conversation, and Walter gave him a look of undiluted dislike.

"John Andover? Nice try, Bryce Delaney. You were supposed to die back at my house."

Bryce grinned. "I never do what I'm supposed to do."

"Now we have the pleasantries out of the way, let's get to the questions I want to ask you—" Steffi held up a hand as Walter began to protest "—and hear me out. Who knows, you may find they're not so difficult to answer after all." He stared back at her in silence. "First of all, why were you so keen to be part of the decision-making process about who my adoptive parents were? Why did it matter to you, Walter?"

When he didn't answer, she continued. "There was a family that was prepared to adopt Greg and me together, but you put a stop to it. Why was that? And, even when you got your way and placed me with June and Todd, why did you refuse their offer to take Greg, as well?"

Walter remained silent. "On that recording, you said you made me. I know you sent me gifts and that you provided the money so that I could attend performing arts school. Why was that? Guilty conscience? If so, it was an expensive one." Steffi withdrew the cell phone from her purse, swinging it between her fingertips. "But the burning question, Walter, the one I really want the answer to, is, what did you do at the end of this recording? What made Greg cry out in shock just before you walked away?"

Walter moved toward her so suddenly that Bryce rose

from his seat. Resting his hands flat on the desk, Walter loomed over her. "You want answers to your questions, Stefanya? You want to know what Gregori saw to make him cry out? It is the thing that answers all your questions." She'd never noticed it before, but those strange, dark eyes lacked the ability to glitter.

Reaching up, Walter pulled down the lower eyelid on his left eye. Sliding his index finger across his eye, he removed a contact lens he wore before repeating the process with his right eye. Stunned, Steffi gazed up into his eyes. Without the dark contact lenses he usually wore, Walter's cat's eye irises were identical to her own.

"When I said I made you, I didn't just mean I molded your career. You are my daughter. Ekaterina and I started our affair in Russia and continued it after Aleksander moved his family and his business to America. If she had done as I asked and left him, she wouldn't have died that night." Reaching over, he withdrew the cell phone from her lifeless fingers and slid it into his inside pocket. "And your expression is identical to the one your brother—or I should say half brother, since Gregori was Aleksander's son—wore when I revealed our little family secret to him."

With a laugh that ripped a hole in her heart, Walter pushed past Bryce and walked out of the room.

"You knew, didn't you?" Steffi rested her forehead on Bryce's shoulder as he came around the desk and knelt before her. "That's why you asked if my eye condition was hereditary."

"I had a hunch, that's all. I couldn't come right out and tell you because it was too shocking." He held her slender body against his own. "It was what he said about

Ekaterina in the recording. He told Greg she hadn't been loyal to him. When Greg questioned him, Walter didn't answer, but it got me thinking about why he would expect loyalty from your mother."

"He didn't show her any loyalty." Steffi's eyes were anguished as she raised them to his face. "No matter what they may have once been to each other, he murdered Ekaterina."

"What do you want to do now? You've just sustained a terrible shock. We can forget the rest of the plan, call Laurie up here, have her arrest you and get this whole mess over with."

He watched her face as she weighed the options. Then she straightened her spine. "No. Let's do this the way we arranged it. I don't want Walter to be able to wriggle his way out of another court case."

His heart expanded with love and pride. After what had just happened, most people would still be trying to pick themselves up from the floor. Not Steffi. She gave him a shaky smile, took a borrowed compact out of her borrowed purse, checked her makeup, made a couple of minor adjustments and got to her feet.

"I'm ready."

When they left the office, Vincente was just outside with Toby Murray. Bryce had met Toby a few times at Cameron's place and liked him. *Another of the good guys.* They needed all the help they could get. He doubted Walter's men would be inside the building during a function of this type, but they wouldn't be far away.

Vincente avoided the main staircase, taking them down a back way that, judging by the brushes and buckets stored at the bottom, was used by cleaners. From there, he led them along a corridor and into the curtained area at the rear of the stage that occupied one end of the memorial hall.

"Cameron is about to give his speech. The podium on which he's standing is on the stage, directly in front of these curtains. You'll be able to hear what's going on from here without being seen. When the moment comes, all you need to do is simply step out from behind the curtains," Vincente said to Steffi. He had spent the afternoon carefully choreographing the scene.

"Once Cameron starts talking, we need to go," Bryce said. "Are you sure you'll be okay on your own?"

Steffi gave a soft laugh. "There are hundreds of people on the other side of that curtain. If Walter finds me and tries anything, I'll come bursting right on through. It'll be the most memorable fund-raiser this town has ever seen."

"I have a feeling that's how it will turn out anyway." They could hear the sound system being tested, then Cameron's voice welcoming the guests to the fund-raiser. "That's our cue." Bryce pressed a quick kiss onto Steffi's forehead. "See you on the other side."

With Vincente and Toby flanking him, he made his way to the edge of the curtained area, glancing back once at Steffi. In the high-ceilinged area, she looked tiny and so heartbreakingly beautiful. He wanted to turn back and wrap his arms around her, but Cameron had warned them his speech wouldn't take long.

Bryce could never enter the memorial hall without experiencing a feeling of awe. Apart from the fact that the hall was named after his great-grandfather, this was Stillwater at its best. Serving many different purposes, the huge room was used as a theater, function room and community hub. The decor was elegant with a tiled floor, plaster columns and chandeliers that harked back to another era. This was where Stillwater held its barn dances, rock concerts, bake sales and children's Christmas parties. When part of the roof collapsed a few years ago, there had been talk of closing the place down. It was just too expensive to maintain, some people had suggested. Did a modern town really need a turn-of-the-century relic? Yes, it did. That had been Stillwater's resounding response. Lose the Clarence Delaney Memorial Hall? It would be like ripping the heart out of the town.

As Bryce walked in, he felt Cameron's eyes flick to his face, even though his brother was getting into his speech. A quick glance around showed him Walter was standing close to the stage, looking up at the podium. Perfect. In one corner, a few members of the press were gathered. Newspaper reporters were recording Cameron's speech, and the local TV station was filming him. Bryce nodded to Vincente, who moved into place by the sound system. Laurie was near the fire exit talking to Dino. Bryce and Toby remained in position by the closed double doors. There were no other exits.

"We have with us tonight a man who needs no introduction." The hall was crowded and Cameron's voice carried through the microphone to every part of the vast hall. "Walter Sullivan—" he indicated Walter with a wave of his hand "—has made his Stillwater roots a central part of his bid to become a Wyoming senator. Decency, honesty, belief in family, loyalty and humility. Those, to me, are the values it takes to be a true son of Stillwater."

Cameron paused, ensuring he had the attention of every person in the room. "You have to hand it to him,"

Toby murmured. "He knows how to do this for maximum effect."

"Tonight we have a special guest. Someone who is going to explain exactly why Walter Sullivan doesn't demonstrate any of those values." There was a murmur of confusion. A ripple of nervous laughter. People were looking from Cameron to Walter—whose face was shifting from smiley to thunderous—waiting for the punch line.

Cameron stepped slightly to one side. "Our special guest, ladies and gentlemen... Anya Moretti."

As Steffi stepped out from behind the curtain, Bryce could hear the whispers from those closest to him.

"Isn't she the one who...?"

"It can't be? Can it?"

He saw Laurie's boss, Chief Wilkinson, across the room. The police chief didn't make a move and Bryce guessed Laurie had already briefed him on what was going to happen. His sister-in-law would not have left the situation to chance and he offered up a silent thank-you for her organizational skills. Chief Wilkinson was due to retire in a few months and Laurie was widely tipped to be his replacement.

Steffi waited calmly until the room was silent. She removed something from her purse and placed it next to the microphone. Even from a distance, Bryce could tell what it was. It was the photograph of Greg and Bliss. Steffi was doing this for them, as well.

She looked stunning. Even in a gathering such as this, where everyone had gone the extra mile, her star quality shone through. Raising the microphone with an expertise born of many such occasions, she began to speak. "I probably don't need to tell you the background to my story. Most of you will already know that, three months ago, an actor called Greg Spence was murdered in his Los Angeles apartment together with an unnamed woman and that I have been on the run from the police ever since."

Bryce glanced around. Most people were gazing at her as though struck dumb. The press contingent was going wild, many of them on their cell phones, doubtless trying to get this story to their national counterparts. And Walter? How was he taking this new development? After a quick glance at the exits, his face had settled into a mask of fury as he turned back to watch Steffi.

"What you don't know is that Greg Spence was my brother. His real name was Gregori Anton. My real name is Stefanya Anton. Our father was a Russian mob boss who was murdered, along with our mother, here in Wyoming, when we were very young. Greg and the woman who was with him—a bright, beautiful young woman called Bliss Burton—were murdered by the same man who killed our parents."

Steffi's calm, beautiful voice, the voice that had graced dozens of popular movies, somehow made the words sound even worse. As she finished speaking, Vincente started up the sound system and Walter's voice took over through the speakers. The damning recording of his conversation with Greg filled the room. No one moved as they listened. No one commented. The TV cameras kept rolling and several of the reporters kept their phones trained on Walter's face.

When the recording finished, Steffi spoke into the microphone. "Walter Sullivan killed my parents. He killed Greg Spence and Bliss Burton." She looked down at Walter's upturned face for the first time. "I found out tonight that Walter Sullivan is my biological father. I've been fortunate. I've had two real fathers. Aleksander Anton did some bad things to other people, but he cared for me. Then a man called Todd Grantham took over and became my real dad." There was a note of pity in her voice. "Walter wouldn't know the meaning of the word."

It seemed to be the cue to galvanize Walter. Pushing past the people around him, he strode toward the doors. Bryce and Toby moved closer together, blocking his way. As Walter pulled a gun from his inside pocket, a woman nearby screamed.

"You know I've been waiting for an excuse to kill you," Walter snarled at Bryce. "Get out of my way."

"You seriously think that's going to happen?" Bryce stepped forward to grapple with him. As he caught hold of Walter's right arm, the other man ducked. Bryce muttered a curse and tried to land a punch that would knock Walter out. He wasn't fast enough and the sound of the gunshot coincided with the searing pain in his left thigh. As his vision clouded, he was conscious of Vincente and Toby forcing Walter to the floor.

Chapter 20

Steffi had remained still with her head bent over the microphone as she gazed at the photograph of Greg and Bliss. She had played some emotional roles during her career, parts that had drained her and tugged at the depths of her comfort zone. But nothing had come close to the way that speech had made her feel. She knew why, of course. It was real and raw. Although keeping her cool had involved playing a part, the words had been the truth. She had just lowered the protective barriers around her heart and exposed her life to a room full of strangers.

Gradually, she became aware of a scuffle taking place across the room. From her raised vantage point, she looked up just in time to see Walter pull a gun on Bryce.

"No." The word came out as a croak.

Everything happened too fast. As Bryce stepped forward and grabbed Walter's arm, Walter dodged out of his way. Even though he couldn't raise the gun high enough to shoot Bryce in the head or the chest, he fired anyway. Steffi broke into a run as Bryce began to fall, her high heels slowing her down as she clattered across the stage, down the steps and through the horrified crowd. Bryce was unconscious when she reached him, an ominous pool of blood forming beneath his injured left leg. Vincente had Walter by the throat up against the wall, and Toby had removed the gun from his grasp.

"Please…" Steffi looked around the faces that were crowding in on them as she cradled Bryce's head on her lap. Where was Cameron? Laurie? Somebody who could help them? Sobs tore at her throat, making it difficult to get the words out. "He's losing too much blood."

Leon dropped to his knees beside her, loosening his belt. "I need to apply a tourniquet to stop the bleeding."

As Leon got to work, Steffi felt a hand on her shoulder. Turning her head, she saw Laurie standing behind her with tears pouring down her face. "I'm sorry, Steffi. It's time to go."

"No." Steffi shook her head. "Not now. Please…not when I don't know if he's going to be okay."

"It's the only way we can do this." Laurie held out a pair of handcuffs. "I've informed the Los Angeles police that you are here in Stillwater, and they've instructed me to arrest you." A sob escaped her before she got her voice under control. "Stefanya Grantham, I am arresting you on suspicion of the murder of Gregori Spence. You have the right to remain silent…"

The television news crew pushed its way forward as Steffi got to her feet. Laurie read her the rest of her rights and snapped the handcuffs closed.

A microphone was thrust in her face. "Anya, do you

have any comment to make about what just happened here?"

She kept her head down, ignoring their questions. Leon was working on Bryce, tightening the belt around his thigh and giving orders to get everyone back out of his way. If only Bryce didn't look so pale. If only he would open his eyes and look at her. If only she could tell him she loved him...

Taking hold of Steffi's upper arm with her hand, Laurie led her from the room. Chief Wilkinson accompanied them as they left the building. The shock hit Steffi at the same time as the night air. Cold, numbing sweat broke out all over her body and she began to shiver so violently her teeth chattered. The edges of her vision began to darken and she felt light-headed. The Stillwater Police Department was located in an annex to the main building and, as Laurie began to walk her along the path toward it, Steffi stumbled.

"Easy." Laurie caught hold of her, easing her down gently onto the low wall that bordered the path. Chief Wilkinson stood nearby. "Do you feel nauseated?"

Unable to speak, Steffi shook her head. She didn't know what she felt. Everything inside her had stopped working. Her thoughts were frozen. The only thing in her head was an image of Bryce lying on the floor, his face like marble, and that widening pool of blood around his leg.

"Oh, dear God." Without warning, everything started up again and crushing pain caught her in the chest. She doubled over, fighting to find her next breath.

"Let's get you inside." Laurie slid an arm around her waist. "I don't want the press coming after us."

She was barely aware of her surroundings as they led her into the police headquarters.

"You need to get her into a cell. I've called Detective Wright and Deputy Marsh. They're both on their way over here now. I'm going back over to the memorial hall to arrest Walter Sullivan." There was a sympathetic note in Chief Wilkinson's voice. "You don't want her meeting him again tonight."

"I need to speak to the investigating officers in Los Angeles about what we do next." Laurie's voice was quiet. "Although they told me to arrest her, I'm not sure how they'll want to proceed once they hear that recording."

"We are going to be under the spotlight over the next few days. Just play it by the book." Steffi saw the chief's big hand come down briefly on Laurie's shoulder before he walked away.

"I'm so sorry, Steffi." Laurie took a set of keys from a cupboard behind the counter and led her to a cell. "At least I don't have to pat you down. I know you can't conceal anything under that dress."

The next few hours took on a surreal quality. There was a narrow bunk in the cell and a scratchy blanket that didn't really keep her warm. Steffi removed her shoes and lay down, but her mind insisted on replaying the events of the evening on a continuous loop. Pacing up and down the cell didn't help. She alternated between sitting and pacing until Laurie reappeared.

"Is he okay?"

"Bryce is alive. They're operating on him now." Laurie's expression was grave.

"What is it?" Steffi clasped her hands together so hard it hurt. "Tell me he'll walk again."

"It's not about Bryce. Before the chief got back to the hall, Walter managed to snatch his gun back from Toby. He killed himself, Steffi. Your father is dead."

Steffi was quiet for a few moments, absorbing what Laurie had told her. "No," she said at last. "My father is Todd Grantham, and he has gone away for a few days."

Apparently satisfied that she would be okay, Laurie left her alone to several more hours of boredom. Dawn was making an appearance through the high, barred window of the cell when Laurie returned, by which time Steffi was close to delirium. Not knowing what was happening with Bryce, with the investigation, with *anything*, was driving her crazy. She judged about seven hours must have elapsed since she left the memorial hall.

"I've been speaking to the detectives who are leading the inquiry in Los Angeles, and they have a few questions they want me to ask you." Laurie led her to an office where a uniformed officer was seated behind a desk. "This is my colleague, Deputy Marsh. First of all, can I get you a coffee?"

Steffi nodded as she took a seat on the opposite side of the desk. When Laurie handed her the plastic cup of coffee, she wrapped her hands around it gratefully. "Do I need my attorney present?"

"Both your manager and your attorney arrived in Stillwater an hour ago," Laurie said. "By all means, I can ask your lawyer to attend this meeting, but I'm pleased to tell you that you are no longer under arrest." A smile lit her eyes. "I'm interviewing you as a witness in the murder of your brother and his girlfriend, Steffi. You are no longer a suspect. Once you have given me your statement, you are free to go."

* * *

The pain in Bryce's leg was nothing to the ache in his chest. During the operation, the surgeon had removed the bullet and pinned the bone in his thigh. Now he had a cage around it and, despite the painkillers, every movement was agony. Vincente had been at his bedside when he awoke and remained with him since. Bryce had come around from the anesthetic a few hours earlier and his first request had been for a TV set to be brought into his room. There was only one news story he wanted to watch.

"Walter killed himself?" Bryce frowned as his befuddled brain attempted to process what he was hearing.

"In full view of all the guests. The camera crew filmed the whole thing, but it was way too gory to be shown on TV."

"What happened to Steffi? Tell me she didn't have to see that." Bryce attempted to sit up straighter. The action sent a jolt of pain through his leg and he collapsed back again, a sheen of sweat coating his brow.

"No. Laurie had already arrested her and taken her to the cells before it happened," Vincente said.

Bryce swore under his breath at the thought of Steffi in a cell. *I wasn't there for her.* He watched the screen avidly, desperate to hear what was happening with her. There was plenty of speculation. The story dominated every news channel. In the absence of any developments, footage from Steffi's films was played alongside images of her, Greg and Walter.

"Miss Moretti's manager, Paul Conway, and her attorney, Gina Bailey, have just arrived in Stillwater. Seen here entering the police department offices, Mr. Conway has said his client will be making a full statement in the coming days and weeks. In the meantime, he has stressed that the important thing will be to get her home to Los Angeles where she belongs."

Where she belongs. That was it. It was over. The closest he'd gotten to saying goodbye had been in bed the previous day. And maybe that was the best way. They'd always done their best talking with their bodies.

"We're going over to our reporter in Stillwater where something seems to be happening." On the screen, the familiar image of city hall appeared. The crowd of reporters parted as a tall man—presumably her manager—escorted Steffi to a waiting car. She looked tiny as, with her head down, she ducked into the waiting vehicle. As soon as she was settled in the rear seat, the car drove away.

"In a statement just issued, Paul Conway, Anya Moretti's agent, has confirmed that all charges against his client have been dropped. He has asked the press to respect her feelings and to grant her privacy at this time." In the studio, there was speculation about Anya Moretti's next moves. A period of rest followed by a book deal? Straight into a new movie?

"Switch it off." Bryce had almost forgotten Vincente was still there. "Torturing yourself won't do any good. I'm going to stop by the office for an hour or two—try to get some rest while I'm gone."

Vincente was right. Continuing to watch the speculation and gossip, culminating in Steffi's return to Los Angeles, wasn't going to do his well-being any good. He pointed the remote control at the TV. But rest? He didn't think that was likely to happen.

Surprisingly, the effects of the anesthetic in his system meant he did doze on and off. He even dreamed. Vividly. He was walking along the beach at Leucadia.

It was sunset and Steffi's hand was in his. His imagination was working overtime. He could smell Steffi's perfume, that light, summery scent that was uniquely hers. He could even feel the clasp of her hand in his. When he felt the press of her lips on his cheek it was so perfect he sighed.

"If you are going to stay asleep when I have just fired my manager and announced to the world that I am retiring from making movies, it doesn't look good for the future." There was a trace of amusement in her voice that had to be real.

The beach scene faded and he opened one eye. The bland hospital room came into view and Steffi was sitting in the chair recently vacated by Vincente. "Am I still dreaming?"

"If you are, I am, too." The smile in her eyes warmed every inch of his body.

"What did you just say about retiring?"

She looked a little nervous. "Did you miss my press conference? It was on all the news channels. Chief Wilkinson wouldn't allow the press into the police department, so I had my manager hire a room at the Stillwater Heights Hotel. I've had enough of the celebrity lifestyle."

"What will you do instead?" His heart had commenced an irregular, heavy beat.

"That depends on you." Although her cheeks were flushed, her eyes were steady on his. And loving. He wasn't wrong about that. He'd grown used to reading the expression in her eyes. There was love in those golden depths. "On what you want to do next."

He grinned. "My leg won't let me show you *exactly* what I want to do next, but come a little closer and I'll give you a preview." She leaned over him and he tucked a hand behind her neck, pulling her down so he could kiss her long and hard. "That will have to do. For now. But we have the rest of our lives to do everything we want. Together."

"I love you, Bryce." The words were a sigh against his lips. "I never knew it was possible to feel this way."

"And I love you. I wasn't living when I met you. I was barely functioning. You've made me whole again. When I saw the footage of you driving away from city hall, I thought I was losing you and I couldn't think straight." His arm moved lower, tightening around her waist. "I am never letting you go again."

Leucadia Beach at sunset. Steffi couldn't imagine a more idyllic setting. She would have been happy for the marriage ceremony to have taken place anywhere. In the little chapel on Lakeside Drive in Stillwater. In city hall…although maybe she would draw the line at the memorial hall. On the Stillwater Trail. In a field. Even in the Wilderness Lake Trailer Park.

This had been Bryce's idea. The screensaver on Greg's cell phone had taken hold of his imagination. Greg and Bliss couldn't be at their wedding, but this was one way they could include their memory in the ceremony. And he had been right. It was the perfect way to end the first chapter of their story and begin the next one.

Four months had passed since that awful night in the Clarence Delaney Memorial Hall. Months during which Bryce had recovered slowly, and they had taken their time with their romance. The things they had once missed out on had become their priorities. They went on dates, held hands and kissed in public, spent time really getting to know each other. Fell even deeper in love…if that was possible.

Cameron had completed the necessary formalities and was licensed to be a deputy marriage commissioner for the day. He gave the occasion just the right amount of gravity, but also injected a touch of his own charm if the mood seemed inclined to stray downward. Not that it did too often. The bride and groom were too happy for that.

June and Nancy clung to each other's hands and cried constantly throughout the service, while Todd and Tanner looked on with twin expressions of bemusement. Although they exchanged the what's-this-about glances that men gave on these occasions, Steffi caught a glimpse of moisture in her dad's eyes when he placed her hand in Bryce's. It was there again when Cameron pronounced them married.

Laurie, who had lived most of her life in San Diego, was excited at the prospect of vacationing in California, but confessed to a feeling of regret that the wedding had not been a full-on Beverly Hills celebration.

She eyed Steffi's simple white lace dress and bare feet with her head on one side. "But you look incredible."

Laurie's disappointment at the lack of glamour was compensated for when Steffi handed her the keys to her house in Beverly Hills. "It's yours for the next two weeks. My housekeeper has instructions to make sure you have the vacation of a lifetime."

Once Laurie and Cameron left, the house would be placed on the market. The real estate agent, buoyed up by the recent publicity, had talked of holding out for an inflated price. Steffi had shaken her head and told him to get the place sold quickly. She wanted to cut her ties with Los Angeles as soon as possible. Stillwater would be her home from now on.

The only person she would leave behind with any regret was Elsa, but she had given her housekeeper a generous settlement package and references that would ensure she could walk into any job. Laughing, Elsa had told her the offers were flooding in.

"They all want to know what happened with you," the little housekeeper had said. "Don't worry. I'll never tell." Steffi believed her.

Before the reception Tanner took them out on the boat along the darkening coastline. Leaning on the rail, Steffi watched the white waves churning in the boat's wake.

Todd came to stand next to her. "Is this where I'm supposed to say something fatherly about the rough waves you can see behind you representing the past and the smooth water ahead being the future?"

"That's actually very poetic." She smiled up at him.

He turned to look at where Bryce was talking to Vincente. "You chose a very good man."

Steffi felt her smile widen. "I know."

"I wish there were things we'd done differently." The words seemed to have been dragged from somewhere deep within him.

Placing a hand on his shoulder, she rose on the tips of her toes to press a kiss to his cheek. "I expect every parent says that."

"Maybe with less reason?" His smile asked for acceptance, and she was happy to give it.

"Not every parent had Walter Sullivan to contend with."

Moving away, she made her way to Bryce's side, catching the tail end of his conversation with Vincente.

"No matter how happy I am for you and Steffi, times

like this remind me that I still don't know what happened to her." Vincente's voice was low and wretched.

"There's still no news?" Bryce asked.

"Nothing. Laurie said the police haven't found her body. They've taken out advertisements asking her to come forward but there's been no response. It's the not knowing that's the worst." When Vincente saw Steffi standing close by, he forced a smile and relinquished his place at Bryce's side. "I'm going up ahead to ask Tanner if I can take the wheel."

"What was that all about?" Steffi slid her arms around Bryce's waist, tilting her face up to his.

"Vincente's girlfriend—on-off girlfriend—Beth, went missing around the time the Red Rose Killer, Grant Becker, was murdering women in Stillwater. We don't know if she was one of the victims."

"That explains it." Steffi watched Vincente as he walked away.

"Explains what?"

"Why Vincente looks so sad sometimes."

He held her tight against his side. Although he had dispensed with his crutches for the day, she knew it annoyed him that he still wasn't able to swing her up into his arms. Yet. "Enough about other people. It's about time you kissed me again, Mrs. Delaney."

Steffi obliged. Sometime later, when she was finally able to speak again, she tilted her head to one side. "Mrs. Delaney. Steffi Delaney. I've had enough different names in my life. That's the one I'm sticking with from now on."

* * * * *

Get 2 Free Books,

Plus 2 Free Gifts—

just for trying the Reader Service!

HARLEQUIN
ROMANTIC suspense

"Want to come in for a cup of coffee?" Jade asked.

If he went inside with her, he would have a hard time
tearing himself away and going home. "I have a meeting in
Odessa tomorrow. I have to leave early in the morning to
make it in time."

"On a weekend?" Jade asked.

"Unfortunately," Declan said.

The disappointment in her face was unmistakable.
"Another time, then."

Jade stepped out of the car and Declan followed her up
the steps to her front door. A gentleman walked his lady to
the door, a simple and kind gesture to ensure she was safe.

At the door, Jade turned.

"I'll ask again. Want to come in?" she said.

She turned and unlocked her door. Declan followed
her inside, pushing the door closed and locking it. He had
declined her offer, but he wanted to be with her. He should

keep a travel bag with him. It wasn't like the bed-and-breakfast was home. He was living on the road.

The air-conditioning cooled his skin, the humidity of the air disappearing inside the house. In a tangle of arms and legs, they stumbled to the couch. The couch was good. Better than the bedroom. Being in the bedroom would lead to one thing. As it was, this was inviting. Declan pivoted, pulling Jade on top of him.

He had several inches on her, but their bodies lined up, her softness fitting against him. The right friction and pressure made Declan want to peel her clothes away and finish this the right way. But he would wait.

She leaned over him, bracing a leg on the floor. Her hair swung to one side and he ran his fingers through it. Her blue-and-white dress was spread over them and lifting the fabric of the skirt ran through his mind.

Jade sat up. "Did you hear something?"

Declan shook his head. "Nothing." His heart was racing and his breath was fast.

"Like a creak on the porch. Like the wood shifting beneath someone's feet."

Worry speared him. Declan moved Jade off his lap and rolled to his feet. "I'll walk the perimeter and have a look."

Jade fisted his shirt in her hand, stopping him. "Maybe that's not a good idea. My mother has no compunction about killing or hurting people. I could be next. We could be next."

Don't miss
CAPTURING A COLTON by C.J. Miller,
available August 2017 wherever
Harlequin® Romantic Suspense books
and ebooks are sold.

www.Harlequin.com

Reward the book lover in you!

9423

Earn points from all your Harlequin book purchases from wherever you shop.

Turn your points into *FREE BOOKS* of your choice
OR
EXCLUSIVE GIFTS from your favorite authors or series.

Join for FREE today at
www.HarlequinMyRewards.com.

Harlequin My Rewards is a free program (no fees) without any commitments or obligations.

MYR17